RESOLUTION: BOOK TWO OF RESILIENCE DUET

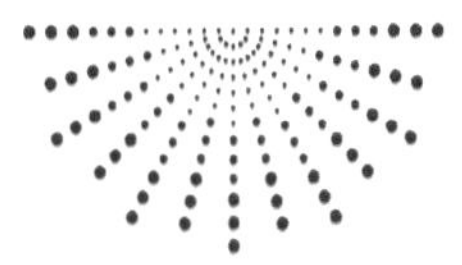

AMANDA SHELLEY

ISBN
E-book: 978-1-951947-02-6
Paperback: 978-1-951947-03-3

Editor: Sue Soares
SJS Editorial Services
https://www.facebook.com/sue.soares71
Proof Reader: Julie Deaton
Deaton Author Services
http://jdproofs.wixsite.com/jddeaton
Cover Design: Amy Queau
QDesign
https://www.qcoverdesign.com

This is a work of fiction. Names, characters, organizations, places, events, and incidents are either products of the author's imagination or are used fictitiously. Any resemblance to actual persons, living or dead, events, or locales is entirely coincidental. The author acknowledges the trademarked status and trademark owners of various products referenced in this work of fiction, which have been used without permission. The publication/use of these trademarks isn't authorized, associated with, or sponsored by the trademark owners.

Visit my website at
www.amandashelley.com

CONNECT WITH
AMANDA SHELLEY

Want to be the first to know about upcoming sales and new releases? Make sure you sign up for my newsletter as well as connect with me on social media and your favorite retail store.

Website:

www.amandashelley.com

Newsletter:

https://geni.us/AmandaShelleyNL

Facebook:

https://www.facebook.com/authoramandashelley/

Instagram:

https://www.instagram.com/authoramandashelley/

Reader's Group:

https://www.facebook.com/groups/AmandasArmyofReaders/

Amazon:

https://www.amazon.com/author/amandashelley

Goodreads:

https://www.goodreads.com/author/show/19713563.Aman
da_Shelley

Book Bub:

https://www.bookbub.com/profile/amanda-shelley

ABOUT THE BOOK

With Enzo returning to Germany, distance has its hardships.

Settling down or having a family had never been on his radar before Samantha. Now her quick wit and sexy smile has him contemplating his life choices. She and her kids have burrowed their way deep into his heart, and he knows he cannot let go.

Samantha never imagined she would fall so hard for the man who broke through her defenses and took her world by surprise. She's looking forward to their carefree vacation. However, fate has other plans, which potentially will bring them closer together or rip them apart.

Will Enzo and Samantha get the resolution they desire?

SAMANTHA

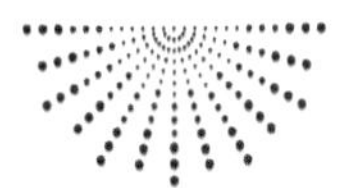

"LADIES AND GENTLEMEN, OUR FINAL DESTINATION IS approaching. We should reach Frankfurt, Germany, in thirty minutes. The local time is nine thirty-eight a.m. The weather is thirty-nine degrees Fahrenheit, which is four degrees Celsius, and clear. It's pretty but cold. Be sure to wear your coats," the captain announces. Then it's translated into German and French before the announcements are made about storing our belongings and putting our seats and trays in the upright positions. Butterflies flip in my stomach as I hear this. I've been traveling for over fifteen hours and can't wait to land.

Never in a million years did I think I'd be doing this. Here I am at age thirty-eight, on a plane to see my *boyfriend* in Germany. *Germany, as in the one on the other side of the world from Portland, Oregon.* If you'd asked me just three months ago if I'd be doing this, I would have told you, you're crazy. First, there's the fact I now have a boyfriend. Second, there's the whole issue of flying around the world. But when Enzo Harper walked into my house that fateful day to surprise his dad, we were both in for the surprise of our lives.

From the moment I saw Enzo walk into my disheveled kitchen, my life hasn't been the same. It feels like it was yesterday. I was simply sitting there, minding my own business, while a work crew remodeled my kitchen. In walks a man I didn't recognize, but was instantly attracted to. He was well over six feet tall with short, tousled, dark-blond hair. He was easily in his mid-thirties. He had an athletic build and glorious green eyes that sparkled with delight.

From the very start, I thought he was sex on a stick. I didn't think any man could ever be that good looking in real life. He's the type of man women spend billions on each year to buy as their next book boyfriend. I should know, I publish and market said books on a daily basis. I make it my business to know what sells, and the stranger before me was a mint in the making.

At the time, I could tell Enzo was up to something when he walked into my house, but I couldn't figure out what it was. When he motioned for me to "shhh" as he winked, I was locked in my spot waiting to see what would happen next. He approached Lorenzo Harper, my contractor, who had been talking on the phone to someone. The minute he hung up, Lorenzo was swept into a bear hug, which was no small feat. Lorenzo had been nearly as bulky as the mysterious man in front of me.

Of course, I was quickly introduced to Lorenzo's son, Enzo. Then, as he showed him the progress his crew was making on my home, I felt a magnetic pull to Enzo, even after just a few short moments. It's something I'd never experienced before. Of course, after they left, I went about my business, though there were frequent thoughts about the sexy man I had met earlier in the day.

As I left my house to get dinner that evening, I was happily surprised to find him outside retrieving his car after spending the afternoon with his dad. To my utter shock, I actually asked him to join me for dinner. Yes, me, Samantha O'Reilly, the single mother of three, got up the courage to ask him out. I hadn't even kissed a man in three years. No one I dated after my divorce was even worth a second date. I felt pretty courageous asking him. There was something about that sexy man with the swoon-worthy dimple, that gave me my mojo back.

Lorenzo Harper's a pilot for pararescue in the Air Force. He can fly just about anything he's given the chance to. He was home on leave, contemplating his career decisions. Should he retire? Should he switch to Air National Guard? Or should he move to the civilian side and work with private contractors for security? Thank God, he chose option three, which keeps him in Portland, Oregon. Now, he has less than two months left in the Air Force and will be returning home, for good. Sure, he'll have to travel with work, but his home base is near me, so who am I to complain?

To say our relationship's been a whirlwind is putting it mildly. I almost blush at the heat and chemistry we instantly displayed. No, I didn't sleep with him that first night, but when we did, the intensity was beyond anything I'd ever experienced. Enzo brings out a side of me I never knew existed and I can't wait to see what the future has in store for us.

Yes, I've been married before, and I've obviously had sex before. I do have three wonderful kids with my ex, Devin. But nothing could prepare me for Enzo Harper. I'd like to say I feel ashamed I want to strip naked the moment the man enters a room, but that would be a lie. After having my heart closed off for so long, due to indiscretions in one form or another, it's a glorious feeling to have someone accept me for who I am and loves me wholeheartedly. I've never been happier.

That's Enzo in a nutshell. Since he's practically been married to the Air Force for the last twenty years, having never found someone to settle down with, I think he's just as shocked to experience this, too. Years earlier, there had been one woman, but soon after his first deployment, he received a 'Dear John' letter from her, forcing him to keep his heart closed... that is, until he met me.

Boy, did I luck out. He's thoughtful, kind, and wonderful to my three kids. My youngest, Frankie, who's eight, simply adores him. Declan, my ten-year-old, also gets along with him well. Ever since Enzo rescued Maddie while she was on her first date with a flat tire, she's befriended him, too.

When he returned to Germany six weeks ago, there was three months left on his contract with the Air Force. It's been a long six weeks, almost torturous at times. Sure, we talk as much as we can when he isn't out on a mission, but he's literally been all over the world. I don't even know about the *where* of his location until it's already happened. It sucks not knowing, but that's how he's kept safe, so I understand and force myself to accept it. We've managed countless talks over the phone, and there may have been some sexy video messaging as well, which has been kind of fun, if I'm being honest.

I bring myself back to reality as I feel our descent, and the Frankfurt Airport comes into view. These last thirty minutes have been pure torture. I can't believe I'm so close, yet so far from Enzo. *God! Can't this plane go any faster?* I don't want to be away from him any longer. My body's a bundle of nerves and I feel as if we'll never make it there.

We finally touch down with a huge bump, coming to a careening stop, before the end of a runway. Thank God, Enzo put me in a first-class sleeper. I'm well rested and eager to see him.

It takes FOREVER for the cabin doors to open and the crew to let us off the plane. I make my way through customs and into the airport. Suddenly, the sexy man I have been dreaming about night and day, for the last six weeks, stands in front of me. He's still just as tall and handsome as ever. Being six-foot-six, he stands out among the crowd. His blond hair's shorter than before. High and tight, like a military cut, but upon further inspection, there should still be just enough to get my hands into. The thought alone makes my mouth water. Enzo's in civilian clothes, wearing dark jeans, dark sweater, and I can tell there's a collared shirt underneath. The moment he spots me, he closes the distance. A large bouquet of flowers is in his hands, but that doesn't stop him from swooping me up into his arms to kiss the life out of me.

Fuck, if we weren't in a crowded airport, I'd beg him to take me right now. But I'm an adult, so I can practice some patience. *I hope.*

"God, I've missed you, beautiful," he whispers into my ear as he sets me down.

"I've missed you, too," flutters against one last kiss.

Like the gentleman he is, he grabs my carry-on bag, leaving me only my purse to carry, leading me to the baggage claim.

After getting my luggage, we walk hand in hand to the parking garage. His large hand warms mine, making me feel secure and safe with him.

"Are you hungry?" he asks as we get into his silver Land Rover.

Taking in the sights around me, I finally answer, "I could eat." I've been a ball of nerves and haven't eaten since last night. My stomach feels a little off, but flying will do that to me from time to time.

We get on a highway and drive for a while. I'm in awe of actually being here, in Germany. With Enzo. This is so far from my life in Portland, Oregon. I've traveled abroad a little, but never to Germany. Enzo keeps his hand on my thigh and I hold it, keeping me grounded in reality, even though it's still hard to process I'm really here. My mind reels with possibilities. I'm relieved to find the electric pulses that flow between us haven't eased in our absence. If anything, they're stronger. *How's that even possible?*

Eventually, Enzo pulls off the highway into a little town I didn't catch the name of. It's lined with what I would imagine most German towns are like. The houses and buildings are a Bavarian design, like rustic chalets. My only experience with Germany before this was going to Leavenworth, Washington; a town that mimics Germany in its architecture and tourism, but that hardly does this beautiful town justice.

Enzo pulls into a parking spot in front of some shops. There's one in particular that draws my attention, so I ask, "Oh, can we go in there? I'd love to bring home an ornament to remember this trip."

"Let's go, beautiful." He takes my hand, and before we can make it to the storefront, he pulls me in for a kiss that could lead to so much more, if we weren't in public. This man makes me weak at the knees. Every nerve ending comes alive and I'm completely caught up in the moment. Eventually, all good things must come to an end, and he reminds me when he says, "Let's see what's inside," before giving me one last, chaste kiss.

I'm in Christmas Heaven. Christmas, hands down, is my favorite holiday. I love decorating and making memories with my family. I peruse up and down the aisles, peering at everything on the shelves. This place is amazing. I could spend an eternity here and never get bored. Enzo's a champ, taking it all in with me.

When I finally see a hand-carved Santa ornament with St. Nicholas Day and this year's date, I hold it up for Enzo to see. "Oh, Enzo! Look at this. Do you realize that your birthday is on St. Nicholas Day?" His birthday is December sixth. This ornament would be a perfect way to remember not only his birthday, but this incredible experience.

"Yeah, I know," he says modestly, as he holds out his hand to further inspect it. "You should get this. It's beautiful."

The next shelf catches me a bit off guard, I can't help but notice there's lots of pickles. And I mean *a lot.* It's stacked higher than me, full of pickles in varying sizes, made with different materials. *What in the world do pickles have to do with Christmas?* "Uh, Enzo?"

"Yeah?"

"What's up with the pickles? They seem to be everywhere." I hold one up for him to see.

His eyes light up with delight. "Ha! For St. Nicholas Day, here in Germany, the parents decorate the tree. Then the first time the kids look at it, they search for the pickle. The first one to find the pickle gets an extra present under the tree."

"Well, we should get one of those, too. It'd be a fun tradition to start." I wink at him to show just how much he means to me.

He winks back at me as he whispers, "Would you like to find *my* pickle?" I can't help the blush that creeps over me. God, I love him, horniness and all.

The thought of starting new traditions with Enzo is exciting. I spend some time picking one out for our tree at home. Enzo gives me his input, and before we know it, we're moving on to the next shelves. Unfortunately, Enzo won't be home this Christmas. *But there's always next year.* Besides, St. Nicholas Day is only a few days away.

We finish with our purchases, then head to a restaurant nearby. I'm slightly impressed when Enzo speaks in German to our waitress. He's kind enough to ask me what I'd prefer, and since I'm still a little queasy from the flight, I order something light, with a large coffee. He orders it effortlessly, then we slip into an easy conversation.

I tell him about the events of the last few days, getting my three kids ready to go to their dad's this week. I'm sure my kids will miss me like crazy, just like I'll miss them, but they're excited that I'm visiting Enzo. They know it's been hard for us to be apart. They didn't even complain about spending the ten days with their dad.

Devin and I have officially been divorced for the past year, but separated for much longer than that. We agreed to joint custody, so every other weekend, as well as Wednesday nights, the kids are with him. He lives relatively close, so the kids can still ride the bus to school from either house.

Personally, I've made every effort I can to get along with Devin. We may no longer be marriage material, but we chose to have three kids together. They are what's important, and we try to put them first. Though it's definitely easier said than done, sometimes. But I love my kids and will do just about anything for their happiness.

While I update him on the kids, Enzo suggests I call them before it gets too late. He offers his phone since it has international rates and it won't cost me a fortune. We video conference from the table, while we wait for the food. Frankie's eager to see us and chats a mile a minute about her day. I think she mentions wanting a souvenir at least three times in our short conversation. Declan is growing up before my eyes. I can tell he's happy to see me. He's doing homework, so he doesn't talk long. Maddie, my fourteen-year-old, tells me about going on another date with Soren Silva, the same young man who Enzo had helped change his tire a few months ago.

It melts my heart when Enzo pipes in and asks, "He has a jack now, right?" referring to their incident.

Maddie grins with delight. "Yep, though I hope he won't need it anytime soon."

We try to get off the video call as soon as our food

arrives. Frankie insists on seeing around the restaurant as well as what our food looks like before she will let us go.

To ensure we're both on the screen, Enzo scoots to my side of the table to drape an arm around me. I love the fact that he stays that way throughout the rest of our meal. Being apart from him has been hard, and I don't want to let him go anytime soon either. Unfortunately, I know my time here will fly by and I will have to leave all too soon. Then we will have about seven weeks before he returns home for good.

As soon as we get back in the car, the heat stirs around me and fatigue sets in. I'm not sure if it's my travels, my full stomach, or being close to Enzo, but I completely relax. The next thing I know, Enzo's outside my door and we're at a small house. "Shit, I fell asleep. Are we here?" My arms and legs feel like dead weights, so I must have been knocked out.

"Relax, beautiful. You didn't miss much. I'll take you sightseeing another time."

I let out a deep yawn. "Now that I've rested, what do you want to do this afternoon?" I get out of the car and take his hand.

He leads me to the ground-level apartment. "Let's get you settled, then we can decide." He looks in the direction of where we're going and pauses. "I hope you aren't expecting anything fancy. It's basically a basement that has been converted into an apartment. There's a three-bedroom flat above me, which is also rented out. Three guys live in it. All are stationed at Ramstein, though not in my unit. We get along okay."

He looks a little nervous to show me. His eyes dart around and he looks anywhere but at me. "I'm sure it will be fine,

Enzo. Don't worry." To reassure him, I lean up to quickly kiss him.

He rubs the back of his neck nervously when I pull away. "I've warned you that I'm not home much, right? I just got this place so I could come and go as I please, have some privacy, and stay out of base housing. It's nice to get away from it all, if you know what I mean."

I stop outside the door and put my hands on my hips, to make a point before entering his home. "Enzo, I couldn't care less what it looks like. I didn't come here to stay at the Ritz. I came here to see you."

"If you don't like it, I can get a hotel for the week you're here," he offers.

What a crazy idea. Why would we waste money like that? He just bought first-class tickets for me, and that was more than generous. His apartment can't be that bad. "Don't be ridiculous. Does it have a clean bed and a shower?"

"Yes," he sighs. "It's not a dump, just tight quarters. You're used to living in a big, beautiful home. I don't want you to go without."

I laugh. I can't help it. *What does he think I am, a pampered princess?* "As long as I have you, I'm fine."

With that, he opens the door and lets me in. I see a modest living room with an open floor plan and a kitchen along one wall. He quickly shows me that one door leads to the bathroom, while another one leads to his bedroom. He takes my things into the bedroom and says, "If you'd like to hang anything up, feel free. There's plenty of room in the closet."

"Thanks. Do you mind if I take a shower?" I ask, realizing I must have grime on me from traveling.

"Sure. You can grab your things through that door. There's another door which opens to the living room, so if you don't want the neighbors to see, be sure to shut it," he ends teasingly.

I quickly use the facilities and do my business. After inspecting the shower to see if there's room for two, a plan forms quickly and a smile spreads across my face. I undress in record time and as casually as I can manage, I call out, "Enzo, can you help me with something?"

Within moments, he's at the door asking, "What do you need?" He peers around the room, looking eager to be of assistance.

God, I want this man right now. Why the hell is he waiting? "Only you," I say, making my intentions clear. His eyes lock onto mine before sweeping up and down the full length of my body.

Thank the fucking Lord, he takes my hint. He's undressed in record time, clothes flying everywhere. Before I know it, he bends down and swoops me into his arms. Seconds later, I'm being placed on the bed.

"Took you long enough," I pant. *God. I've been wanting him to do this since I laid eyes on him at the airport.*

"I was giving you some space, beautiful. I've wanted to attack you since you stepped into my arms from the plane. I'm *trying* to be a gentleman." The way he emphasizes that last statement has my insides doing flips off a mountain.

Not wanting there to be any misinterpretation, I tell him, "Have your wicked way with me, Enzo. I can't wait any longer." The beautiful man before me reads my signals loud and clear and spends the next few hours worshiping my entire body, the only way he knows how. His delicious mouth nips, sucks, and licks his way across my body, getting fully reacquainted. I don't think I have ever been this insatiable, but he gives me everything he has and then some.

Hours later, when his stomach rumbles, we force ourselves to the kitchen to make dinner. But our break doesn't last long. Let's just say, naked picnics have their advantages. We pass out from exhaustion, wrapped in each other's arms, from pure orgasmic bliss.

I'm not sure what time it is when I wake, but it's still dark outside. Nature calls my name with urgency. As much as I want to stay entwined with Enzo, there's no way I can ignore it much longer. I untangle myself from Enzo and sit up slowly. The minute my feet hit the floor, a wave of nausea hits and it's all I can do to run to the bathroom to make it to the toilet in time.

Yep. That's where the sex god himself, finds me. Praying to the porcelain throne, giving her all I've got. He's all sexy with rumpled hair and still entirely naked. Meanwhile, I'm lying on the floor, camped out between the wall and toilet, trying to keep my head in the vicinity of the bowl, so I don't make an even bigger mess.

"You okay?" he anxiously asks, worry etched in his voice. "Anything I can get you?"

"Go away, I don't want you to catch this," I croak in humility.

"Not happening, beautiful," is, of course, his perfect response.

He gets a wet washcloth and places it on my forehead. He also grabs a towel from the counter and wraps me in it. I think

I thank him, but all I can do is lay my head against the rim of the, *thankfully clean*, toilet seat once I stop dry heaving.

"Do you think you're done puking now?" *God, just let me die.* Why does he have to witness my humility? This is awful. No one should witness this, let alone the sexy man of my dreams.

All I can manage is a nod. I don't have the energy to do much else. Strong arms suddenly envelop me and I find myself airborne. Enzo walks me over to the bed, then covers me with the blankets.

I must drift off for a moment; the next thing I know, he's there standing in his boxers, offering me a t-shirt and boxers to wear. When I don't do anything but stare at him, he dresses me like an infant. I'd like to say I try to protest, but I just don't have the energy to give a fuck. I'm miserable. I can't believe he even brings me a large pot to puke in. I don't remember the last time anyone helped me when I was sick. The thought alone has my heartstrings being plucked rapidly. Emotion overwhelms me. But all that ends abruptly, when he crawls into bed with me. I protest with a croak, "Enzo, I don't want to get you sick."

"Samantha, we've swapped enough DNA since last night. If I'm going to get sick, I'm already exposed." He laughs a little at the end, but then his tone changes. "Beautiful, I just want to hold you. Please let me do this. I feel helpless right now. Not to mention, there's no way I'm going in the other room after spending the last six weeks apart." Who am I to resist the face he gives me?

A few hours later, I wake again. This time, feeling much better. I make it to the bathroom, brush my hair and nasty teeth, as well as use the facilities, without any further sickness. *Thank goodness for small miracles*

I hear, "Are you feeling better?" through the door.

I take pity on him and don't make him wait for my answer. "So much better. I'm a little hungry. Do you have any toast?"

I walk out into the living room to find Enzo making toast, as well as getting a blanket for me to snuggle with on the couch.

"I don't know what I did to deserve you," I whisper as he tucks me in.

"I'm the lucky one," he says as he brushes a kiss on my forehead.

Then I realize I've said my thoughts aloud again and mutter, "Damn filter."

"I love you, Samantha, lack of filter and all."

I try to be angry that he finds my lack of filter endearing. "You're lucky I love you, too, Enzo."

"Damn right, I am." The smile on his face nearly melts my heart entirely. This man's so loving. I wouldn't want to be anywhere else right now. I'm in heaven when he sits beside me and wraps me in his arms to snuggle.

We rest for a while, but eventually, I get restless. I feel so much better and I'm in a foreign country after all. Why would I want my only view to be from this couch?

Though when I look at Enzo, I realize it is quite a view. But still. I don't want to be sick and helpless on the couch all day.

A little while later, I convince Enzo I'm well enough to see some sights. He reluctantly agrees to drive me around Ramstein Air Force Base. He shows me where he works, where he likes to shop, and where he works out. We do this all from the car so I don't expose anyone to my germs, in case I'm contagious.

After a while, we pick up something to eat from a deli. Unfortunately, I quickly find that I can't hold anything down. I find myself begging Enzo to pull over so I can relieve myself in the bushes. Like a perfect gentleman, he doesn't complain once. He simply takes me back to his apartment and we spend the rest of the evening resting on the couch, watching movies and snuggling. I'm thankful to keep some chicken broth down before going to bed for the night.

Fuck! The next morning's a repeat of the day before. Like the movie 'Groundhog Day,' it totally sucks. To make matters worse, I'm so weak Enzo has to help me shower. I spend the entire day in bed sleeping and just trying to be in the land of the living. I must say, the man's a saint. There's not a wish I have that he doesn't answer. If I actually had the ability to care, I'd be mortified for being such an invalid.

Thank the Lord, I feel alive again the next morning. Not feeling like death warmed over is almost like a miracle. I'm eager to make the most of our limited time together. Today's Enzo's birthday and I can tell he's relieved that I'm on the mend. We get dressed and I decide to wear the green dress he bought me, but this time I wear knee-high boots and tights to keep my legs warm. My jacket's thick, so I have no worries about being chilly.

Within a few minutes of being in the car, Enzo takes me to the Nanstein Castle. It was built in 1162. I'm eager to get out and walk around the grounds of the castle itself. After being stuck in bed, it's a relief to walk about and enjoy the culture and history. I soon learn this castle was built after the Holy Roman Empire. Fredrick demanded its construction as an additional defense for the Palatinate, which is the area we are in. I dig out my camera and take as many pictures as I can of the architecture and view of the city below us. I also insist Enzo and I take a few selfies together, since it's his birthday after all. You don't turn thirty-eight every day. He teases me the entire time about being a cougar trying to steal his virtue. Yes, I'm nearly a year older than him, but it's not that big of a deal. Age is just a number anyway, not something that defines you.

We stop at a café for a late breakfast. Still scared of being sick again, I only get a light pastry and coffee. Then we make our way to another beautiful castle in Thallichtenberg, Germany. This one is the biggest castle ruins in all of Germany. It overlooks the outskirts of town and looks much more rustic than the previous one we toured.

As we walk the grounds, I'm in complete awe. It feels like something fairytales are made of. I can't believe I get to experience this. You don't see something this old in the United States. Not only do I get to share this magnificent experience with an amazing man, I get to learn more about the history of Germany as well. I'll never forget this trip with Enzo. I take it all in, trying to engrain this experience in my memory.

Enzo whispers in my ear while I'm lost in thought, "Does this make me Prince Charming?" My only response is to kiss him senseless and make this a dream come true.

On our way to the third castle for the day, my stomach starts to quiver. *Fuck! I know I'm going to be sick again.* I beg

Enzo to pull over, and I relieve myself on the side of the road. This time, after he's assured that I'm done puking, he insists on taking me to the hospital. I'm feeling so fucking weak again, I can hardly protest. *This isn't how I wanted to spend my fucking vacation. I'm a single mother of three, can't I catch a break? I just want to spend time with the man I love, explore a new country, and enjoy this once in a lifetime opportunity. What the hell is wrong with the universe? I should not be sick right now.*

In sheer exhaustion, I fall asleep cursing the universe, only to be woken when we arrive at a hospital. Since all my energy has been zapped out of me and I can barely stand, the nurse insists on me being in a wheelchair. *Great. Now I'm an invalid as well as a puking monster. What must Enzo think? I sure know how to live it up while I'm with him. Geesh!*

When the nurse asks if Enzo is family, he says, "I'm her fiancé." I don't give it much thought. There's no way I want to go through those doors alone. I'm sicker than I've ever been, and I'm beginning to worry about the possibilities of what might be wrong as well.

A nurse comes in to take my vitals. She draws some blood and asks a series of questions. After a while, the doctor comes in and does a quick exam. Well, *quick* may be an oxymoron. *Nothing* seems quick when I'm feeling this miserable. He throws around words like appendicitis, gallbladder, kidney infection, sending Enzo and me into heightened tension, as we await the results. Neither of us says much, but I can tell we're both more anxious as time slowly passes. A nurse comes back in and asks if I can give a urine sample and thank God, she offers to help me. *Enzo has been a godsend, but that might be pushing our love too far.*

As soon as I get settled in the hospital bed, Enzo takes my hands. He kneels beside me on the bed and he almost shouts, "Samantha!"

Surprised by his sudden enthusiasm, I ask, "Yes?" wondering what has him so worked up.

In a much calmer tone and demeanor, he states, "I need you to know how much I love you."

I'm not dying. Just really sick. He doesn't need to get so worked up over this. "I love you, too," I soothingly say as I place my hand on his forearm to calm him.

He clears his throat and begins again, this time his words coming out as a caress. "Samantha, I need you to know how much I love you. I've never met anyone like you. You've become the most important person in my life."

Okay, now he has my attention. Where's he going with this? I don't respond to let him continue.

"Samantha, no matter what those test results say, I will be with you in sickness and in health. I want you to know that I will always have your best interests at heart. I'm sure there will be times you're going to have to put me in my place. I can be a little thick headed."

Gee... you think? I still don't know where he's going with this, but I can't help but laugh at the last statement. Thankfully, he joins me as well.

Once we stop, he continues, "But know that I will always do it out of love."

He takes a deep breath to collect his thoughts. I nod at him to continue. Something about the way he just said, 'in sickness and in health' and he's professing his love for me, has piqued my curiosity.

Oh My God! Could he be...???

"These past six weeks of being apart has made me a miserable bastard. I don't want to spend another day without you being mine."

Oh My God, he is...

I can't help it, I'm a nervous laugher. I pull him to me and give him a quick kiss, not caring that I have vomit breath. I'm too caught up in the moment.

He pulls away and continues, this time capturing my entire heart, "Samantha Elizabeth O'Reilly, would you do me the honor of being my wife? Will you marry me and make me the happiest man alive?"

He reaches into his pocket and pulls out an exquisite white-gold diamond ring. It's a three-diamond setting that represents the past, present, and future, the largest being in the middle. I'm nearly in tears. This is the last thing I expected.

When he looks me in the eye, I know without a doubt what my answer will be. He's everything I could ever dream of. Although I'm sick as a dog, he loves me. He loves me no matter what.

I nod profusely because I can't talk. Tears stream down my cheeks and I'm certain I've terrified him.

He eyes me warily to get my full reaction. *Why can't this be one of the times my filter doesn't work? I need to tell him yes, but I can't even speak. Emotion consumes me.*

"Is that a yes, Samantha?"

"Yes!" I gasp through tears. "Yes, I'll marry you!"

He stands to lean over me in the bed, embracing me with everything he has and nearly squeezes the life out of me.

"Samantha, you just made me the happiest man on earth. I love you so much!"

"I love you, Enzo," I say as he pulls back to look me in the eye.

He takes a look around the room, then he lets out a laugh. "I know this isn't the most romantic place, but I've been wanting to ask you to marry me since you stepped off that plane."

He did? "You did?" I practically stutter. I'm shocked.

"Yes, being apart from you put things into perspective. I've never let myself get close to anyone, but our time apart has made me realize you're it for me. I'll move heaven and earth to make things work with you."

"Wow," is all I can whisper. I know we have a lot to work out, like how to tell the kids, when we'll tell them, and most importantly, how will they react?

Enzo continues, "What do you say we get you better first, then we call the kids and tell them the news?"

It's as if he's reading my mind.

A few minutes later, the doctor comes back in.

He looks at each of us, then takes a deep breath. "It looks like we can't do the CT scans at this time."

Oh. My. God! What's wrong with me?

Enzo barks, "Why the fuck not? She's been sick for days."

"Well..." The man before us doesn't cower in Enzo's sudden anger. The doctor stands a good six inches under Enzo and calmly says, "I already know the reason for her sickness."

Enzo's vein on his neck pops and he's enraged, barely holding it together. "Are you a New Age doctor who has premonitions? Why aren't you giving her the tests?" I almost feel sorry for the man in white.

Once again, calm as can be, "Sir, I have. Calm down and I'll explain."

Tension rolls off Enzo in waves. I feel it as it stretches across the room. I reach for his hand and he immediately calms. *I love knowing that I have that effect on him.*

I squeeze his hand, causing him to look at me. "I love you," I whisper.

"I love you, too." He bends down to kiss me on the forehead, then we look to the doctor for further explanation.

"Go ahead," I say.

The doctor looks sheepishly for a moment, which seems a bit out of place, then steels his features and simply states, "You're pregnant."

What. The. Fuck.

I can't get pregnant!

"Excuse me? I tried for years. Nothing happened. I thought I couldn't get pregnant."

"Well, you apparently can." The doctor smiles. "I'll have an ultrasound brought in. From your hormone levels, you appear to be pretty far along."

I gasp and count back the weeks from my last period. "But, I've had my period not that long ago."

"We'll find out more with an ultrasound, Mrs. O'Reilly."

I finally turn to Enzo, who has been unusually quiet this entire time. When his eyes lock with mine, the expression on his face is complete and utter shock. *Oh my God, he's going to think I've trapped him.*

What the fuck am I going to do? I'm thirty-eight years old,

for crying out loud. I already have three kids, and Maddie's almost fifteen. People are going to think *she's* the mother, not me. I'm going to be asked if I'm this child's grandma. I'm going to be a laughingstock.

How the hell am I even pregnant? *Well, I know how.* But Devin and I tried for years. *Years!* I remember month after month hoping for it to happen, getting to the point where I utterly hated my period. How did I not get pregnant then? What's different now?

Enzo. That's what. I turn to look at the man next to me. His beautiful features are like stone. For once, I can't read his expression. It scares the shit out of me.

Enzo's kind, loving, and has spent his entire life being single. He's never settled down or been with anyone serious. Being with my family and me is one thing. Adding a baby to the mix? He's going to run for the hills the first chance he gets.

2

ENZO

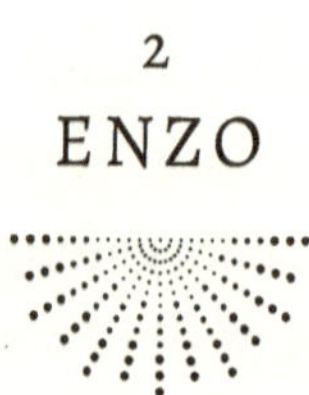

Yes, I'm scared shitless. Yes, this is completely unexpected. But when I look at the woman before me who looks utterly freaked out, I'm at a loss for what to do. I love her no matter what, but what if she doesn't want this? What if she doesn't want any more kids? Would I be okay with letting her make that decision for us? I wish I could find a way to take the look of terror off her face. It's my fault we never use condoms. It's my fault she's going through this now.

The doctor and nurse return, wheeling in a large machine. It has a wand-like thing and a monitor. There's also a long stick thingy on the side, next to where the wand for the ultrasound is.

The doctor presses his hands across Samantha's belly. It's light, but it makes me nervous. *What if he hurts the baby?* Samantha's already in a hospital gown since she was expecting to take a series of other tests, not an ultrasound for pregnancy.

The doctor adjusts the sheet so she's covered and opens up

24

her gown to expose her stomach. He squirts some gel onto the wand, then moves it around. For a few minutes, there's nothing.

"I was afraid of this," he says ominously. *What. The. Fuck. Is. Wrong? We just found out she's pregnant.*

"What?" Samantha squeaks.

"I'm afraid I'm going to have to use the vaginal wand," the doctor says as an explanation.

Samantha lets out a sigh and I still don't have a fucking clue as to what's going on. I finally ask, since no one says anything else, "What does that mean, Doc?" I feel the muscles in my jaw clench.

The doctor looks at me with kind eyes, and I relax a little. "It means she's likely not that far along and I'll have to do a vaginal ultrasound since it's too small to see at this point."

Samantha reaches for my hand. "Don't worry, Enzo. I did this with my other pregnancies. All turned out fine."

Her touch soothes me, along with her words. I feel myself relax.

The doctor wipes the gel off her stomach. "Would you like me to step out of the room while you remove your underwear?"

Samantha sighs and shakes her head. "What's the point? You're going to see it all anyway. There's no modesty in pregnancy, right?"

Meanwhile, I'm over here thinking, *What the fuck is she talking about? I don't want any man looking at her vagina, but me.*

Before I can say anything, Samantha shimmies out of her underwear and hands them to me. She manages to stay covered, but *what am I supposed to do with them? Shit.* I don't want to look like a fool, so I stuff them in my pocket. That takes care of one problem.

The doctor picks up this long-handled thing and squirts gel onto the end. *He's going to stick that… where?* Then it dawns on me and I can't help that I'm suddenly thinking of dildos. *Jesus Christ, I'm about to see my child for the first time and I'm thinking about dildos. Great! What a great dad I'll be. Thank God, she can't hear what I'm thinking. This woman's carrying my baby and here I am acting like a randy teenager. What the fuck is wrong with me?*

"Oh, that's cold." Samantha gasps, breaking me out of my revelry.

On the monitor, there's a blur of motion. Suddenly, I hear a birdlike drumbeat. It's soft and fast.

"There's the heartbeat," the doctor announces to the room.

I. Am. In. Awe. I can hear my child's heartbeat. I look to Samantha, who has tears welling in her eyes. She's the most gorgeous woman in the world, and she's carrying my baby. I'm a lucky bastard.

"I love you, Samantha," I whisper to her. If I speak any louder, my voice will break.

When the doctor moves the wand around, I hear something different. This time it's louder and slower.

"What's that?" I ask.

"That's Samantha's heartbeat."

"Here." The doctor points to a place on the screen. "You can see the heartbeat on the screen. See the flitter? There it is."

But I see more than one flitter.

"Um, Doc?" I'm about to ask more when Samantha beats me to it.

"Do I see two heartbeats on that screen?" Her voice is high at the end.

The doctor beams with excitement and his nurse says, "Congratulations!"

"Yes," the doctor confirms. "You're having twins!"

"Holy shit!" Samantha exclaims. She looks to me and adds, "You not only knocked me up, but you gave me twins?" She seems a little bewildered at the end.

I'm pretty sure her filter has left the building. I laugh aloud.

I look at her with shock written all over my face, I'm sure. "Twins, beautiful. We're having twins."

The most beautiful smile spreads across her face, and I nearly melt.

3

SAMANTHA

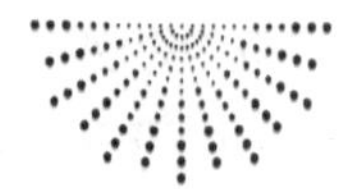

THE MOMENT I HEAR MY UNBORN CHILD'S HEARTBEAT I'M already in love. Tears roll down my face as I'm overwhelmed with joy. I realize, no matter what fears I've had before, I can get past them. I have a baby to care for. The light strum of the heartbeat brings a calming sensation over me. Though, that calmness is short lived. When I see there are two heartbeats, I go into utter shock. *What. The. Ever. Loving. Fuckity. Fuck!!! This can't be happening!*

Enzo's face is almost humorous as it's the perfect mixture of shock and awe. I can't help but smile when his dimple pops. The damn thing gets me every time.

The two of us remain silent as we stare at one another. Soon, the nurse and doctor excuse themselves and it's just us. They mention something about bringing a prescription for anti-nausea medicine and prenatal vitamins, but I can only focus on the man before me. *I wish he would tell me what he's thinking.*

He places his hand on mine and the inevitable pull we seem to share is back in full force. It calms me, even though there's a storm inside my head at the moment. Like a cyclone, I have ten thousand thoughts swirling through my mind. I wish I could catch one and voice it aloud. I wish I had the words to put his worried look at ease.

Just as I'm about to say something, a nurse comes in and gives me instructions for the medication. She takes the IV out of my arm that they had put in for dehydration when I first arrived. I laugh and shake my head at the thought of worrying about a gallbladder, kidney, or my appendix. Instead, the news I received today has totally knocked my world off its axis.

Soon, we'll be released from the hospital, though our lives will never be the same. We came in as Enzo and Samantha. We're leaving as Enzo, Samantha, plus two.

I continue to be lost in my head during the short car ride to Enzo's apartment. Not surprisingly, he's a gentleman through and through. He's held my hand through it all and not gone running for the hills, yet. Though, I wouldn't blame him if he did, with my freak out at the hospital. I'm dying to ask him if we're okay, but I'm mortified of what his answer will be. What if he doesn't really want kids of his own? We've never talked about this before. Now that I think about it, there's still so much about him I don't know.

We go inside, and Enzo remains unusually silent as he makes dinner. Making sure I eat properly was one of the doctor's suggestions. I can't help but find it endearing that Enzo still wants to take care of me.

I make a quick trip to the bathroom, then curl up on the couch, and snuggle under the blanket. I'm exhausted from all the puking, as well as the emotional whirlwind of the day, but a part of me can't help but be a little excited. The initial shock is wearing off and the thought of having another baby—correction—*babies*, makes me a little giddy.

Holy crap, I'm going to be the mother of twins. I know that having one baby is a rollercoaster ride of its own, but I can't imagine what it will be like with two. I really hope I haven't scared Enzo off. I don't want to do this alone. I know I can, but God, I hope his silence is just him processing this information, not him trying to find the words to let me down easy.

Apparently, I'm lost in thought. The next thing I know, he's bringing me dinner and it smells delicious. Thank God, the doctor gave me anti-nausea medicine. I still have about a week left in Germany and I want to see more than the inside of a toilet. I almost feel human again.

Once I've eaten, I set my plate down on the coffee table. I notice Enzo hasn't eaten a bite. The man always eats, so something must be wrong. *Fuck, how did I miss this?*

"Are you okay?" I ask hesitantly.

"The more important question is, are you?" Enzo locks eyes with me and it's as if he's peering deep into my soul.

"I'm okay. I'm apparently pregnant, but okay," I whisper as I cradle my belly in my hands. "I can't believe this happened. With twins. It's a lot to take in." I inhale a deep breath and release it slowly.

"Yeah, it is," he whispers, still holding my gaze. I can't get a read on him, and the unknown is enough to do me in for good.

I take a deep breath and steel myself for what I need to tell him. This uncertainty has gone on long enough. It's time I let him off the hook and deal with whatever reality may bring. Tears prick my eyes as I start, "Enzo, I understand if you... I mean, I really didn't think I could get pregnant..." I stammer.

Before I can say anything more, his deep voice fills the room, "I meant what I said. I want to marry you. Now, we'll just do it sooner. I can't wait to have these babies with you." The pensive look on his face still has me completely unsettled.

I let out a shaky breath. "Are you sure? Babies change a lot," I say, giving him an out. I don't want him to feel trapped. He didn't sign up for this.

Enzo looks at me with kind eyes and says, "Samantha Elizabeth O'Reilly-soon-to-be-Harper." *Oh, I like the sound of that.* "Get this through your head. I. Love. You. I want to be with you. Having children with you is a dream I didn't know could exist, but now, I'm ecstatic to have it become a reality." The sincerity on his face gives me hope. He cocks a light smile and that damn dimple pops, making me swoon.

His words calm me, but only for a moment, before another thought pops in my head. "What about my other children?" I ask, panicking. Crap, how could I forget about Maddie, Dec, and Frankie? I didn't forget. No, I just hadn't considered he was already taking them on. These twins are certainly throwing me off. Can pregnancy brain be blamed, this early in the game?

Enzo releases a deep belly laugh, letting that delicious dimple pop once again. It stops me in my tracks, keeping my panic at bay.

"Samantha, beautiful. I already love your children. Otherwise, I wouldn't have asked you to marry me. Don't think for one second that I will love them any less. I have room in my heart for all of you."

"You do?" I stupidly ask, not knowing what else to say.

He takes my hands in his. "I didn't know what I'd been missing until I met you. You've made my meager existence thrive. I can't imagine my life without you and your kids now. Correction—*our* kids. Now we'll just have more to love."

Relief washes over me to know that he thinks of my kids as his own. "You're right," I sigh. "I love you for pointing that out."

"Anytime, beautiful, anytime."

"What if people call us grandparents?" Another worry wiggles its way out of my mouth.

Enzo chuckles. "No one's going to call you a grandma anytime soon. You're far too sexy for that. Besides, people have babies in their forties all the time. You'll only be thirty-nine; it's not like it's *that* unusual."

"Great, now people are going to be calling me the cradle-robbing grandma. Just what I need." I pretend to pout.

"Samantha, I just turned thirty-eight today. You're still thirty-eight for another six months. You're not that much older than I." His laughter does wonderful things to my insides.

"Happy Birthday, Enzo!" I exclaim in pure joy, then tease, "I guess I don't have to give you a birthday present now, do I?"

Enzo's smile spreads even wider across his face. "Happy Birthday to me, indeed. Thank you for the most wonderful gift." He kisses me on the lips.

"*Gifts*," I remind. "Although, you might not be thanking me at this time next year when neither of us is getting any sleep."

"Best birthday, EVER!" he emphasizes by rearranging us

on the couch, so that we're both able to fit and bends down to kiss me again. Maybe it's the extra hormones I have flowing through me, maybe it's just Enzo, but suddenly, I only want to focus on him.

4

ENZO

Samantha feels much better now that the anti-nausea medicine has kicked in. A look mixed of hunger and lust suddenly fills her face and I couldn't care less that I've yet to eat the dinner on the table in front of me. I'm just so fucking happy that she's healthy and not upset about being pregnant.

The car ride home was brutal. For once, her filter stayed intact and I had no clue what was going through her mind. Of course, I was silent as well, but it's not every day I find out I'm going to be a father. I also wanted to give her some time to process this new information. I know I needed it.

Twins. That's a hell of a lot to take in. Samantha already has three wonderful children, but now she's going to be a mother of five. *Fuck! Talk about an instant family.* I already love her children as much as I love her, and I hope they at least like me a little. It's all pretty new, but I have never felt as close to anyone as the way I feel about Samantha. And those babies inside her, I'm already in love with them, too.

34

I honestly never thought I'd be a father. I love kids, but with my age and the fact that I've never settled down, I just didn't think kids would be in the cards for me. Hell, I'm thirty-eight years old. Haven't been in a serious relationship in nearly twenty years. *What makes me qualified to be a dad?* Give me something to fly out of any type of danger zone imaginable, I'm your man. But toting tiny tots that are mine?

Samantha distracts my hurricane of thoughts and suddenly has my sole focus, when she straddles my lap. The second her hands run through what little hair I have on my head, thanks to my high and tight haircut from being back on duty, my senses are on overload. When her lips graze mine, I can barely contain myself. I force myself to let her take the lead. It takes every bit of effort I have to sit back and enjoy her every move. My instinct is to stand and take her to the bedroom, but for now, I'll just see what she has in mind.

"I love you, Enzo," she whispers as she kisses across my jawline and down my neck. Her hand roams down my chest and pulls at the hem of my shirt. I lean forward and quickly remove it with one hand, barely breaking our contact.

"I love you more than ever, beautiful," comes out huskier than expected.

She resumes kissing down my jawline to my neck, then chest, sending my body on fire. My hands seem to have minds of their own as I reach under her shirt, connecting with her silky-smooth skin. Electricity zings through me, making my nerve endings come to life. One hand reaches around her back to pull her closer while the other caresses her breast through her bra. *This just won't do.* With a practiced move, I release her bra with one hand and cup her full, smooth breast, causing her to make the most beautiful moan I've ever heard.

"That's right, beautiful. Tell me what you want." Fuck, I just want to lay her on this couch and completely have my way with her.

"You," she says in a groan as she goes for the fly of my jeans. "I just want you."

I can't take it anymore. I stand and she wraps those sexy as fuck legs around my waist. I walk to the bedroom and set her down in front of the bed. The minute her feet hit the floor, she's undoing her pants and sliding them down. I take her lead and shed myself from my own clothing briskly. I can't even assist her in removing her shirt because as I take a step toward her, she rips it over her head, sending it flying through the air, across the room.

Now that we're both naked as the day we were born, I close the gap between us, kissing her with everything I have. I grip her ass firmly in both hands and lift her gently onto the bed, as my mouth devours hers. She tastes slightly of marinara sauce and something that is entirely Samantha. I break our kiss, making my way down her body, making sure I pay close attention to all the places that I've learned drive her wild. I kiss that spot behind her ear, which sends her toes and fists grasping the sheets. I trail down her neck and worship each breast the best way I know how. Her body writhes as if it's ready for release. I reach with one hand between her legs and find she's exactly as I thought. Wet and ready for me. I barely press my thumb against her clit, slip a finger inside of her, and she detonates. Her core clamps around my finger and pulsates fervently as I pull on one nipple with my teeth, playing with her other taut nipple with my free hand. I continue to assault her senses as she rides her high to completion.

The moment her body's calm and sated, I remove my fingers and kiss down to her belly. It's still flat and sexy as hell. I can see faint stretch marks from previous pregnancies, and I can't help but wonder what she will look like, round with my children inside her. I can't help but whisper to Samantha's belly button, "I love you already, little ones. Be good to your ma and let her stay healthy for you. We're going to do everything we can to give you the best future we can."

I look up at Samantha, who has tears threatening to fall, as they pool at her lashes. "Oh, Enzo." Her voice cracks at the end of my name. "You'll be the most amazing dad."

Pride soars through my heart, feeling as if it could burst out of my chest. I don't know shit about being a dad, but that look of confidence Samantha has on her face, makes me feel as if I can conquer anything. "I sure hope so, Sam. You're already a pro and I'm just a rookie. I'm sure I'll make lots of mistakes." Honesty pours from my soul as her tears release and a smile takes over her face.

"Enzo, honey," she sighs and a light laugh escapes as she rubs her hand through my hair. "No one is perfect. We all make mistakes. Trust me. I'm nowhere near perfect. The key is to make the best decision for the situation and hope like hell it all turns out in the end."

"You make it sound so easy," I say as she pulls me to her for a quick kiss. My treacherous dick makes its presence known. I groan and pull back, not wanting to make her feel any pressure. She has been sick for days and I want this to be about her. *Yeah, I want her just like a dying man wants his next breath, but I can show some restraint.*

Apparently, she doesn't want me to pull away as she reaches out and strokes me. I'm still hesitant. I know what I want, but, *what if I hurt her or our children? Is it even safe to have sex?!?!?*

She sees my hesitation and a flash of concern crosses her face. "What's wrong, Enzo?"

How should I say this? I don't want her to think I don't want her. I obviously do, but now's not the time to be thinking with *that* head. He's what got us into this situation, to begin with. "Um..." Fuck. I'm a grown man. Why can't I ask this simple question? "Are you sure you want this?"

"Enzo..." She looks between our naked bodies and gives my cock another tug toward her. "I want this." Her desire is evident and makes my hesitation even more unbearable.

"Are you... Are you sure I won't hurt you or the babies?" I watch her closely to see if there's anything left unsaid.

She laughs. Not just a little chuckle or a smirk, but full-on belly laughs. She shakes her head, showing no empathy as she takes my hand and pulls me closer to her. Why is she laughing?

"Enzo, sweetheart." She takes in a deep breath before continuing, "There's nothing you can do to me that will harm me or the babies."

"Are you sure? There are two living beings in your belly. I don't want to do anything that could harm either of them. Or you for that matter." I look away, feeling slightly ashamed for jumping to this conclusion. I've never been with a pregnant woman before. I don't know the protocol for this. I just want to do right by her.

"Enzo... Sweetheart. Look at me." My eyes immediately lock with hers as her voice is suddenly urgent. "I'm safe and the kids are safe. Pregnant women have sex all the time. It's perfectly safe and acceptable. In fact, if my memory serves correctly, in just a few short weeks, I'm going to be demanding it on a regular basis. Once I hit the second trimester with all my kids, I practically craved it." A devilish grin appears on her face before she continues, "With you... Since I even want you when I don't feel at my best..." A loud groan escapes her, "Heaven help you if I want to jump you from the moment we wake up, until the moment I pass out at night..." She pulls me closer to make her point and kisses me like she's never kissed me before. I could fuckin' die, right here, right now, and I could say I've lived a blissful existence.

After all too short of time, I pull back, "Well, if you insist... who am I to resist?" I quickly resume kissing her and work my way to completely making love to her until we both pass out from pure exhaustion.

The next morning, Samantha wakes with energy, thanks to the anti-nausea medicine the doctor gave her. She actually beats me out of bed and is in the kitchen making an enormous breakfast wearing nothing but my Air Force t-shirt. Her dark mahogany hair's in a messy bun, and she's swaying to the music playing from her phone. Her back is to me as I enter the room and I can't help but just stop and watch her enjoy herself. I recognize the song as Justin Timberlake's "SexyBack." *Yeah, she has no problem bringing sexy back. It never left her.* I know I should let her know I'm here—*it'd be the polite thing to do*—but I'm simply too mesmerized. Samantha's the sexiest woman I've ever met, and when she lets loose and enjoys the world, nothing's better than the sight before me.

The song ends and Ed Sheeran's "Shape of You" begins and I can't help but grin. To me, this has been 'Our' song, since our first dance together. Every time it plays on the radio, flashbacks of that night come to mind. There's no way I'm letting her dance alone with those words filling the room. I walk up to hold her from behind and dance with her like our night at Allure, the club my friend Rowan owns in Portland. She continues flipping pancakes, even as our bodies sway together. Once they're done, she turns to finish the song by dancing in my arms.

"I could get used to waking up like this," I say as she finally faces me.

"Good morning, Enzo."

She places her arms around my neck and kisses me.

"Mornin', beautiful."

She pulls back to look me in the eyes. "After breakfast, let's go to Frankfurt and see the sights. I want to make the most of my time here, now that I'm not puking my guts out. That medicine is a lifesaver, really. I can't wait to see more of Germany."

"Your wish is my command," I tease as I kiss her lightly on the lips.

"Don't get carried away," Samantha warns with a tease. "I love your place, but I want to see more of Germany."

Although I'd rather get carried away with her, I release Samantha to get the plates from the cupboard. "Let's eat then."

We spend the day being tourists. I drive her through Frankfurt, and she loves the skyscrapers and the buzz of the busy city. She recognizes the Euro symbol as we pass the European Central Bank and asks to stop to take photos there. It's right next to the S-Bahn Station, so we decide if we're going to be tourists, we might as well ride the street cars.

Another of Samantha's favorite places is Eiserner Steg. It's an older iron pedestrian bridge across the River Main, which connects the center of Frankfurt to the district of Sachsenhausen. It was originally built in 1868, bombed in World War II, by Hitler's troops near the end of the war, and rebuilt for pedestrians afterward. We arrive there right as the sun is setting. I manage to get some spectacular shots of Samantha. We also capture some of my favorite pictures of us on the bridge, thanks to a couple who offers to take our photos.

By the time we get back to my place, Samantha looks dead on her feet. We'd eaten out at one of the local restaurants, and I'm so relieved Samantha has her energy back, as well as her appetite.

5

SAMANTHA

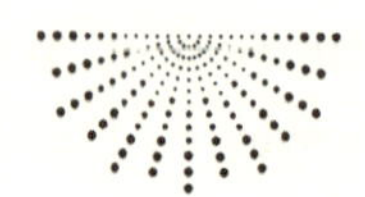

THANK GOD, I'M FEELING BETTER. I'M FULLY CONVINCED THE doctors gave me miracle medicine. Sure, I'm tired but that is to be expected with any pregnancy. I have to say, now that I'm not nauseous, I love the local foods, such as the fresh bread rolls with fruit marmalade. Give me that with some eggs for breakfast, and I'm set for the day. I also love schnitzel, spätzle, and bratwurst with local vegetables. Now that I can eat, I seem to be devouring everything in sight. *God, I hope I don't gain a hundred pounds in this pregnancy. But, I'm eating for three, right?!?!*

Enzo, unfortunately, has to return to work for a couple of days during the last week of my visit. He manages to stay on base, so he's home at night. I spend my days either reading or touring locally. Enzo lets me drive his Land Rover, which makes it so I can go to the City Museum in Ramstein. It's interesting to learn about the local history. I also venture to Trier, Germany, which is one of the oldest cities in the country.

It's heavily influenced by the Romans. If Enzo and I have time before I leave, I'd like to return here to visit one of the Roman bathhouses with him.

The best part about my time with Enzo is the evenings. I just love being with him, in his element. I'm getting used to making love through the night and waking up in his arms. I can't wait until we can do this every day.

It's going to suck when I have to leave on Monday, and he has to stay for two more months. I do my best not to think about it now; long-distance relationships have taken their toll on my life. When these horrific thoughts make their way into my mind, I try to squash them like a bug. Enzo isn't Devin, plain and simple. He knows firsthand how devastating it was to have someone move on while he was away. There's no doubt in my mind that he won't stray in the slightest. He's head over heels for me and these babies growing inside me. I know from the bottom of my heart he feels the same way I do, though it doesn't hurt that he makes the time to assure me of this each and every day I've been here. I think I love this man more than I've ever loved anyone. There's just no comparison.

Yes, of course, I miss my kids at home like crazy. I video-chat with them daily. Seeing them on the screen makes me miss them more. I don't remember the last time I've been away from them this long. After a lengthy conversation, Enzo and I decided not to tell them about my pregnancy until I'm through my first trimester, which is after he returns from Germany. We want to tell them together, in person. I just hope these babies will let me keep this secret until he gets home. Between morning sickness and the fact I'll likely start showing sooner with twins, I'm keeping my fingers crossed.

Today's Friday and Enzo's expected home in the early afternoon. He's off for the weekend, so I stayed in for the day and let him take his car. I've finished reading a manuscript I brought with me and spent the day responding to emails from work. With the time difference, it's easier to keep in contact with clients via email.

I'm deep in concentration when I hear the door handle rattle with the sound of keys. I look up to find Enzo walking through the door. He's dressed in his uniform, which consists of a dark green jumpsuit and combat boots. Holy Hell, is he hot. In a well-practiced move, he removes his cap and stuffs it into his pocket on his pants leg. The smile that lights up his face has me melting in seconds. That damn dimple will have me spontaneously combusting on the spot if he continues to use it at full force. His deep timbre greets me, "Hey, beautiful. How was your day?"

I try my best to clear my laptop and the mound of papers around me so I can get up to greet him. He laughs at my distress and closes the distance between us within seconds. He reaches for my computer and sets it beside me on the coffee table. I reach my hand out to him and he effortlessly assists me into a standing position. I manage to get, "Great, how was yours?" out before my lips are crushed by his.

Damn! He tastes delicious. I don't think I will ever get used to the backflips the butterflies in my stomach like to perform when he appears. I wrap my hands around his neck and pull back to look into his glorious, green eyes. For a few moments, I'm mesmerized by the look of pure pleasure reflected in them.

"I've never been more thankful I get to spend the weekend with you. Since I wasn't off base, my day was a shitstorm of prepping for our mission next week." He pulls me in for another kiss, then bends down to kiss my belly over my clothes and talks to our babies, like he does every day. "Have you been good to your ma today?"

I can't help the giggle that escapes when he nuzzles his slightly scruffy cheek against my abdomen. "That miracle medicine seems to have done the trick. I've been a little tired, but no nausea to speak of," I sigh in relief.

Enzo stands and wraps his arms around me in a hug once again. "Good to hear. I have no fucking clue how I'm going to survive being apart from you when you leave Monday." The tone of his voice by the end nearly slays me. There's a desperate need and desire that nearly rips me to the core.

I take in a deep breath and steel my spine, knowing this is hard on both of us. There's no need for me to make it more difficult for him than I need to. "I know. I feel the same."

"Will you do me a favor?" Enzo asks as he pulls away from our embrace to look me in the eye.

"Anything," I say without hesitation because there's nothing I won't do for the man.

"Will you send me a belly shot each day?"

Belly Shot? I cock my head to the side and look at him, wanting to make sure I understand him correctly.

Before I can respond, he says, "Send me a picture of a side profile, so I can see them grow and not miss any of the changes that happen during your pregnancy."

Understanding washes over me and I smile. "Of course, I'll do that. Though, the changes will be very subtle every day. You know that, right?"

"Sam, I don't want to miss anything. I hate that I'm not

going to be there with you. There'll also be times when I'm out in the field, and I won't get to contact you each day. The photos will be something I cherish." Enzo seems to be in deep thought for a moment, then all of a sudden, he chuckles. "I used to harass the guys who lived for their daily photos from home. Now, I'm going crazy just thinking about you leaving." He strokes his hands down my back as he pulls me in for a tight embrace.

"If I didn't have kids to attend to, you know I'd rather be here so you wouldn't miss anything, right?" I try to assure him. "Besides, you'll be home in less than two months. We won't be apart for that long." I'm not sure if I'm trying to convince him or myself that this won't be too difficult.

"How do you think we should tell your kids we're engaged, let alone having twins?" Enzo sighs, catching me off guard.

"I've been wondering the same thing." I haven't come up with a good plan yet, but maybe we can come up with one together.

"What if we video-call them tonight and let them know I proposed to you? Then, when I come home for good, we can tell them about their new brothers or sisters."

"What if we have one of each?" I ask in wonder. This still doesn't seem real and I've known for almost a week.

"As long as you're *all* healthy, I don't care what we have. I just want you all to be safe." He pulls me toward his bedroom. "I need to change. Come with me, so we can continue to talk."

He turns and walks to his bedroom and I follow. "So, how do you think we should tell them?" Though the minute I see him shed his clothes, I'm no longer focused on the kids.

Enzo completely catches me off guard when he

nonchalantly says, "I've already told Declan and Maddie my intentions to ask you to marry me."

What?!?!?

"You have?" I ask, my words almost coming out as a shriek. Enzo gives me a dubious grin while that fucking dimple pops out, making me weak in the knees.

"Um, Sam." He suddenly looks sheepishly at me. "I spoke to each of them separately before I left for Germany."

"You did?" *When could he have done that?!?! How could they have kept it a secret for so long??? God, I wonder what their reaction was? Oh, to be a fly on the wall.*

The laugh that escapes Enzo lets me know my filter has gone amuck again. *Great.* "Samantha, I wouldn't have asked you if they weren't on board with it. They kept the secret because they wanted this to be a surprise for you. We all agreed that Frankie wouldn't keep it, though, so she, unfortunately, isn't in the know."

"Are they really okay with this? With you and me getting married? Us living together?" *I'm on sensory overload. There's no way this could go so easily.* I've been fretting about how to tell them, but I wanted to stay in this blissful bubble for as long as I could.

Enzo goes into specific details about each of his conversations with Maddie and Declan. I can tell he doesn't leave anything out because he cringes, as well as laughs, throughout his explanation. He admits they were both hesitant and maybe even shocked by their conversations. But once he had explained that he'd never felt this way about anyone before, they seemed to be more open to the idea.

I think the clincher for both Declan and Maddie was the

fact Enzo readily admitted his ultimate goal is to make me happy and be a part of our lives. He wants to spend as much time with us as possible when he returns to the States, and for the first time in his life, he wants a family of his own.

Having the twins will likely cause shock to my entire family, but I can't worry about that now. It's a bridge we'll have to cross later.

Enzo has me in stitches when he explains how serious Declan was in their conversation. Apparently, Dec alluded to the possibility of injuring Enzo, if he ever hurts me. I absolutely love that Enzo's response to Declan's attempt at a threat was, "I'll happily help you, should that ever happen. I never want to see your mom hurt." This, evidently, defused Declan's worries.

After I settle down from envisioning my ten-year-old puffing out his chest, posing a serious threat to the glorious man before me, Enzo continues to tell me how he promised them he wasn't trying to replace their father. He assures me that he let both Maddie and Dec know that he thinks Devin has always been a great dad to them, but he wants to find his place in their lives as well. This got both kids on board, which is a huge relief. I can't imagine telling our news to them without any forewarning. I guess I've been so wrapped up in our blissful bubble, I hadn't thought about the aftereffects.

Maddie was more resistant to the idea of us getting married at first, bringing up the fact it was too soon. In typical teenage fashion, she seemed standoffish and told him she didn't need another dad. Enzo further explains how he wore her down by telling her all the things he loves about me. This part makes me swoon, if I'm being honest. His charms seemed to work on her as well. Eventually, she told him she noticed how happy I'd been since he came into our lives, and she hoped he would keep the smile on my face.

When he's done with his explanation, Enzo lets out a huge breath. "So, what do you think about calling them later this evening? I know Maddie's dying to hear your response." He waggles his eyebrows and makes me fall in love with him even more.

"That sounds like a plan," I say as I wrap my arms around his neck, pulling him in for a hug. With Enzo being the sexy man that he is, it doesn't take long before I'm desperately wanting more.

6

ENZO

THE MINUTE SAMANTHA SAYS, "GUESS WHAT, KIDS?" TO ALL three faces on the screen of our video chat, Maddie immediately screams with excitement.

"You said YES!" Maddie enthusiastically concludes.

"Yep," I say before Samantha can respond. I couldn't be happier to share this news. I glance at Samantha and the excitement's evident on her face as well.

"I knew it." Maddie's smile is wider than I could have imagined. "When will it happen?"

"What happen?" Frankie asks everyone on her end of the screen.

"Congrats," quietly comes from Declan, ignoring Frankie's question. His arms are crossed against his chest and his face looks as if he's bored with this conversation. Not exactly how I pictured this moment, but he's not looking upset, so I'll take it.

"Thanks, Dec. Well, Frankie." Samantha takes a deep

breath and squeezes my hand out of sight of the camera for support. "Enzo asked me to marry him."

The look of pure astonishment has me wondering if I should have included her in my conversation with Maddie and Declan. I know she's only eight, but she seems a little put out by the fact her brother and sister were *'in the know'* and she was not. *Fuck. Did I mess up here?*

"Really?!?!" Frankie still seems dumbfounded. Her eyes are wide and her mouth hangs open until she asks, "You're getting married?"

I look to Samantha to see how we should proceed, but she just gives me a slight shrug and lifts her eyebrows. *Why couldn't her filter be broken at this moment?* I'm dying here. Fuck, I have no clue if Frankie's excited or pissed! Jesus. What should I do? How can I fix this?

I glance over at Samantha once again and she's scrutinizing the screen to gauge Frankie's reaction as well. I can't take the silence any longer, so I break in by saying, "Yeah, sweetheart, we are."

Frankie looks far too serious for an eight-year-old. Damn, she could put my CO to shame for her pensiveness. The mask she wears on her unresponsive face has my stomach dropping to my feet. *Shit. Damn. Fuck. I screwed up.* I love Samantha more than anything, but not knowing if her kids will accept me is worse than the thought of being captured by insurgents. There's no way I want to live without any of them in my life. But I can't marry her if her family isn't on board.

"Frankie?" Samantha quietly says as she reaches for the screen. Her desire to comfort her child is evident.

"What's wrong, Franks?" Maddie asks as she puts her arm

around her little sister. I can tell by the look on Samantha's face it's killing her not to be there comforting Frankie herself. Hell, *I'd* give anything to be there to comfort her, if I could.

"I…" Frankie gasps, taking in a big breath of air. My blood turns to ice as I await her response. "I…"

"What is it, Frankie? You can tell us anything," Samantha coaxes as she reaches out and places a vise grip on my leg beside her.

Through the screen, I can see tears well up at the corners of Frankie's eyes. I might as well be sliced through the heart with a dull tablespoon, this pain caused by her reaction is immeasurable.

"I… missed it?" Frankie asks in disbelief, causing more confusion than anguish to wash over me.

"Missed what, Sweetheart?" I attempt to get her to clarify.

"I—" *gasp*—"missed—" *sniffle*—"the…wedding?"

Relief washes through both Samantha and me immediately. I can physically feel each of us relax, as we realize her misconception. "No, Frankie. You haven't missed anything." Samantha lets out a low laugh. "Enzo only has *asked* me to marry him. We will include all of you in the ceremony!"

Suddenly, Frankie beams with delight. It's as if she hadn't been about to fall apart just moments ago. "Really, I get to be in it?"

With tears filling her eyes, Samantha nods. She attempts to say something, but it gets stuck in her throat. I break the silence by saying, "Frankie, we couldn't get married without you."

"Wheeeee!" Frankie shouts, "Do I get a fancy dress and everything?"

"Goofball," Maddie chides as she rumples her sister's hair.

"Does this mean we *all* have to dress up?" Declan asks as if he seems really put out by the idea. The look of pure disgust is almost comical. I can't say I wouldn't have said the same thing at his age.

I glance to Samantha since we haven't discussed any of the details yet. I would marry her today if we were all in one place. I have no idea what kind of wedding she wants. If I'm being honest, I couldn't care less. I just want to spend the rest of my life by her side.

"Of course, we're going to dress up, dork," Maddie says in disbelief as she gives her brother the stink-eye, as only a big sister can. "This is Mom's wedding. It's a special occasion."

I hear Declan groan quietly and can't help the grin that forms on my face.

"We won't torture you too much," I assure him.

When Samantha asks what's new with everyone, the subject naturally changes. We chat for a while longer, with each of them telling us what they have been doing for the past day or so. Of course, we don't tell them Samantha's been in the hospital, or that they are about to have two new siblings. That's something that needs to be done in person. This has already been more of a roller coaster ride than I could have ever imagined. One thing's for sure, I'll never underestimate Frankie's need to feel included again. Just the thought of her feeling completely left out and rejected sends shivers down my spine. Lesson learned.

Unfortunately, the rest of our weekend passes much too quickly. Samantha and I spend every moment possible wrapped in each other's arms. We manage to tour more around Frankfurt and the surrounding areas. She even convinces me to spend an afternoon at a Roman bathhouse. It was a relaxing and unique experience. I would certainly never have done anything like that without Samantha's encouragement. She makes being a tourist an art form. I'll never forget this experience with her. It's as if her mere presence brings vibrant colors to my life, that had once been only contrasting shades of gray.

I know she's exhausted with the pregnancy, but Samantha has more than enough energy to show her true feelings toward me. Of course, the highlights for me include making love to her until we both fall asleep from pure bliss and utter exhaustion. I have no fucking clue as to how I'm going to spend a day apart from her, let alone six weeks.

Thankfully, I know I'll be busy after she leaves. Not only do I have to work, but I have to pack my apartment and ship things back to the States within the next few weeks. I've scheduled the movers to be here in two weeks. Then I'll live in the barracks on post until I complete my contract, since I'm shipping my car home as well.

Since Samantha packed only one bag to travel, I've decided to send another bag with her when she returns. That way I'll have some of my civilian things with me when I return as well as some of the photo albums and a few mementos I've collected over the years. Who knows how long it'll be until I get the remainder of my things. Sometimes it's taken weeks or even a month or more for things to get reunited with me when I've been relocated. Yeah, I don't need more than my "Go" bag, but the comforts of home are nice once I get settled in a new place and are a luxury to have.

As much as I love spending the weekend with Samantha, the dreaded day has arrived. Samantha's set to leave tomorrow morning. My gut twists and turns at the thought of letting her go. I can't believe how, in such a short time, she has become everything my world is tethered to.

Samantha and I talked earlier this morning, and contrary to her typical behavior, she insists, just for today, she simply wants to live in the moment. She can't focus on leaving tomorrow, or she won't enjoy the rest of our time. She knows it's going to be extremely difficult for her to leave. I'm doing my best to make that happen. Fuck, it's hard not to speak of the inevitable. I plan to keep her "in the moment," while making memories that'll last a lifetime.

After giving it some considerable thought, I decide to take her to Metz, France. Not only will it put another stamp on her passport, but it'll give us a memorable destination for her last full day with me. I pack some snacks and encourage her to get ready after agonizingly removing her beautiful body from my comfortable bed. I'd much rather spend the day in bed with her, but I force myself to remember that we'll have a lifetime ahead of us.

It doesn't take long to cross the border into France. Within a few hours, we arrive at our destination. Samantha loves the view from the passenger seat as we drive. Once in Metz, I park near the train station. Though we won't be traveling by train, the architecture inside Cara de Metz is beyond impressive and I can't wait to show it to her.

As I suspect, Samantha falls in love with the building as soon as it comes into view. There's a gigantic Christmas tree decorated with lights as we approach the massive building, as well as impressive, lifelike statues that seem to come off the wall. This building's designed by Jurgen Kroger in 1905 and he did a magnificent job.

"Enzo, this town is what fairytales are made of." Samantha gasps as she spins in a slow circle to take in the town. Her eyes shine bright, filled with wonder. *God, can she get any more beautiful?* "I love the narrow cobblestone streets and the massive buildings around it. Thank you so much for bringing me here." She nibbles on her lower lip as if she's still processing everything around her.

"Let's go inside for a better view," I suggest.

The moment we pass through the entryway, her eyes are drawn toward the vastness of the large room. "This might be bigger than Grand Central Station! I love the dark beams that inlay the ceiling and all the unique, almost lifelike sculptures."

"Come here." I motion for her to go down one of my favorite walkways. I was blown away by my first impression, I can't wait to share it with her. "I want to show you something." I lead her down a hallway that's substantially brighter than the areas around us. The ceiling's made of stained-glass squares, illuminating in the sunlight. It's a magnificent view and I'm dying to show Samantha.

I fell in love with this the first time I went through this station as a passenger.

"Oh, wow!" Samantha gasps as she appreciates the new view. She pulls out her phone and snaps picture after picture. "This is so amazing." She seems lost in thought as she takes everything in.

"Here, why don't you stand over there." I point to a lifelike statue coming out of the wall. "I'll take your picture so you can remember it."

Samantha absolutely glows in this light. Her smile's infectious and I can't help but enjoy this moment. I honestly don't think I could love her any more than I do right now. She's not only captured my heart but will be the mother of my children. My wife. How the hell am I going to watch her get on a plane tomorrow? As much as I want to say something, I choose not to. I promised her fun and adventure today. I hope I've shown her just how much she means to me.

After I've taken quite a few pictures of Samantha, I feel a tap on my shoulder. I turn to see an older woman greeting me with a smile, motioning to my phone and then to Samantha. "Puis-je prendre votre photo?"

"Oui, merci." I nod. "Appuyez simplement sur cette, Madame."

I walk over to Samantha and place an arm around her. I can't help myself as I graze my lips along her cheek and tuck her in front of me. Samantha melts into me, and I grip her even tighter. I could hold this woman for the rest of my life, and it will never be enough.

After the woman takes our photo, she walks over to hand my phone back to me. "Merci beaucoup," I thank her.

She pats me on the arm, nodding her head with a smile shining across her wrinkled face. She brushes her short, graying hair and says, "Je vous en prie. Prenez soin de cette femme. Soyez bénis."

I nod, indicating I'll take care of Samantha before she walks away. Her blessing was kind.

Samantha whispers, "Just how many languages do you speak?" The look on her face is priceless. It's a mix between wanting to kick my ass for showing off and astonishment. I'm not sure which one will win out in the end, and that in and of itself is the beauty of Samantha O'Reilly.

"A few." I shrug in an attempt to be humble. I only speak English, French, Spanish, and a bit of Russian, as well as German. Mostly enough to get by in public.

She rolls her eyes and elbows me in the side as I attempt to back away from her, but I was too late in realizing her intent. She gets me firm in the ribs and a huff as what's left of my breath escapes me in a rush as she says, "Sure, just a few... And I'm only a *little* pregnant."

Samantha cocks her chin to the side and raises an eyebrow in my direction. "Are you going to fill me in on the conversation you just had?"

I chuckle. "Um, she said to take good care of you."

Samantha's eyes shine with delight as she grins. We spend more time walking around the train station. When we're done, we walk around the town of Metz. Samantha and I enjoy the narrow, cobblestone streets and looking in the various shops. We make our way over to the well-known cathedral in town. It's another phenomenal structure that's completely awe-worthy.

By the time we arrive back at my apartment, it's nearly eight p.m. Samantha fell asleep on the way home, so hopefully she'll be well rested. I know the long flight tomorrow will wear her out.

As soon as we enter my apartment, I'm surprised when Samantha wraps her arms around my shoulders. Her fingers lace behind my head as she leans up on her tiptoes. "In case I've forgotten to tell you, I've had the most wonderful time here, Enzo." Her voice comes out like a purr, setting my senses on fire.

"Me, too, beautiful. I'm so glad you came." God, I wish she wasn't leaving. I have the morning off so I can take her to the airport, but it will suck ass, having her away from me. The weeks before she arrived were practically unbearable. I can't imagine how it will be now, knowing I'm half of a world away from the woman I love and our children growing inside of her.

She pulls my neck toward her and I kiss her sensually. Samantha boldly quickens our pace when she reaches between us to undo my belt. It's like she has hands with lightning speed. My pants drop down my thighs at a moment's notice.

I don't get a chance to respond before she drops to her knees and her mouth's on me. "Fuck," I growl. "You're going to be the death of me, beautiful." In tandem movements, her hand fists my shaft, as her mouth applies the perfect amount of pressure. When she reaches up with her other hand to find that sensitive spot behind my balls, *fuck!* I. See. Stars. My spine tingles and I can't help the roar that escapes from the unexpected orgasm that rips through me. Holy fucking shit. What the hell was that?

As I open my eyes to refocus on her, there's a look of pure contentment with a mix of pride filling her features as she milks every last drop out of me. *Fuck, this woman knows just how to do me in.*

Though I nearly die on the spot, *and God, what a way to go,* I somehow muster up the energy to haul Samantha into my arms and crush my lips to hers. I can't get close enough. When my brain registers my desperate need, I toe off my shoes and kick my jeans off as they fall to my feet. I somehow manage to do this all while kissing the living hell out of Samantha. I lift her, and her legs curl around my hips as if she were made for me. I intend on finishing this in my bed.

After a few steps, I realize the bedroom is just too far away. I set her feet down on the floor, and in one fell swoop, I have removed her jeans and underwear before hoisting her again. I take the two necessary steps to place her on the small island in my kitchen.

I continue to pepper her with kisses as my greedy fingers make their way down her body to find that magical place that has her writhing in seconds. First, I slide my fingers along her folds, teasing... testing... to see what she needs. Her deep pants and subtle moans tell me everything. I insert two fingers to really work the woman before me.

My kisses pepper her jaw, behind her ear, along her lobe, where I nibble before I whisper, "I love you, Samantha," as I make my way down her body. I break apart for a moment to literally tear her thin t-shirt from her body. I'm not sure who's more shocked, her or me, when the fabric's torn. There's a moment of laughter, but it's soon replaced with deep desire. Our mouths fuse together again, and my fingers intimately inspect the inner workings of Samantha's body. Like a road I could navigate with my eyes closed, I know exactly what Samantha needs. I instinctively do what it takes to make her pleasure mine. Within seconds, I feel her inner walls tighten. The moment my thumb brushes her clit, she detonates and the pure bliss that crosses her face is the most beautiful fucking thing I've ever seen. *God, I love this woman and her responsiveness.*

Of course, I'm a greedy bastard, and I want to see just how many times I can make this happen. I drop my lips to her inner thighs, teasing and tasting with the perfect combination of fingers and tongue. As soon as she has ridden her high to completion again, I feast on her desire to see if I can bring her there once more.

Just as she's about to light off like the Fourth of July, I reach down and stroke my dick. I give my balls a tug, so they won't crawl up my throat before she's finished. The second she quakes, I quickly stand and thrust deep inside her. I feel myself bottom out with ease from the slickness of her desire. I pull out and urgently thrust deep within her, setting a pace I know she enjoys. She comes gloriously around my cock and with a few more thrusts, I follow her right over the edge into heaven. I lean over her body, completely spread out on the counter before me. Her dark, mahogany hair is fanned around her face, her pants eventually slowing, as her breathing returns to normal. I kiss her jaw, neck, and make my way to her breasts, still covered by her bra.

She pulls at my shirt and I break our contact to haul it over my head in a mere instant, our bodies still connected. The next thing I know, there's a clamping sensation around my cock. The moment I look into Samantha's eyes, I realize she's laughing.

"You're really going to start laughing with me still inside you?" I growl.

She looks around us and her mouth quivers more. "I definitely would say we got a bit carried away." She reaches out and touches a scrap of the t-shirt I ripped off her.

Fuck. Did I really just do that?

"Oh my God, Samantha." I pull her into an embrace and oddly enough, my dick chooses that moment to surge again inside her. "I'm so sorry about your shirt." I kiss her cheek, her eyelids, and place a tender kiss on her mouth, to show her how much I love her.

She pulls me down into a deep kiss that somehow reignites my desire. I've never been able to recover as fast as I do with her. And somehow, I think she feels the same way.

Somewhere in the middle of the night, as we cuddle in bed, reality seeps in. "Enzo, how the hell am I going to live without you for the next six weeks?"

"Beautiful, I feel the same way," I whisper, cherishing this moment. "We've been apart a long time already. We can do this. I love you and I will do everything in my power to contact you when I'm able. This sucks for all of us, but just think, it's only temporary."

We talk about how we will call, text, and video chat. Of course, me being a guy and all, this leads to me prompting about how much I'm looking forward to sexy video chats.

Being apart has its disadvantages, but even from thousands of miles away, there's nothing I like more than to watch her come apart, thinking of me. The thought of Samantha pleasuring herself has me hard in an instant, but I do my best to dismiss it, so we can continue our playful banter and conversation. Samantha's mouth nearly hits the floor when I ask, "So, do you have a vibrator?"

Eventually, she closes her mouth. Opens it to say something, but then closes it again. After a few moments, she asks somewhat hesitantly, "W… W… Why would I need one of those?" *Obviously, she doesn't have one. If she did, I'm sure she would have used it in our earlier conversations.*

Since our bodies are entwined, I snuggle her close and nip at her neck. "I'm just curious. We've never talked about it, so I thought I'd ask." I'm a bit surprised about the blush that crosses her features. After spending as much time with her as I have, I wouldn't think much would embarrass her anymore.

"I… uh… have one, but never use it," she stammers, then looks away.

"Why not?" I ask intrigued.

"Well… The battery's never charged and doesn't last," she rushes out in a blur.

She's adorable. "Beautiful, there's no need to be embarrassed." I chuckle lightly as I snuggle closer. "I thought it would be fun to watch you get off, that's all. You mentioned before you have needs while you're pregnant." I waggle my eyebrows at her and she giggles before I add, "Since I won't be there to help you, I want to make sure you're not left hanging…"

She gasps and shakes her head. "Enzo. I've gone years

without so much as a kiss. I'm sure I can manage a few weeks without you... even with pregnancy hormones."

Suddenly, a flash of something unreadable crosses her features. It's something like desire and intrigue, but it's gone in an instant. If I hadn't been paying attention, I might have missed it. *Hmmm... I might have to remedy this.* Obviously, this is something she has an interest in. Her expression drastically changes, catching me off guard.

"Where will you live when you return?" she suddenly blurts out, catching me off guard. We haven't talked about the details, but I assume since we're getting married, moving in together is something we would eventually do. I know I certainly don't want to be away from her, and with the babies coming, I have no intention of being far from her for long.

"Where do you want me to?" I say in a teasing tone, but in my mind, there's only one place I want to be.

I'm met with silence, which is unusual for Samantha. She seems lost in thought and I can't read her expression to save my damn life. There's no way I'm letting her clam up like she did in the hospital. "Beautiful, talk to me," I almost plead. "I'll be wherever you want me."

"But where do *you* want to live, Enzo?"

"Um, with my wife and kids." I raise an eyebrow to get my point across.

"Do you think we should live together before getting married? What about my kids? Would that be setting a good example to them?"

Christ. I hadn't thought about that. "Samantha, I plan on marrying you the minute you're ready. I would've taken you to a chapel this week, but that wouldn't have been fair to your kids. Unless you change your mind, my vote is to get married as soon as possible, when I return to Portland."

Samantha's dark eyebrows shoot up and her mouth forms an 'O.' She squeaks out, "Are you serious?"

"As a heart attack. I've gone a lifetime without you and the past six weeks have been hell being away from you. I want nothing more than to have you as my wife and start a life together. I'll wait until you're ready, but you're it for me, Samantha. Why wait any longer?"

"Okay... But what should we do until we get married?"

"I can stay with my parents or get a place of my own until you're ready to get married. Then, as long as I'm with you, I couldn't care less where we live."

"Enzo, renting a place is just plain silly. I meant, would you like to move in with me? Or would you prefer to get a new place together?"

I smile at Samantha, loving the fact she's putting so much thought into our future together. "Beautiful, I will move to Timbuktu if that's where you want to live. Seriously. I. Don't. Care. A house is just a house. I want to be with you and our children, and that's about it."

"I did just remodel my house to make it into my dream home, and the kids would have one less adjustment if we stay put." Samantha bites on her lower lip and it takes all my restraint not to remove it and kiss her senseless.

"Then it's decided. I'll move in with you. Now, for the bigger decision. When will I get to officially call you my wife?" I bring my thumb to her mouth and release her lower lip. I can't help but outline her features with my thumb as she contemplates.

"What kind of wedding did you envision for yourself?" she asks.

"Uh…" I've never actually thought about it. "Well…I guess the kind where we simply say I do and be married."

"Enzo, I'm being serious. You've never been married before and I want you to have your dream wedding," Samantha pleads.

My heart melts at her thoughtfulness. "Beautiful, so long as you're there, it is my dream wedding."

"But what about our friends and family? Do you want a big or small wedding?"

I can see where she's going with this. I should have known better. I remember the infinite details of my sister's wedding. I'd better stop this freight train before it gets rolling out of control. "Samantha… How about this… We can have a small ceremony with our family and close friends. Besides you, your kids, and your family, I just want my family there. That's all I need. Nothing big."

A look of relief washes over Samantha's face, telling me she's content with a small wedding as well. "You say you want to get married right away. Are we talking weeks, months, this summer?"

"There's no fucking way I'm waiting until summer," I practically growl. "Honestly, even waiting until I get stateside is a lot to ask. Why don't we plan something for the week or so after I get back? I don't want you to worry about that much. Just give me a date and what you want, and I'll hire someone to take care of the details." There. That should do it.

Samantha shakes her head and rolls her eyes. "Enzo, you know nothing about weddings and brides."

"All I care about is *this* bride and making her *mine*." I pull her close to me and plant a chaste kiss on her lips. "Please tell me we can do it ASAP?"

"Enzo, weddings take time..." she pleads for my understanding.

"What do we need besides you, me, and our families?" I shrug as if it's not a big deal.

She lets out a deep breath, shaking her head. She ticks things off on her fingers as she says, "Well... There's a dress, a venue, food, and guest lists. Not to mention a photographer, cake, flowers, and music."

Geesh, that list's fucking huge. "That's for a small wedding?" I ask in assurance. Of course, she nods and I cut her off before she can say anything else. "How about this... You take care of your dress and clothes for the kids, and I will take care of the rest. I promise to run things by you before I make a final decision, but this has to be possible, right? I don't want you to stress out about anything. Your focus needs to be on staying healthy, nothing else."

"But, Enzo..." she starts, but I stop her with a finger over her beautiful pouty lips.

"Samantha, all I care about is being married to you. Give me a week or so and I'll have some ideas to run by you. My sister's friend is a wedding planner and I'm sure if I ask her, she would be willing to help us. Or at the very least, point us in the right direction."

"Okay, Enzo." Samantha slowly exhales. "I trust you. I've already done the big wedding before, and the thought of something like that again has me breaking out in hives. I just need you. It doesn't have to be elaborate, but it does have to be what you want. This is your first wedding and I don't want you to miss out on anything, just to do it quickly."

"Oh, beautiful. It will be epic. Simple, but epic. I will be marrying the woman of my dreams. I couldn't give two shits about the specific details, but I will do this right by you. I love you and want to start our life together right." I kiss her deeply to show just how much she means to me, which ends most of our conversation for the rest of the night. I spend the remaining hours we have left together memorizing her body, cherishing it and making sure she doesn't forget me while we are apart.

7

SAMANTHA

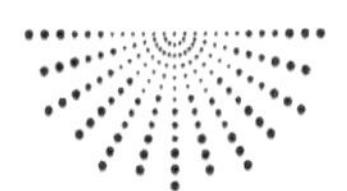

GETTING ON THAT PLANE IS PROBABLY ONE OF THE HARDEST things I have ever done. Though my life and family are in Portland, there's no way I wanted to leave Enzo. My body aches in glorious ways, and I can't help but smile when I think about the love and attention Enzo showed me. It is agonizing to actually say the words, "goodbye." Though I'm proud of myself for not breaking into tears until I actually have to say it.

Enzo's just as wrecked as I am. He takes the time to walk me into the airport and help me get my luggage settled. Since I'm taking his extra bag back, he claims he needs to ensure I don't have any problems or have to lift anything unnecessarily. I keep reminding him I'm pregnant, not an invalid. But if I'm being honest, it's really sweet of him to care so much.

He was stoic the entire trip to the airport. But when I begin sobbing as I embrace him one last time, he breaks down, too. His eyes well up with tears as he whispers, "Beautiful, I'll be home before you know it. I love you so much and I can't wait to meet these beautiful babies growing inside of you."

Then he takes me completely off guard, kneeling down on one knee in front of me to softly say, "You take care of your ma until I can get to you all. I love you all so much. I'll be there as soon as I can." He kisses my belly and holds me close before standing to kiss me senseless once again. I don't care that we're in a crowded airport, in front of everyone to see. I love this man, and though a part of my heart is being left with him, his love for me is what gets me on that plane and sends me home.

As I take my seat and make myself comfortable for the nine-hour flight to New York, I glance down at the beautiful ring on my finger and shake my head at the thought of how he insists on taking over the wedding plans. Devin never had any interest in planning our wedding, so to have Enzo say he only wants me to worry about my dress and clothes for the kids, seems unbelievable. I hope he knows what he's getting into. He's set the bar pretty high for himself.

I've never been more thankful for first class than I am right now. I'm not sure if it's the pregnancy or my lack of sleep from last night, but I feel as if I'm about to drop at any moment. Thank God for the anti-nausea medicine. I haven't been sick since I was in the hospital earlier this week. I watch out the window as the plane taxis away from the terminal, and I feel my eyes getting heavier as we make our ascent into the sky. I take one last glance out the window at Frankfurt and can't believe how much my life has changed in less than two short weeks. Drifting off to sleep, I know I'll never forget this experience for as long as I live. All of it was incredible. Thanks to Enzo.

As I finally touch down in Portland, Oregon, I'm relieved to feel refreshed after traveling for nearly twenty hours. My layover in New York went off without a hitch and I managed to get plenty of rest on my two flights. Thanks to being in first class, I didn't have a single whim that went unnoticed. It helps I was able to walk around the cabin when I got stiff, have quick access to the bathroom, and I stayed well hydrated and fed during the trip. I've been wide awake for most of this last leg of my journey, having slept nearly the entire flight from Frankfurt to New York.

I've never been more relieved to see Mount Hood as I am now. Eager to see my kids, I'm practically bouncing in my seat when I hear the final call for landing. I haven't been away from Maddie, Frankie, or Declan like this in ages. I miss them more than ever. I'm dying to tell them everything, and I have no idea how I'm going to keep this pregnancy a secret for the next six weeks.

Since the kids are still in school, Lexi, my best friend, and co-owner of our company, insists on picking me up from the airport. Normally, I catch a cab or Uber it home, but after finding out I was engaged, she cleared her schedule, determined to meet me in person. Knowing Lexi, she just wants the juicy details about Enzo, and I have to say, I'm excited to share them with her. *After all, what are best friends for?*

I don't even make it through security at PDX before I hear her scream of excitement. She pounces on me like paparazzi looking for their next big break. I whirl to the sound of her voice and make my way over to her. Her brown, curly hair and dark-rimmed glasses make her appear to have a bigger personality than ever. As she weaves through the crowd, her hair bobs and springs into action, taking on a life of its own as she hightails it directly toward me. I don't even get a word of greeting out before I'm being squeezed like a vise.

"Sam, I'm so excited for you!" Lexi exclaims. "I've missed you so much."

I manage to say, "You, too," before she pulls back and studies me further.

"Love looks great on you. You're simply glowing." She eyes me up and down and stops on my left hand, a telling smile pulls at her lips. I know what's coming next. "Okay, show me the ring!"

I can't contain my excitement. I eagerly show off the perfect ring Enzo picked out. I love how our past, present, and future is symbolized. I gush over the details as I tell Lexi as much. Once she's done ogling my ring, we make our way to baggage claim.

Lexi and I spend the time catching up as we wait for the luggage to funnel onto the conveyer belt. She tells me about some of our clients' needs, and I tell her more about Germany. She insists we take the afternoon off and go to lunch before my kids get home.

Once we settle into a booth at our favorite Mexican restaurant, Lexi orders her usual margarita. Her jaw nearly drops to the floor when I don't follow suit, sticking with water. She doesn't say anything, but I can tell her wheels are spinning. *Maybe she will buy my jet lag excuse? Highly doubtful.*

Just as I take a huge bite of my chicken enchilada, her

silence breaks. "Okay, so what's the plan for when Enzo returns?"

"What do you mean?" I play being obtuse for a moment, trying to see where she's going with this.

"Where's he going to live? When will you get married?" Lexi eyes me dubiously in that knowing look, only a best friend can give. "You know... all the deets!"

"Well..." I swallow, then rush to say, "We're getting married, he's moving in, and we're having babies." Once I finish, I take another bite of the mouthwatering food before me. For some reason, I'm starving. The fact that it keeps me occupied while I wait for her reaction to the bombs I've just delivered, doesn't hurt either.

"When's the wedding?" she asks, but then gasps as if she has just inhaled all of the air from the room. "Baby... did you say, baby?"

Hmmm... Is it getting hot in here? I squirm a little as I slowly finish chewing and take a long drink of water.

"You misheard me," I say with as little emotion as I can muster. I love catching Lexi off guard, and this will be priceless. "We're getting married soon after he returns."

"Um, I swear I heard you say *baby*..." she trails off, appearing as if she's replaying the scene in her head over and over again.

"Well, I didn't," I calmly state. I wait until she's looking at me directly in the eyes and her curly hair has stopped bobbing with excitement. "I said *babies*," I whisper.

Her jaw drops almost to the table. She starts to talk, gets out a muffled sound, then clamps her mouth shut again. *God, it's taking all my inner strength not to laugh at her reaction.* Like a fish out of water, a rattled Lexi's something to be seen.

"I'm pregnant with twins. Apparently, I got pregnant before he left, and he has super sperm." Her eyes nearly bug out and I lose my composure by bursting into laughter. "Oh My God, Lex, I'm going to be a mother at thirty-nine years old! Can you believe it?"

"But you tried for years with Devin! I thought you couldn't get pregnant?"

"Me, too," I sigh. "Like I said, super sperm."

"Have you told the kids?"

"No, we're waiting until Enzo comes home to do it in person. They apparently knew he was going to propose before he left for Germany, so we thought one change, for now, is good enough. He proposed before we even knew what was wrong with me."

"Wrong with you, what do you mean?" she asks with confusion.

I launch into the story about being sick for days and not being able to hold anything down. She soon becomes just as smitten with Enzo as I am when I tell her how amazing he was at taking care of me. She can't believe he proposed in the hospital and that he had been carrying the ring around the entire time I'd been there. We both agree Enzo's amazing. Soon, we are talking about wedding plans, and the best friend that she is, insists on helping with anything I need. I'm so lucky to have a friend like her.

When the alarm goes off the next morning, I have to drag myself out of bed. The kids all have school, so I know I have to get up to help them. *Those are the perks of being a mom.* I have no idea if it's the jet lag or the pregnancy, but I certainly don't want to get up, and I'm clearly dragging this morning.

I reach out to check my phone. Sure enough, there's a text from Enzo. A smile immediately forms on my face, as my day just got better. We had spoken last night, but he's heading out on a mission at some point today.

> **Enzo: Morning, beautiful. I'm heading out. Will call or text when I can. I'll have to be radio silent for a while though, so don't worry. Take pictures of the babies and know that I love you all. Counting the days until I see you again! (Kiss emoji)**

My heart swoons at how thoughtful he is. I can't help but squeeze the phone to my chest tightly and wish it were him in person. I take a moment to look through some of our photos together from my trip. I select one, making it the background for my phone.

As soon as I'm dressed, I pull out my phone again. I lift up my shirt and snap a side profile of my belly in the mirror. I'm not one to take selfies like this, or at all for that matter, but for Enzo, I'll do just about anything. I text the picture to him.

Me: I miss you like crazy. One day closer. Be safe. Love, us

I rush downstairs to find Frankie eating cereal in the kitchen.

"Hey, Squirt." I give her a quick squeeze and kiss the top of her head. "Did you sleep well?"

"Yeah, I've been up forever."

I glance at the clock. It's barely past seven. She still has nearly forty minutes before she has to leave.

"Have you seen your brother or sister yet this morning?" I ask, wanting to know if I should go up to check on them.

"Yeah." Frankie rolls her eyes before continuing, "Maddie's in her room texting Soren, and Dec's in the shower, I think."

"Good to know you're keeping tabs on them," I tease, then pull out food to make the kids' lunches.

"Mom?" Frankie sounds rather reluctant, so I turn my attention to her.

"Yeah, Franks?"

"If you get married to Enzo, does that mean he's gonna live here?" she asks so innocently, and I can't help but smile. But, if I know my daughter, there's more on her mind.

"Are you okay with that?" I ask, rather than just telling her that he will be.

"Um, yeah." She seems shy all of a sudden and ducks her head to the side as she whispers, "I just miss him and can't wait to see him again."

My heart melts. Right there. "Oh, honey. He misses you, too." I pull out my phone and open a text message. "Here, why don't you tell him. It'll make his day."

"Okay." She smiles as she types. The complete concentration she uses is almost comical. When she's done, she hands me the phone. I can't help but tear up a little as I read her message. She's so sweet. *God, I love this girl!*

Me: Hi Enzo. This is Frankie. How are you? I miss you. I can't wait till you're here. Can you take me ice skating? Also, I want your chocolate chip pancakes. You make them better than Mom-but don't tell her. Write me back soon. Love Frankie

Declan and Maddie barrel into the kitchen on a mission to grab some breakfast before I can say anything more to Frankie. Maddie gets cereal from the pantry while Dec grabs the milk from the fridge. I step out of their way to let them pass and can't help but think how much I missed the simple things like this when I was away.

They hastily eat their meal in silence before Maddie asks, "Hey, Mom, can Soren come over after practice tonight? Neither of us have games and we want to study together."

"Is that what you're calling it these days?" I tease. Soren's been nothing but respectful to me and I have no problem with him being here. They respect our house rule of 'no boys' upstairs. But I love to make Maddie squirm when I can. Parents have rights.

"Mom..." she huffs out in irritation. "I can go to his house instead, if you'd prefer..."

"Relax, Mads, it's fine. I'll plan dinner so we can eat here. How does honey chicken and rice sound to you?"

She exhales and I see her visibly relax. "It's fine." She scarfs down her cereal and rushes out the door. Now that they have been dating for a while, he picks her up for school from time to time, and I have a feeling it hasn't happened much when they were at Devin's house. Maddie was unusually chipper about this as she made arrangements with him last night. *I might need to have "the talk" with her once again to make sure she's being careful.*

As soon as I drop off Declan and Frankie at school, I head to my office. I have a meeting with a client at ten. I want to make sure Lexi and I get back on track for what I need to do, now that I've returned. It's nice to be in business for myself; it gives me flexibility, but I feel out of it after taking the last few weeks off.

As the end of the day approaches, I'm ravenous. Thankfully, while I was in Germany, I kept up with most of my work while Enzo was working, so I'm fairly caught up with everything by the time I'm ready for dinner. Just as I pack up my purse to head out to grab some groceries and the kids, my phone rings. Enzo's beautiful face flashes across the screen.

I quickly sit back down at my desk as I swipe across the screen. I'm greeted with the sexiest voice I never knew I could miss so much. "Hey, beautiful."

I sigh in relief to hear Enzo's safe and sound. "Better now that I'm talking with you."

"Are you settling in okay? How are you feeling? I actually have good WIFI, would you want to video chat?"

"Absolutely," I gush. "Your sexy voice isn't enough. I need to see the real thing!"

Enzo chuckles. "Good to know. I'll call you right back." He ends the call and immediately, there's an incoming call to video chat.

I feel my face flush with heat as my eyes land on the rugged Enzo. His deep, green eyes pierce me on the spot. His eyes crinkle in the corners as a beautiful smile spreads across that chiseled jaw, that's now sporting a few days' growth of dark-blond beard. That damn dimple pops and I still feel my knees go weak. It happens every. Single. Time. *Will I ever get used to his absolute handsomeness? God, I hope not.*

Amusement fills his features. "God, I hope you don't either."

Crap. My filter's been misplaced again.

"Samantha, you are a sight for sore eyes. I've missed you like crazy since you left." The longing in Enzo's eyes is undeniable.

"Me, too. I thought you were going radio silent for a bit. Everything okay?" I knew they were expected to be traveling for most of today and into tomorrow. *Wonder what happened?*

"Well, the men who are supposed to go out on this mission just got called out on something else. While they are prepping for the new orders, I'm here twiddling my thumbs."

I know better than to ask where *here* is. He told me he can't tell me any specifics, so as much as I'm dying to know, I refrain from asking. "I'm so glad to get to talk to you now," I sigh as I touch the side of his face on the screen.

"I'll text you something for Frankie in a bit. Her message was so sweet this morning. I've never wanted to get stateside more than I do right at this moment. Speaking of stateside, I used some of my downtime and talked to my sister about using her friend as a wedding coordinator. Erin says Melanie Hill's amazing. When I spoke to her, she said it was perfect timing since she just had a cancellation, and it'll work out perfectly for our timeframe."

Holy crap, this man's amazing. "You already spoke with her?" I ask in disbelief.

"If you don't like her, we can go with someone else," Enzo

assures me. The look on his face is actually a bit hesitant for once.

"No, I'm sure it will be fine. I'm just surprised you've moved so quickly into the planning."

"Samantha…" Enzo chides. "I've waited my whole life for you. I have no need to wait any longer. Besides, with the babies coming and the fact you also have kids, I want to do this right. I want to be married to the woman I love before I live with her officially."

"Enzo…" I start, but he interrupts, with a gorgeous smile on his face.

"Samantha, I'm a selfish bastard. I want to be with you every chance I can get. There's no way I'm waiting to be with you when I'm finally in close enough proximity to touch you every day." Enzo's eyes are almost emerald green as they darken with obvious desire.

I can't help but shake my head and laugh. "You are too much, Enzo Dean Harper. But I love you all the same."

We spend the next few minutes talking over the plans. Melanie will contact me later today or tomorrow to discuss my thoughts and feelings about the wedding and reception. Enzo assures me that it won't be a problem financially when I offer to help pay. He claims he's had years of overseas missions, and nothing to spend it on.

Right before we get off the video chat, Enzo asks me to show him my belly, which still feels a bit weird. But the man's thousands of miles away serving our country, the least I can do is feel awkward for a few minutes. He asks me to place my phone next to my belly. Thankfully, he can't see when I tear up as I hear him say, "Hey, babies, I'm your daddy. I can't wait to see you. I love you so much. Be good to your ma and I'll be home before you know it."

There's a moment of silence, so I pull the phone up and look him in the eyes. I know he can see the tears, even though I've done my best to wipe them away as he spoke. "Beautiful?" Enzo's voice nearly breaks, "Are you okay?"

"Just pregnancy hormones." I try to laugh it off. "I miss you and that was the sweetest thing ever. I love you so much."

"I love you, more," he says into the phone. He kisses his fingertips and places them on the screen. I can't help but do the same. "I've gotta get going, Sam. Are you sure you're okay?" His face is filled with compassion and concern. I couldn't love him more at this moment if I tried.

"Absolutely. Hurry home, I love you." I whisper, though he's able to hear.

"I'll call when I can. I'll also send a text to Frankie. Tell everyone I miss them, too. Love you, beautiful. Take care of our family for me." His deep, sexy tone completely does me in.

"Will do," I manage to say, then he ends the call.

I sit at my desk as the tears freely flow. I absolutely loved talking with him, but it makes me miss him even more. I'm so thankful for everything I have and can't wait to start my life with him. I sit at my desk in awe.

Of course, this is how Brenda, our receptionist, finds me when she knocks on the door. I'm staring out into space with tears running down my cheeks. She gasps in surprise when she finds me in such distress.

"Oh my God, Sam, are you okay?" She rushes over to a box of tissues I have on my conference table and swoops the entire box up to hand them to me.

"Yeah." I take the tissue and blot at my eyes. "I'm fine."

Brenda raises an eyebrow and eyes me speculatively. "You don't look fine. If you were fine, you wouldn't be crying. This isn't like you. What's going on?"

She's right. I hardly ever cry. "Well, this is the new hormonal me," I suggest as an explanation.

"Hormonal you?" Confusion is clear on her face. "Are you on your period or something?" she suggests as an explanation.

"No," I mutter. "This is apparently, the new pregnant me." I blow my nose and look her in the eyes as I await her response.

Like Lexi, Brenda doesn't disappoint. Her jaw drops and her eyes round to look like saucers. "Excuse me?" she asks as if she couldn't have possibly heard me right. After all, I'm an old lady who already has plenty of kids. Why would she think I'm pregnant?

"You heard me. I'm pregnant. With twins, no less." There's no sense in keeping this a secret. She sees me every day, and if crying jags are something she's going to experience, I might as well prepare her. I don't recall being this emotional with my other kids, but with Enzo being gone and his super sperm giving me twins, I just might be in for a rude awakening.

"Wow." Brenda gasps as she rounds the corner of my desk. I stand and she embraces me in the biggest hug we have ever experienced together. "Congratulations?" she questions to make sure I'm on board with celebrating.

"Enzo and I couldn't be happier," I tell her. "With him being gone, I think I just miss him, too much. Hopefully, I'll have my emotions in check when he comes home."

"Congratulations on your engagement as well. You guys sure know how to move fast," Brenda teases.

I can't help but roll my eyes. "That's an understatement, but with Enzo, I wouldn't have it any other way." I glance at the clock on my wall. "Crap. I need to get moving if I'm going to get to the grocery store and pick up the kids on time. Was there something you needed?" I say when I realize I never did find out what she came in here for.

She looks a bit perplexed for a minute and shakes her head. "I can't remember. Apparently, it isn't that important. You should get going and when I remember, I'll message you." She hugs me once more, then walks to the door. I grab my purse and jacket and follow right behind her. We walk out to the main office together and say our goodbyes.

I quickly make my way to the grocery store to pick up everything I need for dinner. Since Soren's coming over, I stop by the bakery section and pick up a cheesecake for dessert. I haven't been major grocery shopping since I've returned from Germany, so when I realize I have plenty of time, I get a few more things than I had originally come for.

As I load the conveyer belt, I realize one thing. *I should never shop while I'm hungry or pregnant, apparently.* Ice cream, cheesecake, pretzels, pickles, tortilla chips, cheese, avocados, and sour cream are just the first items I unload from my cart. Of course, I've got everything I need for dinner, but when I look at the combination of items placed on the conveyer belt, I wonder if anyone will wonder if I'm pregnant or just think I'm weird.

By the time I pick up everyone from school and drop them off at practice, I have a little less than an hour to make dinner. Thankfully, Maddie's catching a ride with Soren, and Devin brings Declan from practice, so there'll be no interruptions.

Frankie's upstairs doing her reading homework. I make my way to the kitchen and start the rice for later. I chop up some vegetables and set them in a pot to steam. Just as I begin cutting the chicken, a wave of unexpected nausea comes over me. *Oh, shit. Not again.*

It seems different from before. I don't think I will get sick, but I sit and rest my head in my arms on the counter, anyway. I slowly take deep breaths and soon the wave passes. When I feel like it has passed, I force myself to get up and attempt to make dinner a second time. I manage to cut all of the chicken and am just about to start cooking it when another round of nausea hits.

This cannot be happening. I don't have time for this shit. I glance at the clock and realize I have another twenty minutes or so before the kids will be home. After a few minutes, I realize I might need to eat something to calm my stomach. I walk to the pantry and pull out some crackers and 7-UP I keep on hand for when the kids are sick. I snack on them as I make my way to the couch in the family room, just off the kitchen. After a few more bites and a small sip of soda, I lay myself down, covering my eyes with one arm. *Much better. The world has stopped spinning for a moment and I can finally relax.*

The next thing I know, I hear the front door opening and voices coming from the hall. *Crap. I must have fallen asleep.* I soon realize the voices are coming from Declan and Devin. I make it as far as a sitting position before they stop talking and notice me.

Declan greets me with, "Hi, Mom. What's for dinner?"

I stand and stretch off the sleep that just consumed me. I

can't believe I took a nap in the middle of the afternoon. "Honey chicken," comes out in a yawn.

A grin lights up Declan's face. It's his favorite. "Awesome. I'm going to shower. Soccer was muddy." For the first time, I notice that he's indeed covered from head to toe in undeniable dirt. Well, his feet are clean since he obviously changed his shoes before getting into the car.

"Sure thing, Dec. See you in a few," I offer to his backside as he darts out of the room.

Devin looks around the room and eyes the crackers and 7-UP. He doesn't say anything but asks, "So, how was Germany? I hear you had an exciting trip."

"It was wonderful." I turn to start the chicken again. *Thank goodness, no nausea. Must remember to eat and be well rested before cooking again.*

"The kids said you got engaged. Congratulations," Devin offers as he sits at one of the barstools at the island next to me. "When's the big day?"

"Well, we're actually going to be married shortly after Enzo returns from Germany." I might as well lay it out on the table. He has every right to know since it'll affect the kids as well.

Devin takes in a big breath and slowly releases it. Evidence of shock flashes across his face, but he recovers. "Wow... That's soon."

I shrug. Not that it's any of his business. "Well, there's no reason to prolong an engagement. We think it is important to be married before living together." I make eye contact with Devin to ensure he gets that I'm doing it to set an example for our kids as well. *Though, if I'm being honest, I just want Enzo and I could care less if there was an official paper stating we were together. But with the babies coming...* "It makes sense to do it right away. There's no use in him getting his own place and just have to move a few months later."

He takes a moment to process what I said. In the short time Enzo was here, Devin and he actually spent a bit of time together. With Devin and I wanting to be an active part of our kids' lives, we're usually both at their activities. Devin knows Enzo's a decent guy who cares about our kids. I don't think they'll ever be best friends, but they tolerate each other the best they can.

I can tell the moment it clicks into place. He shrugs and says, "It makes sense. I guess... If you're happy, I'm happy for you."

"Thanks. I appreciate it." I go back to adding spices and honey, as I turn up the heat to caramelize the chicken.

Devin's quiet for a moment. Long enough for me to look his way to see what he's thinking. When I glance over, he's looking at the sleeve of saltine crackers and 7-Up. Knowing Devin like I do, he appears as if he's going to say something else but closes his mouth before anything comes out. His expression changes as if he changes his mind and instead says, "Well, I'd better get going. Let me know if you need help picking up the kids this week."

We say our goodbyes, and just as dinner is ready, the door opens again. This time it's Maddie and Soren. I'm still not used to seeing them holding hands as they enter, but I guess there could be far worse things for them to be doing. It's weird watching my baby grow up. It feels like it was yesterday when she came into the house with pigtails and dirt on her face, claiming boys were disgusting and there's no way she would ever have a boyfriend. Times sure have changed.

"Hey, Mom." She beams as she enters the kitchen. "Smells great. I'm starving." She sets her bag on the floor near the island and takes a seat on the barstool next to it.

"Me, too," Soren says as he rubs his stomach. "Coach had us run lines forever when we kept missing our shots this afternoon."

"Well, if Jack hadn't been mouthing off, I'm sure that would have helped," Maddie snarks out, which is out of character for her. Especially around Soren. "You said he's the one that brags about staying out all night with Anna and kept missing his shots today, right?"

I can't deny my eyebrows aren't shooting through my hairline with this line of talk. *Do kids really stay out all night with one another?* The mom in me acts before I think it all the way through. "By staying out all night... You mean..."

"Mom!" Maddie's cheeks turn pink. "You know what I mean." She shakes her head. "Don't make me say it..."

Soren uses this exact moment to take a long drink from the water bottle he has in his hands and seems rather uncomfortable.

I look back and forth between the two of them. Neither of them will make eye contact with me, but when I scrutinize Maddie, I can tell she's hiding something. *Fuuuck, I don't want to broach this subject. Sometimes it sucks being the responsible adult.* But when neither says more, I guess it's time to put on my big girl britches and face this head on. *Here goes nothing.* "Is this something the two of you intend on doing in the near future?"

Water bursts from Soren's mouth and spews all over the counter. He immediately sucks in a deep breath and begins to cough, as Maddie shouts, "MOOOMMM!" *Well, that was priceless. It takes all I can to keep a straight face.*

I cock a hip against the counter and raise an eyebrow. "What?" I say defensively. "You obviously talk openly about this, so why can't I do the same?"

Not a peep comes from either one of them, but I'm in for a penny, might as well go in for a pound. "Not that I condone the two of you having sex. AT ALL. Only the two of you can decide IF the time is right for you." I glance at Maddie, who's wishing she could vanish into the floor, she's staring at it so intently. *Mission accomplished.*

Soren, on the other hand, takes me seriously, wondering where I'm going with this. I gotta respect the guy for not squirming away from our conversation. Sort of, this is my baby he's dating... so my point needs to be clear here. Time to hike these britches higher and get this show on the road.

I clear my throat and continue with a shrug. "I won't always be there all the time to stop you." I pause for effect. "But just know this... there are steep consequences for your actions. Sure, there's STDs and side effects of having sex. Some can be cured. Some can't." I stop to look directly at both of them before continuing, "Everything is a risk... Then there's the possibility of a baby. Now, as a teenager, I'm not going to say your life will be over because that's a lie. I will say this though..." I take great care to look each one of them in the eye, to drive my point home. "Your life will change. It will no longer be your own. Dreams and goals you have are still achievable, but it'll take a hell of a lot longer to accomplish them. Your life's no longer your own and your child becomes the top priority. Do you understand what I'm trying to say?"

"Yes, ma'am," comes quietly out of Soren's mouth, whereas Maddie's still frozen in shock from my speech. Her mouth hangs on the floor.

To save us all from any more of this conversation I turn to Maddie. "Get your brother and sister. Dinner's ready."

It isn't until bedtime that I finally get a chance to be alone with Maddie. She'd been pretty quiet through dinner and that isn't usual for her, especially with Soren here. I'm pretty sure my little speech had something to do with it. I had just gotten Frankie to bed and Declan upstairs when she approaches me in the kitchen.

"Hey, Mom?" comes quietly from across the room.

"Yeah, Mads?" It feels like this might be a conversation worth sitting for, so I gesture to the couch in the family room and bring the glass of water I had just filled myself over to get comfortable.

She takes a seat in the corner of the couch, propping her legs under her, but she remains facing me. Maddie's usually my most direct child, so I'm a bit surprised she hesitates. I decide to wait her out. It feels like forever. Just when I'm about to ask what's up, she says, "We're not. You know."

Um, what the hell is she talking about? "Not???" I draw out as an attempt to get her to share her thoughts.

"We're not having sex," she says as her cheeks paint a rosy color and she looks away from me.

Well, that's a fucking relief. I hadn't really suspected they were, since we've been pretty open about it. But I wasn't certain when I launched into my tirade this evening. "Okay," I manage to calmly say.

She stays silent. I wonder if there's more she wants to tell me, but I'm charting new waters here. Before when we've talked about the prospect of having sex, it was always about hypothetical people. Soren is about as real as they get.

"I just wanted you to know. I'm... Well, I'm still... a virgin," she sputters as she picks at some invisible lint on the couch.

Okay, still relieved. I take in a deep breath and let it out slowly. Suddenly, there's something I have to know. But, help me God, I don't want to ask it. "Are you wanting to have sex with Soren?" Somehow, this comes out naturally and not at all exposing how I feel about this conversation.

This shocks Maddie. "Oh." She lets out the deep breath she had apparently been holding and shakes her head vehemently. "No. I'm not ready."

"Is Soren pressuring you?" I ask, biting my lower lip. He doesn't seem to be the type, but then again, I'm not the one dating him.

"Oh, no." Maddie smiles. "Not at all. He actually was really impressed with you today. His older sister had a pregnancy scare in college and he wished his parents had been as open about this as you are."

Okay, wow! "Really?" is about all I can manage at this point. I wasn't expecting this conversation.

Maddie sighs and runs a hand through her thick, brown hair. "Yeah, they were pretty pissed. But the funny thing is, they had never even had 'The Talk' with any of their kids.

They just assumed they would abstain or it wouldn't be a problem, I guess."

"Well…" *What can I say to that?* "At least in terms of communication, talking can help. It doesn't mean there won't be pregnancy scares or anything." I shrug, wishing there was a manual to help with situations like these. "There's only one way to prevent that." I look pointedly at her to make sure she comprehends my meaning.

"Yeah," Maddie sighs. "I know."

"You know you can talk to me about anything, right?" I reach out a hand and she grabs it. I give her a squeeze and thankfully, a smile spreads across her face.

"Yeah, I know," she repeats once again, but with a more promising tone.

"Love you, kiddo."

"Love you, too, Mom." She stands and walks to me. Before I know it, she has her arms wrapped around me in a hug. "Thanks, Mom. I'd better get to bed."

"Anytime, sweetheart," I offer to her as she turns to leave the room.

Well, that went better than expected. Where's a manual when you need one?

8

ENZO

Fuck. I'm tired. I've been working nonstop since Samantha left. I've literally flown across two continents and won't be back to Ramstein for another week or so. I'm not sure if it has to do with these being my last weeks in the Air Force and I'm ready to retire, or I'm dying to see Samantha again, but it feels as if time's standing still. The next six weeks are never going to get here.

I've been able to keep minimal contact with Sam, but nothing compares to the real thing. I'm one moody SOB and my buddies have been letting me know it. Gunderson, my life-long friend since Basic has been riding my ass about me actually dating someone seriously. Hell, if our roles were reversed, I'd be doing the same thing.

We're on call, waiting for orders to extract Team 6. Gunderson and I catch up to pass the time. He's recently been on leave and I can't get over the stories he's telling about his trip to London. It seems he had more than one woman catch his attention. Now, I'm not saying he's a man-whore, but the dude likes to have his fun. Ever since his divorce ten years ago, he's sworn off commitment and takes being single to a new level.

"You should've been there, Harps. The club was fantastic. I had to swat women away like flies. It was an epic vacation. I don't think I've ever enjoyed myself more. What did you do on your leave?" Gunderson asks. He takes a long pull on the water bottle he's holding while he waits for my answer.

Christ, I'm not passing judgment, but after being with Samantha, I'm so fucking happy those days are over for me. There's something to be said about spending time with the one you love. Gunderson has no idea I actually proposed to Sam. He's heard the guys razzing me about dating one woman seriously and this is the first time we've been alone or had the time to say anything.

"Samantha came for my birthday and we had quite the celebration." *Boy, did we ever.*

"Really?" he asks in disbelief. "I'll bet it's nowhere near as epic as London."

I attempt to catch him off guard, by understating, "Well, it was epic for me." This catches his attention.

"What happened?" Gunderson asks with more interest.

"Well, for starters, I'm engaged..." I get interrupted before I can say more.

"No. Shit?" Gunderson's frozen in place, awaiting my response. His eyes bulge in disbelief.

"When have you known me to lie?" I raise an eyebrow to prove a point.

"Wow!" He actually seems a bit shocked. "Not to be rude,

but isn't it a little soon? Didn't you just meet this woman a few months ago?"

"When you know, you know." I feel a huge grin spread across my face at the thought of Samantha. "I already had the ring picked out before she got here. I just didn't get around to asking her for a few days since she got sick."

"Oh, man, that sucks. Was she okay?"

I can't help but laugh at the situation now. I was such a wreck not knowing what was wrong with her. That poor doctor. I was such a dick. "Yeah, she's okay. She's pregnant, but okay. Thank God for anti-nausea medicine."

"Oh, shit!" He brings his fist to his face and looks as if he's going to take a bite out of his knuckles. Then Gunderson's quiet for a moment as he studies me. "Fuck, you're serious."

"Dude, you haven't heard the best part yet."

"What's that?" He looks as if I can't say anything else to shock him.

"We're having twins! I'm going to be a fucking father of twins. After Vanessa, I was sure that ship had sailed for me. But not only do I get to be a part of Maddie, Frankie, and Declan's life, but we're having twins. Isn't this fucking fantastic!" I can't control my excitement by the end. I'm going to be a father. I waggle my brows to emphasize my point. *Fuck yeah, I'm excited.*

"Holy shit! You went from being single and carefree to a family with five children in two seconds flat. Aren't you freaking out?" The sincerity on his face shines through. Gunderson's one of my best friends. He genuinely wants to know how I feel about this, all BS aside.

"Not gonna lie. I freaked the fuck out at the hospital.

Samantha had been so sick and the doctor wouldn't tell us what was wrong." Shaking my head at the memory, I continue, "Then, when I saw two flutters as heartbeats across the screen…"

"Fuck, that had to be a sight to see." Gunderson's face could've mirrored mine when I witnessed it firsthand. It's filled with a mixture of shock, awe, and disbelief.

"Aside from Samantha saying yes, it's the best fucking thing I've ever seen in my life, man." Words don't exist for my emotions. Hell, I've known for weeks and I still feel as if I'm on a rollercoaster. But one thing's for sure. I can't wait to be a dad.

"Wow," Gunderson whispers in disbelief as he shakes his head. Then he finds his voice, "Congratulations, man. I'm happy for you. So… When's the big day?"

"As soon as possible. If I had it my way, we'd already be married. But, we want her kids involved."

"So, we're talking later this year sometime?"

"No, man. We're talking as soon as I can get stateside. I don't want to wait another minute not being married to her."

"Uh, Harps, correct me if I'm wrong, but I recall weddings being a big event, which involves lots of planning. That means you're eloping?"

"Nope, we'll have a family affair. My sister's best friend is a wedding coordinator and she just had a cancellation, so if all goes well, we should be married within weeks of me being home."

"Damn, man, your life's changing so fast I can hardly catch up," Gunderson teases, but the pat on my shoulder tells me he's happy for me.

Before I can say anything else, our orders come through.

We need to be wheels up in fifteen minutes to extract the guys in the field. Gunderson and I've already done our preflight check, so within minutes, we're in the cockpit of the helo, ready to move.

When I finally get back to my apartment, I barely have a week to pack and get things ready for the movers. It's hard to believe this is going to be my last move. I'm so fucking ecstatic to be this much closer to being with Samantha and her kids.

I've just spent the last hour going over wedding plans with my sister's friend Melanie. I still can't believe all the shit that goes into planning a wedding, even a relatively simple one like ours. But, I know she's worth every penny it's going to cost me to have our wedding go smooth. I know Sam has a lot on her plate, so I want to lift the burden as much as possible.

When I look at the clock, I realize there's another hour or so until Samantha even wakes up for the day. With it being Saturday and the kids at their dad's, I want to let her sleep in as much as possible. I hop on my computer and pull up a website one of my buddies told me about. I love surprising her, and what I have in mind will definitely be a surprise. After a few clicks, it's being sent. I can't wait to see the look on Samantha's face when she receives it.

Since that took all of ten minutes, I'm left with the dreaded chore of packing. How the hell did I get so much shit after just being here four years? Last night, Samantha and I discussed what I should bring to her house. Since my living room furniture's only a year old and Samantha's furniture in her family room is much older, I'm bringing this along with my bed and dresser. As I look around my kitchen, most of this crap will be donated to a local charity or to one of the guys on base. There's no way we'll need all of this. Samantha's kitchen is already full. But while she was here, she mentioned how much she liked my coffeemaker, electric skillet, and a new set of knives. Knowing she doesn't have a waffle maker, I place that in the box as well as a few kitchen gadgets I can't live without. The rest is put aside to donate.

Just as I'm finishing up the cupboard under the sink, my phone alerts me to a text.

Samantha: Hey, handsome. How was your day?

Me: Good morning, beautiful. Packing kitchen now. Video chat?

Within seconds, Samantha's beautiful face appears on my screen. Her smile drives me wild and she has no idea the effect she has on me. She's still in bed and I can see she has just awoken by the rumpled way her hair lays behind her and the slight haziness of her eyes. She has never looked more beautiful. God, I wish I were there to wake with her each morning. Being apart from her is harder than I ever imagined. Her voice is huskier than normal as she says, "Morning, handsome."

"Good morning, beautiful. How'd you sleep?" I notice her eyes are slightly puffier than normal. I hope she hasn't been sick again.

"Fine. I'm sleepy today. These kiddos sure know how to

kick my ass. I fell asleep watching a movie last night before eight."

"You're kidding me?"

"Nope, I awoke at two a.m. and found myself alone in the dark family room, freezing because my blanket had fallen on the floor." Samantha shakes her head and rolls her eyes. She couldn't look more adorable. I long to reach out and just run my fingers through her hair.

"You've had a long week. You must have been tired," I offer as encouragement.

She heavily sighs and I see her shoulders hunch through the screen. "I'm not sure how much longer I can keep this pregnancy a secret, Enzo. Frankie and Maddie both have asked if I feel all right. I'm already resorting to wearing my 'fat pants' and I won't be able to keep this under wraps if I suddenly decide to pop."

"What the hell are 'fat pants,' Sam? You're nowhere near fat," I ask, confused. She's been wearing her regular clothes in all the pictures she sends to me each day.

I can hear her eyes roll from across the screen. "Uh… Fat pants are clothes you wear when you're feeling fat. You know, when you feel bloated?"

Uh. No. I don't know. But from the look on her face, it's best I don't mention that. "Do you need to go shopping to get a bigger size?" I offer, thinking this is something I can help her with. I've got the one-click shopping thing down to a tee. We can fix this.

"Ugg… With the others, I didn't have to wear maternity clothes until I was nearly twenty weeks. But since there's two in there… I'm guessing it'll be sooner than that." She bites on her lower lip and even from across the world, she still drives me wild.

"Why don't you and Lexi go shopping sometime this week?"

"No. I'm fine for now. I just don't like tight things around my waist. I'll just pull out my baggier clothes and that should do the trick." She then gives me a conspiratorial grin as she says, "Our secrets are safe for now." Her arm vanishes from the screen and I can imagine she's patting her belly.

"So how are the babies today?" I ask, hoping she will show them to me on the screen. Her stomach is a little fuller now, but she barely has a bump. If you didn't know she was pregnant, you could assume she'd just put on some weight in her mid-section. *There's no way in hell I'm mentioning that either.*

"They're doing great." Then in a cooing voice, she says, "They let their mama sleep in today and I haven't felt nauseous in a while. Life is good!" She moves her shirt up over her belly, then says, "Here. Have a look for yourself."

"Mornin', kiddos. Be good to your ma. I love you so much," comes out naturally as if it's not at all crazy to be talking from thousands of miles away to a beautiful belly. I can't help myself, I want my kids to know me. "I can't wait to…" Samantha interrupts me with a loud, uncomfortable groan and suddenly, I'm on instant alert. "What's wrong? Are you okay?"

"Yeah. Relax. I just moved and now I feel like the weight of the world is pressing on my bladder." Her face is now a slight shade of pink as embarrassment spreads across her features. Suddenly, the phone is a blur as she bolts out of bed. "I'll call you right back," is heard with sudden urgency in the distance and the screen goes black.

Oh, fuck. Is she sick again? Please God, let her be okay. Being halfway around the world has never sucked harder than it does at this instant. I hate not being there for Samantha.

Thankfully, my thoughts don't get too far out of control before my phone notifies me of a video call coming through. I'm greeted with a guilt-ridden face. Samantha shrugs as "Sorry," becomes the first thing I hear.

What's she sorry for? "Are you okay?" My mind nearly spins out of control wondering what could have happened to make her end the call so abruptly.

Her face turns a brighter shade of red. Her shoulders are nearly attached to her ears as she states, "Had to pee."

Seriously? I got worked up over that? I burst out with laughter. "Christ, Sam. You had me thinking you were sick again or something was seriously wrong." I laugh some more at my ridiculousness. "Had to pee? Really?"

"Well, yeah... It felt like I wasn't going to make it. I didn't want you hearing me pee." Her face suddenly screws up with a look of disgust. "Or worse, watch me pee."

"Fuck," comes out in another spout of laughter, but I somehow manage to get it under control. Somewhat. "Beautiful, I know I've never been married, so this is new territory for me, but don't you think this is something we ought to get used to?"

"Enzo," comes out almost like a curse.

"Seriously, Sam. Chances are, at some point, I'm going to see or hear you do your business. It's not a big deal."

"Maybe for you it isn't," she pouts defensively. "Nearly

peeing my pants just because I rolled over is embarrassing enough, I think... I'm not even that far along. Wait until I sneeze or cough when I'm *really* pregnant... Besides, I didn't need you to experience it firsthand."

I can't win this argument, so I simply admit, "Even if you did, beautiful, I'd love you anyway. You've got nothing to be embarrassed about."

She's quiet for a moment. Her features have returned to normal and she sighs. "I know."

To change the subject, I state, "You should receive some packages in the next day or so. I bought the kids some presents to put under the tree from me, and there's one being sent to your office. I'd advise you not to open that one until you're home alone." A conspiratorial grin spreads across my face. There's no way I'm giving away her surprise. But I'll give her a warning.

"Enzo. What did you do?" She attempts to use her mom voice with me. But it won't work today.

"Some things are just better left alone," I tease. Dropping the subject, I switch to one she's sure to latch onto, and hopefully forget about her surprise until it arrives. "So, I talked with Melanie today. We hashed out a lot of the details for the wedding. She'll be contacting you today to verify things."

"Oh, really?" She glances at her bedside clock and blanches. "Did you wake her at the ass-crack of dawn or something? Geesh, Enzo. Not everyone likes to know there's two five o'clocks in a day."

I lightly laugh at her reference to my inability to sleep in. "Actually, she called me knowing I'd have time to talk."

We spend the next twenty minutes going over the details

for the wedding. Before long, she has to get off the phone to make it to her hair appointment on time. As I disconnect the call, I can't believe how much I love Samantha and our newly forming family. I'm one lucky SOB to get to have her in my life. Sometimes, I shake my head in disbelief that she actually said yes. I just hope she appreciates me after the gift I'm sending her.

9

SAMANTHA

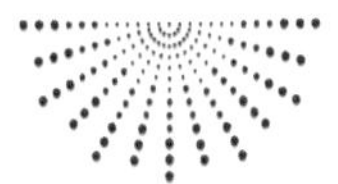

WITH CHRISTMAS BEING LESS THAN A WEEK AWAY, I MAKE THE most of my time to finish last-minute details, while the kids are in school or at Devin's. While I was in Germany, I picked up a few things for Enzo and left them at the top of his closet. They're small and won't take up much space.

I know he's about done packing his apartment, but he'll still be there through Christmas. After that, he'll either bunk with a buddy in a guest room or stay on base in temporary housing, depending how often he's actually at Ramstein. He's been radio silent for a few days, since our last video call. I miss him like crazy, and though he told me to expect this to happen, it doesn't make the distance any easier. He can't tell me where he is, so for now, no news is good news. He seemed to think he'd be back on base by Christmas, so hopefully we will at least talk to one another then.

With Christmas vacation for the kids starting tomorrow, I've arranged my schedule so I won't meet with clients until the New Year. I want to relax and spend time with my family. Though various projects need my attention, I'm relieved not to have work commitments for the next two weeks.

Just as I'm about to leave the office for lunch, I get an unexpected phone call from Sara, Enzo's mother. She greets me warmly, "Hello, dear. Am I catching you at a bad time?"

"Not at all, Sara. How are you?" I ask as I sit back in my chair and stretch my legs out under my desk. For some reason, just the sound of her voice puts me at ease.

"Oh, I can't complain. I've spent the morning with Zoey and she's napping now." Sara lets out a low sigh, then laughs. "Boy, keeping up with a two-year-old is a sure way to stay young at heart. But honestly, I'm not sure who's more ready for a nap, her or me."

I chuckle right along with her at the thought. "I remember those days. Frankie always kept me on my toes..." I almost add, *just wait until we're chasing twins.* But thankfully I catch myself beforehand. *I wonder what she'll think about being a grandma again.* I can't wait until we're past our first trimester and we can tell people. I hate keeping secrets.

"So... Enzo mentioned you're going to be alone on Christmas Day," Sara states as she jumps to the point of her call. I guess Enzo was right when he said his mother never minces words.

"The kids are with me until Christmas morning. Devin's going to pick them up around ten to visit his parents in Seattle for a few days. With this being my niece's first Christmas, my parents are spending this year with my brother Blake in Montana... So yeah, I guess I'll be alone most of the day." This is the first time I haven't spent the holiday with my kids and the thought alone has my heart clenching.

"Well, we'd love to have you come spend the day with us. Everyone does their own thing on Christmas morning, but they all end up here around noon. You're welcome anytime."

Truth be told, I've been dreading spending Christmas alone this year. My plan was to do something to keep my mind off the fact my kids are so far away. Don't even get me started on Enzo. Who knew I could miss someone so much in such a short time? "That's really sweet of you to offer. Is there anything I can bring? I'm used to doing all the cooking, so I'd been wondering how I was going to fill my day since there's no use cooking for just me."

"Oh, you can just bring yourself. Relax and enjoy the holiday for once. Unless there's something you can't live without?" A holiday to sit and relax, what kind of alternate universe have I landed myself in? But I can't show up empty handed.

"I do make a great seven-layer dip I can bring as an appetizer," I offer. "Are there any food allergies I should be aware of?"

"None that we know of." Sara chuckles. "Whatever you like is fine. There will be enough to feed an army, so it's your own fault if you go away hungry."

"I'll keep that in mind." I laugh in return.

"Well, I'd better rest while the wild child does, or I'll be paying for it later. I'll let you get back to work. I'm looking forward to seeing you on Christmas Day, Samantha," Sara kindly states before we say our goodbyes.

Just as I'm leaving for lunch, the package Enzo mentioned

arrives. As much as I want to rip it open now, I know I should do what he said and wait until I'm home alone. Lexi and Brenda have been in and out of my office helping me with all the last-minute things that need to be done before we take our holiday vacations. Who knows what he has up his sleeve. I place it in my bag to take out to the car later.

I spend the rest of the afternoon wrapping up things with clients before rushing out to pick up the kids from school. I've never been more thankful to have an entire unplanned evening ahead of me. I'm dead on my feet, and as soon as dinner is dealt with, I have a date with my couch. A jammies and movie night sounds amazing.

Apparently, word gets out about movie night. The next thing I know, Maddie has Soren over and Dec has invited his friend Jacob for a sleepover. I make things easier on myself and order pizza. I also pull out the air popper to make popcorn. Once the pizza arrives and we have our food and drinks, we all get settled to watch *Guardians of the Galaxy II.*

The atmosphere in the room hums with excitement. Maddie and Soren are on the opposite end of the couch as Frankie. They are close enough to hold hands, but still have enough distance between them to not cause me to worry. I'm sitting in my favorite recliner, and Dec and his friend lounge across the other couch in the room. I'm apparently the only one in the room who has yet to see the movie already, but we're all looking forward to it. I let them turn the lights down and the volume up as the movie begins, and I snuggle into my blanket.

That might as well be my demise.

The next thing I know, the lights are being flicked on and

the kids are all raving about how great the movie was and what their favorite parts are. I didn't even watch any of the credits, the beginning or the end. I glance at the clock and realize nearly two and a half hours have passed. Holy crap! How could I have slept that long?

Soren stands and stretches. "Well, I'd better get going if I'm going to make my curfew on time."

"Okay." Maddie reaches out her hand to have him assist her in standing. "I'll walk you out."

I extract myself from the comforts of my recliner, placing my blanket to the side, as Maddie makes it to her feet. Then Soren turns to me. "So, what did you think of the movie?"

"Uhhh…" What am I supposed to say? I feel embarrassment spread through me as my ears heat.

Maddie lets out a sound that is a cross between a cough and a snort. "Uh, I guess you didn't see her sawing logs… I'm not sure she saw much of the movie." Maddie rolls her eyes as she shakes her head in my direction.

I inwardly cringe, feeling worse that she noticed my unplanned nap. So much for family night. I try to pull it off with a light laugh. "Uh… she's right. I don't think I saw that much of it."

Soren grins wide. "Well, you missed a great movie. You should watch it sometime when you're not so tired. Are you feeling all right?"

Maddie suddenly looks very concerned in my direction. "Yeah, Mom, are you feeling all right? You've seemed really wiped out lately."

Not wanting to give anything away, I brush my hand in the air with denial. "No. I'm fine. Just had a long couple of weeks."

"Are you sure?" Dec chimes in. "You never fall asleep before us."

Great, now they're choosing to be extra observant?

"Guys, what's with the Spanish Inquisition? I was tired and fell asleep. No big deal." *Yeah, I'll keep feeding them that lie and watch it bite me in the ass.*

Thankfully, they let it go when I look over to see Frankie's reaction and realize she's zonked on the couch. She's at that awkward age where if I wake her, she might be up all night. I opt for just covering her with the blanket I'd been using as she stretches and takes up most of the couch. Dec and Jacob say goodnight to Soren and make their way upstairs. Maddie walks Soren to the door, then heads upstairs herself. I'm left with locking up and turning off the lights. I'm still exhausted and ready for more sleep. I drag myself up the stairs and get ready for bed.

Just as I'm about to fall asleep, I hear my text notification. I reach out for my phone on my nightstand and can't help the smile that spreads across my face.

Enzo: Night, beautiful. I can't talk but want you to know I am thinking about you. Love you all.

I tap out a quick response, not knowing if he will receive it.

Me: Love you, too. Night.

With a full heart, I drift off to sleep with thoughts about the man of my dreams.

The next morning is a bit of a blur. I wake up and make pancakes, eggs, and bacon for everyone. I take Maddie and Frankie to the outlet mall to complete our Christmas shopping lists, while Declan spends the day with Jacob and his family. Maddie takes forever to pick out a gift for Soren, while Frankie's eager to be done shortly after arriving. Thankfully, we reach a compromise and split up to complete everything we need within a few hours.

By mid-afternoon, I'm dead on my feet. It's all I can do to make it back to the house and pull a lasagna out of the freezer to cook for dinner. Maddie offers to make no-bake cookies with Frankie and I take this opportunity to go upstairs and catch up on some reading.

As I look in the bag I brought home from work, I'm reminded of my surprise from Enzo. I love the giddy sensation that warms my body when I think of how thoughtful he is. God, I miss him so much. I can't wait until these next few weeks pass and he's here permanently. As I look at the medium-sized, non-descript box, my interest is piqued. He'd specifically told me I should open this alone. *What the hell is he up to now? Why be so secretive?* Before opening the package, I shut my bedroom door to give myself some privacy.

Of course, inside the plain cardboard box is another box. This time it's white with gold-embossed lettering in a language I can't read. I pull off the end since it slides open, but all that comes out is a charging cord, leaving the rest still in the box. *He bought me something electronic and I had to open it in private? My kids will likely know how to use it better than me.* As I pull out the plastic remains of the packaging, I find a pink object with controls and a gold-plated end. I gasp.

Oh, shit. This isn't for my kids. Holy hell, he bought me a vibrator.

Twin emotions course through me. On one hand, I'm mortified. On the other, I'm intrigued and slightly aroused. I'm so relieved I listened and opened this in the privacy of my own room. I can't imagine what would have happened if my kids had seen this.

I pull it out to inspect it further. I feel my body heat and tingle in places I haven't thought about since being with Enzo. I press one of the buttons and it comes to life. A low hum of vibration fills the room. Not knowing what all the buttons do, I press the arrow button again and the pulsation changes to a higher pitch. *Hmmmm... this has possibilities.* A vision of showing Enzo just how much I like this takes hold of my mind as I grasp one end to imagine what it would feel like inside me. I press the arrow again, and I feel simultaneously a new pattern of vibration form, and the wider end warms. *Holy crap. This sucker's heat sensitive. What else can it do?* I press the button again and the vibration speeds to a higher pitch and faster pulse.

Suddenly, I hear running up the stairs and, "Moommm," being called.

I press the down button to turn it off, but the sucker keeps vibrating. No fucking way! "Turn off. Turn off. Turn off." I will the damn thing to oblige. But no such luck. FUCK!

I hear the footsteps getting closer. Another holler of my name. *Where the hell is the off switch?* I rush to my bathroom, slam the door shut, and turn on the fan to mask the noise as I frantically keep pushing that damn arrow button to get it back to the start of the cycle. Holy fucking shit! This thing has no off switch. The sound it makes gets higher and higher, louder and louder.

When I hear Frankie enter my bedroom, I know she's only seconds away from knocking on my bathroom door. I give up. I send the vibrating, traitorous bitch into the linen closet with a hard toss and slam the door. I quickly march to the bathroom door to cut Frankie off at the pass. There's no way I can let her in here. I open the door, nearly out of breath, and shut it as quickly as possible behind me as I enter my bedroom.

"Mom?" Frankie asks with concern etched across her face.

I slowly inhale and release it, trying to steady my breathing and appear less guilty. "What's up?"

"Are you okay? Your face is really red." Frankie eyes me skeptically.

Fuck. This is so wrong. I can still hear the faint hum of the friggin vibrator mixed in with the bathroom fan, and my entire body feels as if it might burst into flames. I have to get her out of here.

Thankfully, I'm able to get my wits about me and say, "Oh, I'm fine, I was just in the bathroom and accidentally turned on the heat lamp instead of the fan when I rushed in." God, I hope she buys it.

"Oookkay," Frankie draws out, but doesn't look as if she's convinced.

"What do you need?" I ask, trying to get the subject off me, and I'm relieved when it works. Her expression changes instantly.

"Oh, Ava just came over and asked if I can play. Can I go?" Frankie asks enthusiastically, seeming to be happily distracted.

"Sure. Be home by six for dinner."

As Frankie rushes out of the room, I sigh heavily. I fall back onto my bed from pure exhaustion and shake my head from embarrassment. I pick up my phone and dial Enzo. It goes straight to voice mail. "A vibrator. Really? Ohmigod!"

As I hang up, I see the directions have fallen to the floor. I pick them up and look for the English explanation of how to turn the fucker off. *Hold any button down for three seconds. Really?!??!?* It could've been that fucking simple?

10

ENZO

It's been way too fucking long since I've been able to talk with Samantha. I've been working non-stop since I last spoke to her. Team 4 almost got their asses handed to them, but I managed to get them to safety. I glance at the clock and curse it again. I've already missed Christmas here, but back in the States, it's still early evening.

I power up my phone after days of no use, and immediately, my text notifications chime. As I look through my voice mails, I see there's only one I want to hear. Samantha's sexy voice is what I've been craving for days. But the minute it comes through, I instantly cringe and my blood chills. "A vibrator. Really? Ohmigod!"

If spoken in a different tone, those words could've been a good thing. But there was zero excitement in her voice. Zero room for interpretation. Unlike my expectation or intent when I purchased her gift, she sounds like she's anything but smiling. Fuck! How could I get things so wrong? I'd been sure

113

she'd at least be intrigued and hopefully aroused like me at the thought of using that badass toy together. Damn, I'm a dick.

I glance at the date on the phone for when I received the call and it's been a nearly a week since she'd left it. "FUUUUUCCCCKKKK!" I growl into my nearly empty living room. I'm so fucking screwed. She hasn't called since. There're multiple text messages, but those will have to wait. I need to talk with her now.

Waiting for our call to connect is almost unbearable. I pace between my couch and bed as I wait. Three, four, five rings later. It goes to voice mail. Fucking voice mail. Her unbelievable sexy voice pulls at my heart, making it both speed up and drop through my stomach as she tells me to leave a message. When the beep finally comes, I want to beg, borrow, and plead for forgiveness. God, what have I done?

"Samantha, beautiful. I'm so sorry. I WILL make this up to you. I love you so much. Please forgive me. Please call me no matter how late you get this message. We need to talk. Give me that chance..." Her voice mail cuts me off. It asks if I want to re-record the message or leave it as is.

Feeling completely defeated, I end the call and sink onto my bed. I cradle my head in my hands as my elbows dig into my knees. I'm exhausted and need a shower. I need to call my family. But that can wait. I have no idea how to reach Samantha if she's not answering her phone. I might as well hop in the shower while I figure out what the fuck I should do to make this right with her. I grab my phone and bring it to the bathroom in hopes I will hear from her soon.

Showers usually relieve my tension. This one, not so much.

I need to hear Samantha's voice. To know we're okay and that we can work past this. I've never seen her pissed and have no fucking clue as to how to make this up to her. If it wasn't Christmas, I think I'd send her flowers or something, but everything is closed at this hour. Being so far away has never sucked so much in my life.

By the time I get out of the shower and get dressed in my favorite pair of sweats, I'm still no better off. I glance at the clock again. It's only been thirty minutes, but it feels like a lifetime. Not wanting to miss my family as they are sure to be eating Christmas dinner about now, I decide to call.

"Hello," Pops' deep voice answers.

"Hey, Pops. Merry Christmas!"

"Merry Christmas to you, too, son! It's good to hear from you. You've caught us at a great time. We've just finished dinner and are all dying to talk with you. I'll pass you to your ma, as she's already chomping at the bit. I'll catch you later as you make your rounds." Pops chuckles, knowing I'll be on the phone for a while with everyone.

"Sounds great, Pops." I settle back onto my bed, getting comfortable.

"Enzo, are you there?"

"It's me, Ma. Merry Christmas."

"I love you, Enzo. I'm so sorry you couldn't be here. But next year, you and Samantha had better plan on being here to share it with us!"

I cringe at the thought of Samantha, and my heart sinks even further. I miss my family, but for some reason, I miss Samantha more. I need her like I've never needed anyone. Why the fuck isn't she returning my call?

"Enzo? Are you there?"

Fuck, I need to get it together. Trying to recall what she said, I stay noncommittal. "We'll see, Ma. It's not up to me to decide."

This makes Mom laugh. "Oh, spoken like a true husband. You always were quick on the uptake. Samantha's going to be one lucky girl."

I sigh heavily. "I don't know, Ma. I'm the lucky one." If she'll ever speak to me again. Christ. She's never gone so long without contacting me. Where the fuck is she?

"She's absolutely beautiful inside and out, Enzo. You sure are lucky. And she makes one hell of a pie."

Wait. Pie? "What do you mean?"

"Well, we're all eating her delicious grasshopper pie and cheesecake she brought over for dessert. I can't believe she made them from scratch. You're going to have to keep working out if you eat this delicious food of hers."

"She's there?" I ask in disbelief.

"Well, of course! We weren't going to let our future daughter-in-law stay home alone for Christmas. What kind of family would that make us?"

A mixture of relief and anxiety flow through me. I'm so fucking thankful to know where she is. She can't be too mad if she's at my parents' for Christmas dinner, but how can I be sure?

"Hey, Ma, can I speak with her?" God, I hope she'll take my call.

"From the look in her eyes, I think she's dying to."

No better words could be heard. My body instantly relaxes and I eagerly anticipate Samantha's beautiful voice. A shuffle can be heard through the phone and I'm almost at a loss for words when her voice reaches my ears.

"Merry Christmas, Enzo," comes out nearly breathless and those three simple words are all I need. The dread I'd been feeling drifts away. Even though she may be mad, I know I've worried for nothing.

"Merry Christmas, beautiful. This will be the only Christmas we're apart," I vow. There's no fucking way I'll be apart from her like this again.

Her beautiful laughter flows through the phone and warms my body from the inside out. "I'll hold you to that." Her saucy voice lingers and clutches my heart further.

"So... You're not mad at me?" I hesitantly ask, not wanting to ruin the moment, but having to know at the same time.

There's a long pause, causing my heart to plunge as I await her response. "No, why would you ask that?"

"Your voice mail. You sounded pissed."

"Voice mail?"

I cringe. Not wanting to bring it up unnecessarily, but having to make sure she isn't mad at me. "You know, about buying you a vibrator?"

Samantha almost snorts as laughter spills from her. "Ohmigod. You're never going to believe the story about that." She takes a deep breath, trying to control her laughter. "I can't tell you about it now. I'm having dinner with your family, but no, I'm not mad. Trust me, I'm anything but mad." More laughter spews out of her and I'm left a little confused.

"Are you sure?" I can't help but clarify. She sounded pissed on the phone earlier, so why the hell is she laughing so hard about it now?

"Yeah. I am." Then she changes the subject. "Are you almost done packing?"

Looking around my nearly empty room, I tell her I am.

"Did you pack those presents I left for you on the top shelf of your closet?"

"No, I left them out, so I could open them on Christmas, like you asked. But I didn't get back until today, so I've missed it."

"Well, it's still Christmas here. Go get them."

Within seconds, I have the presents she'd left in my hands and am eager to rip them open. "Which one first?"

"The square box."

Paper is ripped and the box is open within seconds. Inside is not only a watch, but a special ops watch called the Silencer. It is capable of holding a charge for months, has a compass, a strobe light for emergency signals, and a ton of other features if the box is any indication. "Wow, Sam, this is an amazing gift. A buddy of mine has one of these and they're great watches."

"I'm glad you like it. So…" She hesitates for a moment. "Have you read the inscription?"

I take it out of its box and my heart stutters. She couldn't have known just how much I needed this right now.

No measure of time with you will be enough,
but let's start with forever.
XOXO Sam

"Forever sounds great, beautiful." My throat clogs as I'm filled with emotion. Christ, this woman can bring me to my knees in an instant.

"Open the next one," she eagerly states. "That's from the kids."

I pick up the shoe-sized box and open it. It's filled with an assortment of things. Cards, notes, and a few other items all stuffed inside. What draws my attention is a silver 4X6 frame with the word family written on the bottom. This slays me. Samantha, her kids, and I are hiking at Beacon Rock. Just looking at the photo floods me with emotion, making me want to be in Portland as soon as possible.

"Wow, this is amazing," I say in awe of the love that is given.

I pull out a folded piece of paper and see that it's from Frankie. It's a drawing of a man flying a plane in the sky. Underneath are the words, 'Fly home soon. We miss you. Love, Frankie.' My heart soars.

There's also a card from both Maddie and Declan wishing me both Happy Birthday and Merry Christmas. At the bottom is a multi-color, hand-beaded bracelet with the letters *Love You, Enzo*, spelled out. "Is the bracelet from Frankie?" I ask to clarify my assumption. I can't imagine this being from Dec or Maddie.

"Yeah, it is. Will it even fit you?"

I place it around my wrist and I can't quite tie it together. Damn. "Not really. But it's the thought that counts. I'll be sure to thank her when I talk with her next."

"She can't wait to hear from you. She's at Devin's parents, but will be home in a few days."

"I'll call her when she's home then. So, what have you been up to? Did the kids like the gifts I sent?"

"Yes. Funny you should mention that," she says in her best

mom voice, letting me know I'm about to get a lecture. "You need to know what the word *control* means. You have none. If you buy gifts like this at every occasion, we'll be *broke,* and they'll be *spoiled.* Just because they are the latest and greatest gifts doesn't mean you need to buy them. You don't need to be so excessive."

"Oh." What can I say? I wanted to make sure I didn't fail at picking out their gifts.

She goes into great detail about how even though I went extremely overboard, I hit a home run with each of them. I sent Frankie the latest American Girl doll with all the necessary accessories. I got Declan a helmet with a Go Pro attached so he can record videos when he skateboards or plays soccer. For Maddie, I bought a MacBook Pro, to replace her laptop that died earlier in the month. I thought these were all things they needed. Or so they claimed when I asked for their Christmas wish lists. How was I to know this was too much? It's not like I've had kids before.

"So, does this mean you're mad about the gifts, too?" I wince as I wait for her response.

"Enzo…" she huffs. "If I'm mad at you, you'll know. There won't even be a need to ask. Trust me."

11

SAMANTHA

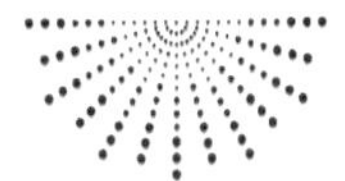

"Lexi, it's been eighteen days. Eighteen days! No text messages. No voice mails. Nothing. He's supposed to be back on base doing only God knows what to officially retire. He mentioned going on one last mission a few days after Christmas, but I haven't heard from him since!" I pace my office as my best friend listens to my rant from the sheer panic attack I'm about to endure.

It had started with a simple question. "How's Enzo?" from Lexi. She meant well, and I'm sure she had no idea I've been barely holding it together, let alone the can of worms she was about to open. I haven't told anyone my worries. With the firm belief in *don't borrow trouble*, I know worrying is just like praying for bad things to happen. Nothing bad can happen to Enzo. It can't. I've done my best to stay positive. I figure no news is good news, but with that simple question, I feel like I'm on the verge of losing my fucking mind.

"Sam." I hear Lexi try to rein me in as only a best friend

can. She walks over and places a hand on my shoulder, in hopes to calm me, I'm sure. But nothing she says or does will pull me back from the frenzy I'm feeling. I attempt to pull away, but she grips my wrist to make me stop pacing.

"Sam, you've got to calm down. This isn't good for you or the babies."

"I know," I moan and do my best to stop fretting for their sake. "Why haven't I heard from him, Lex? Why?"

"I'm sure there's a good explanation for this, Sam. He wouldn't do this to you on purpose."

Letting my worst fears come out, I whisper, "What if something's happened to him?" God. Please don't let anything happen to him. I almost feel guilty for voicing this aloud, but Lexi, of all people, won't judge. "We're not married, so I have no way of knowing. I'm not his next of kin." Fuck. Nothing can happen to him. *Goddammit, Enzo, where the hell are you? Why haven't you contacted me?*

"Sam, if something's happened, his family will let you know," she says, trying to be the voice of reason. "They love you nearly as much as Enzo. They wouldn't keep you in the dark."

"I know," I whisper as I let out a long, slow breath, in an attempt to calm my nerves. It works, a little. I may not be ready to jump off the deep end, but I'm not calm by any means. I'm not a crier, but I feel the prickly sensation begin around the edges of my eyes and I curse. "What the fuck's wrong with me? I can't get my shit together today and I feel like I'm going crazy."

I expect her to say something, but Lexi's silent for a moment, which catches me off guard. When I finally stop my pacing and look her in the eye, I see her head is cocked to the side, her lips are slightly turned up in an almost smile, and she shakes her head slightly. Making me feel even more crazy.

"What?" I almost shout. *How can she be smiling at a time like this?*

"Oh." She chuckles. "That wasn't a rhetorical question?"

"Uh, no."

"Well... Let's see. One, you love him. Two, you haven't heard from him in what seems like forever, and he could possibly be in a dangerous, hostile area..."

I interrupt before she can say more, "Lex! You're not helping!"

"Hear me out, Sam." She comes over and squeezes me with one of her bigger than life hugs, which somehow creates a sense of calm over me.

"Sam, all those are reasons to be losing your shit. Add a baby or two..." She winks and I can't help but smile. "That could push anyone right over the edge."

"I know," I sigh as I wipe a stray tear that has escaped. "But what should I do?"

"Live."

What the fuck? Why would she say that? I am living!

"Sam, calm down. I'm just saying live your life the way you have been. Assume no news is good news. Calm down. Relax and try to get your mind off Enzo being gone. You can only control so many things, and some things are just beyond your control. You're going to worry yourself sick." She's quiet for a moment, then gasps. "I know... let's take the afternoon off and get our nails done."

"But I have work to do, Lex," I protest.

An eyebrow quirks, and her curly hair shakes as she cocks her head to the side to peer at me from behind her dark-rimmed glasses. "Really?" She looks around my office and at my empty desk. "You think you're going to get much done freaking out like this?"

She's got me there. There's no way I'll concentrate on anything important in this frame of mind, so I concede. "Okay, you win."

She claps her hands in triumph and hops in my direction to hug me once more, taking my breath away. "Umph... Lex. Careful, I'm carrying precious cargo here."

She pats my belly and singsongs like she's actually talking with the babies growing inside of me, "See, I know how to get your mama to calm down."

"Oh my God, this feels amazing," I nearly moan as the technician massages my feet and rubs my lower legs with hot stones. Between that and the massaging chair I'm sitting in, I feel myself completely relax. My muscles were much tenser than I'd realized.

"I hate to say I told you so, but..." Lexi trails off as she laughs.

I ignore her comment, but admit, "We need to do this more often."

"Next we're going shopping to get you some new clothes. There's no need for you to look frumpy just because you're preggers."

"Uh... how am I supposed to take that?" I feel my mouth still hanging open.

"Oh, come on, Sam. You're wearing all the clothes you usually wear when you're feeling less than the beautiful woman you are. I know you're trying to hide a baby bump until Enzo returns, but with this being your fourth pregnancy, not to mention the fact you're carrying twins, I'm not sure how much longer you can hide this."

"Lexi..."

She puts her hands up to surrender. "Hey, I was surprised to feel the bump when I teased you earlier. You have to be uncomfortable in tight clothes. I know I always was."

She's got me there. I can only wear so many leggings and sweaters. Thank goodness it's winter, but she's right. I don't think I will last much longer in these clothes. Besides, I'm down to only two skirts and a few pairs of leggings that fit anyway.

"Okay, but nothing that makes me look too pregnant."

"Define *too* pregnant. You've got two babies inside you and they want to be seen by the world. You're absolutely stunning now that you're no longer sick every morning. Why not flaunt it?"

"Lex, I hope I can hold off until Enzo returns. We want to tell the kids together. I have no idea how they're going to react. It's already going to be a big adjustment that I'm getting married in a few weeks, add twins to the mix and they might disown me," I tease.

"They will not," Lexi huffs. Then to change the subject, she asks, "So do you need any help with the wedding?"

I sigh. "No, I've just got to get fitted for my dress the week before and that's about it. Enzo and Melanie have taken care of everything."

"You sure are lucky. What bride only has to show up for her wedding?" she teases. "I'm jealous. Enzo sure is a keeper," Lexi sighs and has a dreamy look on her face.

I'm so fortunate Enzo's taken care of everything. My heart melted when he told me he wanted to get married at the Multnomah Falls Lodge, in memory of our first date. I can't wait to have him here and make this dream become a reality for both of us.

Melanie's been a godsend. She's made all the arrangements, and except for actually trying on dresses, I haven't had to do much. Sure, I've had my opinions and she has helped make those happen in every way possible. I'm sure it helps we're having a small, intimate wedding. Enzo only wanted to invite our families and a few close friends. By the time we sorted the guest list, we have about fifty to seventy-five people invited, but who knows who will actually make it, with our winter weather in the Pacific Northwest.

After our pedicures, Lexi takes me shopping for maternity clothes. Thank God, times have changed and you don't have to look like a tent when you're pregnant. I managed to get some things for work and to relax in at home. They just look a little baggy at the moment, but there's room for growth. I didn't get too many winter things, since spring will be here before we know it.

By the time I get home, I'm exhausted. Even though we got pedicures today, my feet feel tired and swollen from walking around the mall. I somehow manage to get everything unloaded from the car and put away. With the kids at their dad's house this evening, I stealthily hide the clothes from the maternity stores. No need to have snoopy eyes find my secrets.

It's only a little after seven, but my eyes feel like lead bricks, and my body is sluggish. There's nothing to describe this depth of exhaustion. I decide to give into it by going to bed early. It's not often I can do this, so I might as well take advantage. I put on my pajamas and sink into the comforts of my bed. My sheets have never felt more inviting. Within seconds of my head hitting the pillow, I feel myself fall to unconsciousness.

I'm woken by the sound of my favorite ringtone. At first, I think I'm dreaming, but when it continues, I throw myself out of bed and race for my phone I'd left in the bathroom. By the time I get to it, I'm out of breath. "Enzo..." I nearly pant. "Is that really you?"

I hear the most beautiful and sexy laugh come from the other end of the line. "It sure is, beautiful. Did I catch you at a bad time?"

I walk back to my bed and snuggle under the covers, wanting to be as comfortable as I can for any length of time he can give me. "Not at all. I fell asleep and left my phone in the bathroom."

"It's only a little after nine, are you okay?" Enzo's concern is evident in his tone. *But, God, his voice sounds amazing to my ears.*

I fluff my pillow to get more comfortable and chuckle. "Well, Lexi took me shopping and we walked all over the mall. The kids are at Devin's and I'm tired. I took advantage of a night without commitments." But this isn't what I want to talk about. "Enough about me. How are you? Where have you been? Are you okay?" I rush out in a blur.

Another chortle comes out, then I hear, "Slow down, speedy. I've been doing my damnedest to tie up loose ends and have done a bit of traveling."

"Really? Are you able to tell me where?"

Suddenly my doorbell rings.

"Hold on, Enzo, there's someone at the door." *Who the hell would be here at this time of night?*

"Sure." I hear another muffled sound of laughter.

When I get to the bottom of the stairs, I peek out the window near the door and see a large figure on the porch, which makes me cautious.

When I flip on the light, I scream at the top of my lungs as I drop my phone. My pulse hammers, my adrenaline spikes, and suddenly, any bit of exhaustion I've had today disappears.

"Ohmigod! Ohmigod!"

The fucking door won't open.

"Oh, my fucking God! This isn't happening!"

Once I finally get the deadbolt to disengage and fling myself into the strong arms of the handsome man before me, I squeeze him for all he's worth. "Where the hell have you been?"

ENZO

I HEAR A SCREAM FROM THE OTHER SIDE OF THE DOOR. SHE'S realized I'm here. The light flips on and there's a rustle at the door. I hear, "Ohmigod! Ohmigod!"

Then the knob continues to be fiddled with. But the door doesn't open.

I know I shouldn't laugh, but her excitement to get to me sounds so fucking good. I'm just as eager to break through the door to get to her. Just knowing she's on the other side of the door sets a wave of emotions through me. I can't wait to set eyes on her.

Finally, the door flings open and a blur of excitement attacks me. She hugs me for all she's worth, climbing me in the process. As her legs wrap around me, I take in the delicious scent that is entirely Samantha. I have never been more relieved to see her.

These past few weeks have been hell. Not only did I have to fly one last mission, which was a shitstorm that took longer than necessary to right itself, I had to complete all my paperwork to separate and retire from the Air Force. I had started filling them out the minute I made my decision to retire, but there was still some last-minute paperwork, inventory, and things to take care of before I could leave.

My parents will probably have my ass that I didn't invite anyone to my official retirement ceremony, but I just wanted to get stateside. Having everyone travel to Germany would have postponed my departure date. When my CO told me I was free to leave, I got my ass on the next civilian plane out of Germany. It took a lot longer flying stand-by, but I'm so fucking relieved to be here. The sight of Samantha has made it worth every bit of hassle it caused.

Samantha takes me by surprise when she says, "Where the hell have you been?"

"Doing all I could to get to you, beautiful." I nuzzle her neck and pull her tighter.

"You couldn't have called or let me know you were okay?" She pulls back and levels me with a look I hope not to see often in our future.

Fuck. I was so set on getting home to surprise her, I just spent the last two days traveling. I hadn't considered she might be worried. I'm such an ass. How could I do this to her? "I... uh..." Fuck. I don't even know what to say. Nothing will be good enough.

Samantha pulls me close again. "It doesn't matter. You're here now. We can discuss where you've been for the last eighteen days later. Let's get inside so I can greet you properly."

Fuck, this woman's amazing. I pull her in tight and kiss her one last time before saying, "I think I can get on board with that."

She still has my hand as she gestures to the bag near our feet. "Is this all you have?" She looks around for a vehicle and a brow raises skeptically and the unasked question of *'how did you get here?'* crosses her features.

"I took an Uber," I state to get the questioning look off her face. "This is all I have until the rest of my things arrive in the next few weeks." I shoulder my bag on my right while tucking Samantha in on my left. We've been apart for far too long, there's no way I'm going to let her go anytime soon.

We walk through the door and I drop my bag and jacket in the living room, then turn to face her once more. "God, you're so fucking beautiful, Samantha." Now that she's in the light, I can see sleep lines from her pillow and her hair's a rumpled mess, but she has never been more exquisite to me.

"Are you hungry?" she asks.

"Only for you," I growl as I place my hands on her hips and pull her even closer.

"I can work with that," she breathily states, making her intentions clear as her hands find their way under my shirt and slowly move up my back. When it's clear she wants my shirt off, I step back and jerk my Henley over my head.

Samantha's eyes follow my shirt over my body. A low, "You are so freaking sexy," comes out of her mouth and I can't help but laugh. She's absolutely adorable when her filter's missing.

"Not as much as you, beautiful," I say as I step toward her and close the gap between us. I reach out and kiss her soundly as my hands become reacquainted with her body. There's no fucking way I will ever get enough of her. "Let's go upstairs."

I reach out to pick her up, but she shifts out of the way, and with a mischievous look in her eyes, she taunts, "Race you."

Before I can even register her intent, she's sprinting in the direction of the bedroom. I'm right on her trail, but instead of going to her bed as I expect, she races to the bathroom. "Give me a second."

"Oookkkaay," I draw out, wondering why she's going to the bathroom alone and not inviting me in, since she was nearly climbing me downstairs. A few seconds later, my question is answered when I hear the toilet flush, water turn on, then a cupboard door or two be thrown open and slammed shut. "Uh... Sam, everything okay in there?"

"Yep, be right out. Just want to get something."

Within another moment, Samantha walks out and completely leaves me breathless as she stands there in nothing but her naked glory. My eyes slowly roam up and down her body as I take her in, noticing some distinct changes due to pregnancy. Beautiful can no longer be a word that can adequately describe her. I suck in a deep breath before I pass out and continue to take in her features.

Her breasts immediately have my attention as they appear to have grown since last time I saw her. Her areolas have darkened, and her arousal is evident as her nipples pebble in my presence. They're pressed out further than normal because her hands are behind her back, apparently holding something. As I look further, I can see the beautiful swell of a very defined baby bump that I can't wait to cradle and put my hands on. I want to kiss every square inch of her body, devour her in ways I never thought were possible, and never let her go. I lick my lips in anticipation.

She clears her throat. Her face is an unusual shade of pink, as a sly grin forms. "Eyes up here, mister."

Damn, she caught me, but I have no shame. "I know, Sam, but how do you expect me not to take inventory since it's on display?"

"Um...." She appears shy for an instant. *What's she so hesitant about?*

"This is me, Samantha." I try to assure her she has nothing to worry about. "What's going on?"

"I... Uh... Thought we might try something."

Well, this has my attention. What could she possibly want to do that we haven't done?

"What do you have in mind?" I ask, my interest entirely piqued.

"You know that *gift* you bought me?"

From the way she says *gift*, my mind immediately goes to the vibrator, but I don't want to be a complete horndog. "By gift, you mean..."

From behind her back comes the vibrator in question. She hands it to me and lowers her lashes in a sultry way that would make me do just about anything for her. "Wanna play?"

Holy fuck! I was expecting a good old-fashioned ravishing, but she's up to bringing toys into the bedroom. I'd bought it to help get her off while I was gone, but if I'm being honest, I've often fantasized about using it with her as well. I've been dying to bring her to the edge so many times, she begs me to finish.

Before I can utter a word, my body kicks into overdrive and I find myself frantically kicking off my shoes and ridding myself of the rest of my clothes. "You can bet your sweet ass I'm interested in playing, beautiful," I growl when I reach out and pull her mouth to mine. I'm not sure how long we stand here kissing one another, but when she pushes me toward the bed, I take the hint.

Once there, we trade positions so that she's with her back on the bed. She quickly scoots up to lay her head on the pillow and I can't help but climb up after her. I nip and suck at each and every part of her body as I make my way up each sensual curve. My lips trace her inner thighs and she squirms in anticipation. I purposely skip over her center and make my way up to her belly bump. It's small, but it's extremely evident and couldn't be sexier. This woman's pregnant with my children and I'm the lucky bastard she's agreed to marry.

"Hello," I whisper as I get to her belly button. "Daddy's home and he's going to get to see you grow every day now."

"Enzo," Samantha groans. "I know you love our kids. But their mama has needs."

I know she's joking, but I can't help but laugh at the pure desperation in her voice. "Okay, beautiful. I won't keep you waiting."

I trace the frame of her body with my lips as I place an arm above her to brace myself and not put weight on her. Once I reach her neck, I go to the place that drives her wild behind her ear. She squirms, and I know I've met my mark.

With my free hand, I reach over and grope around the spot where I saw Samantha set the vibrator down. I continue to assault her with my lips and drive her wild in the best way I can. It feels like fucking forever, but finally, I find it and bring it to my face so I can peer at the buttons and switch it on. When she hears the vibrator come to life, her entire body jolts and I feel her body arch to reach mine, making me nearly want to forget about the toy in my hand.

"If you press the buttons again, it changes modes," she desperately pants.

What Samantha wants, Samantha gets. I'm just as desperate to fuck her like a wild animal, but if she wants to play first, I'll play with her until her heart's content. I press the button a few times and finally, I hear her breathless declaration. "There. That one. Gets me off like a rocket every time."

Holy fucking shit! Her words alone have me nearly coming undone. The thought of her actually using this to get herself off is a turn-on like no other. I bring it to her clit and gently massage it. I swipe it to her center and bring her wetness up to act as a natural lubricant. The way she simultaneously moans, arches her back, and claws at my biceps lets me know I'm doing something right. I reach down and grab a nipple with my mouth and tug ever so slightly.

"Oh... Enzo. Right. There," is one of the sexiest things I have heard.

I continue this until my need becomes too great. I have to taste her. I pull back on my haunches and press the wand inside of her as I take her clit in my mouth. I don't think she lasts longer than seconds before she detonates around me. Her body thrashes and screams fall from her lips.

"Holy. Fucking. Hell. Are you trying to kill me?" she pants as she pulls my hair to get me to back off. "I can't take any more. Ohmigod. I feel too much. It's sooo fucking good. I never thought I'd say this, but you have to turn it off."

Instantly, I pull the wand out her and leave it still vibrating on the bed. I reach down and press my hand to her slit and I feel the most indescribable tremors racking her body.

"Keep that up, Enzo. Ohmigod. It feels amazing." She places her hand over mine and presses harder, sending wave after wave of aftershocks going through her body. I've never seen anything so erotic in my life. The look of pure bliss that spreads across her face would keep me here for days.

I lie down beside her, keeping my hand in place as I prop my head up with my other one. I reach over and kiss her neck and she turns her face to kiss me. I lose track of time as I get swept up in a kiss. Her body eventually stops shaking and she shifts positions to reach my raging erection. God, if I let her touch me much longer, I will explode.

"Beautiful," I give out a warning and the next thing I know, she's straddling my lower legs as my erection bobs between us. She fists it and strokes me up and down. Her delicate fingers are firm and knowing their effect. A wide grin spreads across her face and I know she's up to something.

"I read about something online." *God, what could she possibly do now?* I'm seconds away from busting a nut and she acts like she wants to go all night long torturing me.

She lifts up to climb on top of me and I hold her hips to keep her steady. *She slides down my shaft until I'm balls deep in her and slowly works her way up.* She feels amazing. Slow and steady will be the death of me, *but what a way to go.*

"Christ, Sam," I growl. "You're killing me."

If I thought slow and steady was going to do me in, I was wrong. She steadies her hand on my chest and reaches over to grab the vibrator. Realizing her intentions, I eye her quizzically. *What's she up to now?*

She switches the speed, causing the pulse to make slow then fast movements and places it on the base of my shaft. Fuuuccckkk, that's the strangest and most amazing sensation I've ever felt. I've never used toys for myself, but holy hell, this takes things to an entirely new level. Each time she bottoms out, she grinds her clit onto it, sending me into the most epic orgasm I've never known to exist. Her breasts bounce in the best way, being etched into my mind forever. I do my damnedest to hold on until I feel her break apart.

I know she's there when she screams, "Enzo, omigod! I'm... I'm..." A large breath of air releases and as soon as she feels me emptying into her, she pulls the vibrator away and collapses onto my chest, panting hard and out of breath.

I lace my arms around her as we come down from whatever universe we'd just entered. I flip us to our sides, still completely seated in her, so she doesn't put any weight on our babies. I rub her back and hear her breathing settle to normal.

Before I know it, her breath is so deep I'm sure she's fallen asleep. The fact I'm still in her twitching like crazy has no effect on her. I pull back slightly and brush her hair from her face. Crap. She's asleep. *What the hell am I supposed to do now?* I can't say this has ever happened before. Talk about a hit to the ego. But I've never orgasmed like that either. I have two options: disentangle and clean us up or deal with the mess later. Her pussy feels like magic and I don't want to let her go for a second. Samantha in my arms is the absolute best fucking feeling in the world. After days of traveling, I'm exhausted, too. I reach over and cover us up with the blankets and drift off to sleep.

13

SAMANTHA

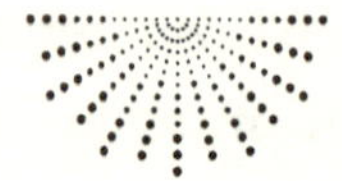

I'M HAVING THE MOST EROTIC DREAM OF MY LIFE. I KNOW IT'S A dream but it feels so amazing and real. I miss Enzo so much, I may never want to wake up. Enzo's finally here and we're snuggled in bed. I have my back to him and he's rubbing my clit in slow, lazy circles. I feel him lift my leg over his outer thigh and he thrusts inside of me. He's buried to the hilt inside of me and kisses my neck as his fingers work their magic. His soft whispers feel phenomenal against my neck as he does his best to make love to me.

His, "I love you so much, Samantha," sounds too real to be just a dream and the hairs on my neck tickle as I feel a warm breath flow over them.

"Oh, Enzo. God. Enzo. Don't stop," I moan and bring my own hand down to touch myself. But instead of feeling myself, I'm met with strong hands.

My eyes bolt open. *Holy crap. This is really happening. Enzo's really here. Last night wasn't just a dream. God, Sam, your imagination runs wild.* I reach up and pull his face closer to mine and turn my head to kiss him for all I'm worth. Reality is so much better than a dream.

By the time we actually surface from the bedroom later that morning, it's nearly eleven. I'd only gotten up once to call Lexi and let her know I wouldn't be in today. Thankfully, I didn't have any meetings with clients, so I'm able to take the day off without any repercussions. I would've taken it off even if I had to reschedule an entire day of meetings. There's no way I'm letting Enzo out of my sight anytime soon. That man has been away from me long enough.

We're settling down for breakfast, well, lunch really, when I ask, "So, what are your plans today?"

"Um…" He smiles around a bite a food and his freaking dimple pops. It gets me every time. I'm glad I'm sitting as I feel myself go weak in the knees. I've spent an entire night with him and I still can't get enough.

"Well…" Enzo wipes his face with a napkin then continues, "I will need to pick up a rental car at some point."

"How long will it be until your things arrive?" I know he said a couple of weeks, but maybe he knows something specific.

"If it goes like it usually has, it could still be a few weeks, possibly a month. My things have to arrive, then they have to clear customs before they're released to me."

"That seems like a long time. Are you sure you want to waste the money on a rental car? I'm sure we can work things out, and you could use mine."

"Samantha," Enzo chastises. "We need two cars. I've seen your crazy schedule and I want to lighten the load. Not add to it."

"Or… Since Maddie's starting driver's ed and my car won't be big enough for the new additions to our family." I involuntarily pat my stomach as I mention the reminder, then continue, "I was considering getting myself another car. We're going to need three within the next year."

"Well, that has possibilities. When does she start driver's ed?"

I laugh as I remember the argument she finally won. "Well, her fifteenth birthday's next week, on the sixth of February. She's miraculously convinced her father she should be enrolled as soon as she is legally allowed, to get as much experience as possible."

"Her birthday's next week, and you've never mentioned it?" He drops his fork to his plate and stares in disbelief.

"In my defense, I didn't think you'd be home. I would have told you, but it's never come up."

Enzo places his hand over his left brow and shakes his head as he looks at the table. I think I hear him mutter, "I'm an ass." But I'm not sure.

"What's wrong, Enzo?" I ask, wondering what he's calling himself an ass for.

"We'll be married in a few weeks, Sam. Don't you think I should know your kids' birthdays? I knew Maddie's was in February, but not the exact date."

I reach my arm out to comfort him. "Enzo. Honey. It's okay. I don't know your family's birthdays either. We have time to learn that." I get up from the table and walk to him and place my arms around his neck.

I kiss him once as his arms snake around my waist. "For the record, Declan's birthday is April fifteenth, and you already know Frankie's is November eighteenth." I kiss him on the nose before adding with a tease, "And so you never get into trouble, mine's June eleventh."

"Okay, smartass. I know that one." He swats me on the ass and pulls me close for a quick kiss. "I guess I just forgot Maddie's. I knew the rest. I've just been busy lately."

"Uh, you could say that again." Just thinking about what he's done in the last few weeks alone has given me hives. I'm glad it was him and not me moving to another continent.

"So what kind of car are you thinking?" His eyebrows waggle, letting me know he's no longer upset.

"Well, we need something that seats at least seven if we're all together."

"Holy shit, our family is huge," he says in disbelief.

"Well, you and your super sperm have seen that we're growing by two, in just a mere matter of months," I tease. "And —Just to be clear, there's no freaking way I'm driving a minivan. You can do it all you want, but I refuse. Even with our ginormous family, I refuse to stoop to that level."

"Um, not that I ever pictured myself rolling up in a minivan, but what do you have against them? Aren't they what all the hip parents are driving these days?"

"Ugh! Not on your life. You just watch when we go to pick up the kids from school today. Everyone has one… It's like they multiply like bunnies. They're everywhere. Nope. No way. Not for me. I like driving on the beach and not worrying about bad weather."

Enzo's expression turns surprised. "Okay. No minivans."

We spend more time talking about the possibility of different vehicles to drive, but never come to a consensus. He agrees that until we find the right vehicle for us, we'll just use my car to get us around. He doesn't have to report for work with Riggs until after our wedding, so it shouldn't be a problem.

Since Enzo's the epitome of punctual, we get out of the car and walk to meet Frankie and Dec at the front of the school, instead of pulling through the drive-thru parking routine, or the DNR as I refer to it each morning when the kids are running late and I have to push them out the door to arrive on time. He hoots with laughter when I inform him DNR refers to Dump-N-Run.

Students file out of the school as Enzo and I take notice of just how many minivans fill the parking lot. He had no idea they even made that many different models of the same car.

A high-pitched scream interrupts our conversation. Before either of us can register who made the noise, Frankie launches herself at Enzo. Thank God, his reflexes are phenomenal. He manages to catch her as she jumps into his arms and squeezes him with all she's got. I've never seen her so excited to see anyone, and her reaction instantly melts my heart. Apparently, I wasn't the only one to miss him so much.

"Enzo!" She pulls back to look him in the eye but doesn't let go. "You're here," comes out in almost a whisper in comparison to the scream she released just seconds ago.

The look of pure joy that spreads across his features makes

my ovaries burst. There's nothing better than seeing the man you love, loving your children as much as you do. Holy hell. The burst of emotion that flows through me nearly has my eyes springing a leak. As I wipe at my lashes, I shake my head and curse. *These damn hormones.*

"I'm here, sugar." Enzo squeezes her once more before placing her on the ground and ruffling her hair. "How was your day at school?"

"It was good. I was on the school news for the Joke of the Day."

"Really? What's the joke?" Enzo asks like he's waiting on pins and needles.

"A farmer had one hundred ninety-six cows in a field. But when he rounded them up, he had two hundred." Frankie laughs so hard at her own joke, we can't help but join her.

When Declan spots us, his pace picks up. "Hey, Enzo, when did you get back?" He, too, surprises me when he hugs Enzo in front of everyone. Enzo should cherish it. I don't even rate like that these days.

"Last night. What do you say to picking up your sister from school and going out to dinner to celebrate?" Enzo eagerly suggests.

As Frankie shouts, "Yes!" Dec has a defeated look cross his face and mumbles, "Can't."

Before I can interject, Enzo notices immediately. "What's wrong, bud?"

Declan kicks a rock on the pavement as he states, "I have soccer tryouts this week. I won't be done until seven."

Enzo nudges his shoulder to gain his attention as they walk side by side. "Dec, we have no problem waiting for you."

"Really? Mom always feeds Frankie while I'm at practice." He looks to Enzo for assurance.

"We can grab you both a snack on the way to practice," I offer, knowing how crushed Declan would be if we celebrated without him.

Relief washes over Enzo's features as he adds, "It wouldn't be a celebration without you, Dec."

When Maddie rushes to the car in the high school parking lot and automatically opens the passenger door to jump in, she's surprised to find me sitting here. She'd been oblivious with her face glued to her phone as she shot off another text to one of her friends. When she sees our driver, she screams, "Oh. My. God! Enzo, you're back!"

His deep chuckle fills the car as he points with his thumb behind him to the one and only empty seat left in the car. "I sure am. Hop in."

Since all three kids rarely sit in the back seat together, I notice what a tight fit it's becoming. Frankie sits in the middle and she bobs up and down with excitement when she fills Maddie in on our plans for the evening. I can't help but feel content when I see how effortless it is to have Enzo as a part of our daily routine.

While we wait for Declan to finish practice, Enzo asks if I'd mind driving by a few car lots to pass the time. He insists we won't buy one, but wants to get an idea of what I am looking for. It gets a little dicey when we let it be known to the sales woman we're looking for vehicles that seat seven or eight. Frankie shouts out, "Why do we need something so big? Is it because Enzo's so tall? He needs more leg room?"

Like a fish, Enzo's mouth opens. He attempts to say

something, then closes it again. He's got to have an answer for everything if he's going to keep up with her.

I burst out laughing and tears threaten to flow as well as some other bodily functions, forcing me to cross my legs as I bend with laughter. *The joys of being pregnant, for the fourth time.* I manage to mutter when I catch my breath, "Enzo... This is all on you." Though I'm referring to his super sperm and cock an eyebrow in his direction, the girls look to him for an answer.

Enzo finds his voice and without skipping a beat, asks, "Don't you like having friends come with you?" *Damn, the man's smooth.*

The girls seem to take it in stride and we move on to look around the lot. Even though we're both perfectly content to purchase a used vehicle with low mileage, Enzo insists on looking at the new vehicles because they have better safety ratings and warranty options. Though we find a few vehicles that would fit our needs, we tell the saleswoman we need more time when we realize it's time to pick up Declan and make our way back to the soccer fields.

As soon as Dec enters the car, he nearly shouts with excitement, "You'll never guess what happened tonight at practice. I made the team!" He bounces in his seat as he fumbles with his seat belt.

I knew he'd make the team. There are three in his age group and plenty of positions to go around. "That's great, Dec!" I encourage.

"No, Mom. You don't get it. I made the top team."

"Wow, Dec. That's awesome." Maddie fist bumps him as Frankie lets out a squeal of excitement.

"I knew you could do it," I state proudly.

Enzo chimes in with, "Now we have something to really celebrate! Why don't you pick where you want to go for dinner?"

Without a second of hesitation, Declan exclaims, "John's Incredible Pizza!"

"Pizza it is." Enzo's smile is infectious as he puts the car in drive.

14

SAMANTHA

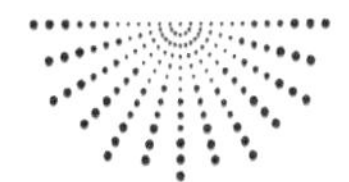

Enzo being home is better than I could have imagined. Waking up in his arms and falling asleep in them every night is more than a dream come true. Between being pregnant and making up for lost time with Enzo, I may be tired but I've never been happier. With Maddie's birthday tomorrow evening and our wedding next weekend, Enzo and I have been in pure planning mode.

Thank God for our wedding coordinator. All I need to do this week for the wedding is try on my dress. I hope like hell it still fits. My boobs are getting out of control and the baby bump is evident, especially if I wear anything remotely fitted. Being in my second trimester usually does this to me, but these twins want their presence known. I can't wait for the wedding to be over with, so everything will be official, and we can tell the kids about the new additions to our family.

As I drive to meet Lexi at the mall to do some last-minute

shopping, I can't help but smile when I think of how sweet Enzo is with our children. He not only continues to go out of his way to get to know Maddie, Dec, and Frankie better, but he has daily conversations with the babies growing inside me. Sure, there's been some stumbling blocks along the way, like Frankie trying to play both of us to get extra dessert before bed, but there hasn't been anything we can't handle.

Lexi meets me outside of our favorite department store and gives me a low whistle.

"What was that for?" I ask, looking around to find what I'm missing out on.

"Your girls." She looks pointedly at my boobs and smirks. "Have they grown overnight? I swear, you wore that shirt last week and looked nothing like you do today."

I feel my eyes roll at her dramatic statement. Sure, they've grown, but I don't think it's too noticeable. Dripping with sarcasm, I reply, "I give new meaning for needing an over-the-shoulder boulder holder, don't I?"

"You've got that right. I'm sure you don't have any complaints from that sexy man of yours, though. You look hot!" She waggles her eyebrows to emphasize her point and I can't help but laugh.

"Enzo certainly has taken a liking to them." I shake my head and look down at my chest. Crap. I can't see my toes since my chest is in the way. "But seriously, I think we need to add shopping for bras to our list today."

"As long as we pick up something sexy for your honeymoon, too."

"Lex, Enzo's seen the goods." I point to my belly and laugh.

"He's sampled them, too, obviously. I'm not even sure something will be considered sexy in the size I'm going to need."

"Now you're being ridiculous, Sam. This is his first night as a married man. You need something sexy as sin that will have his heart beating out of his chest."

The thought alone has me picking up my pace to the boutique. I can't wait to find something that will blow Enzo's mind.

Unfortunately, as soon as I'm back in the dressing room with a bra I thought would be my size, I realize I need to be fitted. These suckers have taken on a life of their own and I have no idea what will contain them. The sales associate comes to fit me, and my jaw drops when she reveals my size. When Lexi hears it, she laughs hysterically.

"What the fuck is E?" I mutter after the saleswoman goes to get some choices in my size.

"E is for enormous," Lexi boldly states, like this is a normal occurrence.

"I didn't even know they went past size D," I complain. Holy Hell, I'm huge. I've always been a C-cup. How the hell did I get this big? "Being a woman, sucks."

"No kidding," Lexi commiserates with me, then adds with a straight face, "No man ever has to measure their parts to get something to fit. Heck, no one even thinks man parts should be supported, except for direct-contact sports."

So many images flash through my mind at her comment. The thought alone of how they would even measure it has me in stitches, making me lean against the wall for support. "Only you would think of that, Lex. Thanks for the mental image I now need to burn from my mind."

Once we contain our laughter, Lexi gets back to business. "Now that we know your size, let's get you something sexy to wear."

By the time I arrive home, I'm dead on my feet. Lexi's a born shopper. She managed to help me find something I can't wait to wear on my honeymoon and finish picking out Maddie's birthday gift. The woman's a shopping queen. I even picked up my ring for Enzo from the jewelers, now that I know his ring size.

The next morning, after getting the kids off to school, Enzo and I do some last-minute preparations for Maddie's birthday party this evening. For some reason, Maddie convinced us having a birthday party on a Friday night would be a good idea, but this means I had to take the day off for preparation. Enzo volunteered to run errands this morning, while I cook some of Maddie's favorite foods. Maddie thinks a taco bar will be a hit. Everyone gets what they want, and I can do a lot of the prep work earlier in the day.

At first, Maddie wanted a sleepover with a few of her closest friends. Then she wanted to invite Soren, a few of his friends, as well as some other guys. Needless to say, nearly thirty teenagers will arrive around seven.

Devin and his girlfriend Aubrey are coming over to help celebrate, as well as be adult reinforcements. This should make Maddie's first boy-girl party interesting. Devin promises to behave, but keeps teasing her about walking around with a ruler when people dance, making sure we have every light on in the house, and that Frankie and Dec will be on patrol. *Heaven help him if he actually follows through with any of this.*

Just as I bend over to reach the pan of seven-layer dip at the bottom of the fridge, I feel two strong arms snake around my waist, making me yelp in surprise. *How the hell can Enzo be so stealthy? Was he a ninja in another life?*

"Hey, beautiful," he whispers into my ear.

"How do you always manage to sneak up on me?" I forget about the food and twist in his arms to face him. His smile makes his dimple pop and my knees go weak. *How can I still feel this way after all this time? Won't I build up an immunity at some point?*

"I simply walked in the room, Sam. Nothing to get worked up about." He nestles into my neck and kisses up to my earlobe. "God, I hope you never get immune to me. I love how responsive you are."

There's a carnal need to be closer to him, but the doorbell rings and we hear feet coming down the stairs, forcing Enzo to pull away. Frankie's the one person who will never sneak up on you in this house. I turn to hide in the fridge for a moment, regaining control of myself. Remembering why I was in here to begin with, I grab the seven-layer dip to place on the center island where I have the rest of the food laid out, ready for the party.

Enzo greets Devin and Aubrey, "Glad you could make it. Come on in. You can put the presents in the family room on the table set up, and I'll put this beer and bottle of wine in the fridge."

Devin reaches out his hand to shake in greeting before he

walks to put the gift out of the way. Aubrey follows Enzo into the kitchen.

"Wow, Sam. You've outdone yourself." She looks around hesitantly. "Is there anything I can do to help you get ready?"

"I've about got it covered. But if you want, you can put some serving spoons in these dishes. The kids should arrive shortly, and we told everyone to bring their appetite." I laugh as I point to the drawer beside her to find the spoons.

Devin walks into the room and looks around. "Looks good, Sam. When will everyone arrive?"

"They'll be here at seven," Frankie pipes in as she picks up a chip to snack on.

Devin looks at his watch. "So, how many boys?"

Of course, he goes there. This is Devin. I shouldn't be surprised. Maddie comes barreling into the kitchen. "Daaad, you promised," she pleads, then looks to me for help. "Mom, you won't let him be mean to my friends, will you?"

Before I say anything, Devin adds, "Don't worry, Mads. I'm teasing." He walks to her and gives her a hug. "A dad has some duties in life. Scaring boys is just part of the fun."

It's hard to contain our laughter but I manage to keep a straight face at least for a few seconds until Maddie turns away. Poor girl. She's been stressed about her dad all afternoon. Hopefully, her friends will arrive soon, so she can get out of the hotspot.

"So, Maddie, did you pass your test to get your learner's permit?" Aubrey changes the subject gracefully and Maddie changes her mood drastically.

If the grin on Maddie's face was any bigger, it would split in half. "Yep!" she draws out, popping the end.

"That's great, sweetheart. I'm happy for you."

"Now, I just need people who are willing to ride with me," Maddie teases as she looks pointedly around the room at each of the adults.

"I'll take you later this week when you come to visit," Devin offers as he attempts to rustle her hair but she dodges his hand.

"Can I stay home?" Frankie pleads. "I'm too young to die," she dramatically adds, making us laugh.

"Cut it out, Frankie." Maddie glowers in her sister's direction. Then points her focus on me, raising a knowing eyebrow.

"Of course, Mads," I offer, but before I can say more, Enzo interrupts.

"Add me to the list. I know the perfect place to practice and no one will be in any danger." He winks at Frankie.

"Wow. It looks like I'll be getting lots of experience."

The doorbell rings and Maddie's friends soon fill our home. Soren's the first to arrive, and more guests immediately follow after him. He greets Maddie with a kiss on the cheek. That's bold with both Devin and Enzo in the room, but he's been doing this for some time. Maybe they're immune? I glance to Devin who narrows his eyes in Maddie's direction. Not everyone is immune to this, apparently. Dads will be dads. He can deal with this. I need to show our guests where the food is and keep the kitchen stocked.

The party's in full swing by the time I take my first break. Presents have been opened, cake has been served, and everyone's eaten. Well, they've been through the kitchen multiple times. If they go hungry, that's on them. I'm not sure the total headcount, but if I had to guess, I'd say there were more than thirty teenagers here. Aubrey, Enzo, and I sit at the island in our kitchen while Devin plays a video game with Declan and Frankie in his room. Enzo sits beside me, stroking my leg absentmindedly as he takes a drink from the beer in his other hand.

Aubrey stands and walks to the fridge. "Want some wine?" she offers as she pulls it out.

"No, thanks," I sigh regretfully when I see the bottle again. I love Latah Creek's huckleberry wine.

She looks at the bottle, and then at me. "Did I get the wrong kind? I swear Devin said this is your favorite."

"No," I exhale, remembering the taste of the Riesling she holds in my direction. The thought alone makes my mouth water. It'll be months before I can relax with that deliciousness again. "He's right. It's my favorite." I stare at the bottle, wishing I could have a taste. It's not like I drink it often, but knowing I can't have it makes me suddenly want it.

"You sure? I feel bad drinking it without you. I can save it for you and drink something else, if you don't want to open it," she offers sincerely. As I've gotten to know Aubrey more this evening, I really do think we could be friends in the future. We seem to have much more in common than I imagined.

My hand instinctively rubs along my growing belly, under the countertop. "No, go ahead and enjoy it. There's no sense in letting it just sit there."

"Really?" Her head tilts to the side, gauging my response.

"Absolutely."

"Here." Enzo reaches for the bottle. "Let me open it for you."

He walks to a drawer on the far side of the kitchen and pulls out the corkscrew to open it for her. I can't help but be mesmerized by his muscular back as he removes the cork from its bottle. Is there anything he does that isn't sexy? Before returning to Aubrey, he pulls out a wine glass from the cabinet and pours it for her.

"Thank you, Enzo," she says, then takes a sip and quietly moans. "Wow. This is so good. I've never had it before."

She brought it just for me? How sweet of her. "It's fantastic," I offer.

Aubrey returns to her chair on our side of the island and glances at my hand rubbing along my stomach and quirks an eyebrow in my direction. "You sure you don't want any?"

"Really, I'm fine. Just relax and enjoy yourself. We'll have to make the rounds soon enough to check on everyone."

Her face fills with a knowing expression and I realize she's staring at my hand caressing my stomach. Crap. There's no denying my actions. I hear Enzo let out a quiet chuckle as he realizes the cat's out of the bag.

Aubrey whispers in our direction, "Are congratulations in order?"

"We want to wait until after the wedding before saying anything," I whisper in return, so that it won't become a rumor spreading throughout the party and the kids find out.

"Wow." Aubrey's eyes turn wistful. "That's amazing. I've always wanted to have kids of my own someday. But that's not in the cards for me."

How sad. Aubrey would make a great mom. The kids seem to love her. "I'm sorry."

"Oh, don't be. It's not like I can't get artificially inseminated, should I choose to."

What the hell is she talking about? Why would she need to do that? Better yet, why is she telling us this?

The puzzled look on my face must make her want to explain further. "Well. You know…" She looks in the direction that Devin left to play with the kids. "With Devin's vasectomy and all. If he and I stay together, I'll have to either accept that I won't have kids of my own, adopt, or since Devin refuses to get it reversed, I could always go to a sperm bank." She giggles a little at the end. *Just how much has she had to drink?*

I feel Enzo tense beside me. I can't look in his direction. I'm shocked by the news of Devin's vasectomy. I try to respond, but my thoughts get stuck in my head. When did he do this?

Without any prompting, Aubrey continues, not realizing she's just dropped a bomb on me. "I can't see him wanting any more than three kids, since that's the reason he got the vasectomy in the first place. Right after Frankie was born."

What. The. Fuck. "Devin's had a vasectomy?" I mumble to myself.

Enzo must hear. He suddenly stands from the stool he was perched on and holds out his hand to me. He glances at Aubrey. "Would you excuse us for a second?"

Aubrey says something, but I have no idea what it is. I feel myself being tugged up the stairs to my bedroom. My mind keeps replaying the last few moments on a loop. I can't even think of how to respond. I'm so stunned Devin's had a vasectomy. *Wait. Right after Frankie was born?* Holy fucking shit! All those months of us trying to get pregnant. Month after month of having my period. Those tears I shed when I started my cycle each month.

As we reach the top of the stairs, I feel like it's getting harder to breathe. My chest tightens and my eyes sting from the prick of tears attempting to fall. What the actual fuck? Devin had a fucking vasectomy years ago and didn't bother to tell me? My vision blurs completely and suddenly, all I see is red.

15

ENZO

I DIDN'T HEAR THAT CORRECTLY. THERE'S NO FUCKING WAY THE fucker got a vasectomy years ago and didn't tell Sam. Who the fuck does that shit to his wife? Or at least, let her be a part of the decision. I can't help but think of when the condom broke in her office. She heartbreakingly explained why she thought she couldn't have kids. It's evident she'd been devastated each and every fucking month. Hell, I'd been decimated for the sheer thought of her loss.

What a cock-sucking bastard. I knew he was selfish. Who the fuck cheats on a woman as amazing as Samantha? Since I've met him, I can't say Devin and I have been close or anything, but we seem to have a mutual respect for one another. We get along for the sake of the kids. Now, I just want to punch his fucking throat out.

The look on her face when the realization hit. I'd murder him right now and spread his body across the continents, if I knew it wouldn't hurt the kids or Samantha even more. I had to get her out of that fucking kitchen as fast as possible. There's no way I would let her implode, or worse, explode in front of Maddie and her friends.

Christ. What the fuck do I say to her? I can tell she's working herself up. I've never seen her mad, but if I were in her shoes, I'd blow a gasket. I'm not even the one who had to deal with having a period month after month, thinking something was wrong with me. Fucking bastard isn't even a strong enough word to describe my loathing for Devin at this moment.

As soon as we're in the privacy of our bedroom, I shut the door, quickly pull her to me, and kiss the top of her head. "It's okay, beautiful. I'm right here. There's nothing you can say that will make me love you any less. Get it off your chest and let's deal with this together." I wrap my arms around her tightly and feel her body taking large breaths, as if to calm herself.

"I... I... I can't even..." she mumbles as she pulls me tighter.

"Shhh, beautiful. It's all right. I'm right here. Just say what's on your mind and let's get it out there."

Her voice is calm, but there's an eeriness when it's barely heard above a whisper. "Enzo. He kept this from me, for years. He mentioned wanting to get one, once. But he never told me he went through with it. I'd told him I wasn't sure if I wanted more kids. I wanted to wait and see how things went with Frankie before any final decisions were made. When she was about a year old, I realized I wanted a little brother or sister for her. Maddie's so much older than Dec, it's like she was an only child. There's always an odd man out."

I don't say anything but hold her closer.

"Devin started working more trips out of town to help

cover the costs of the new baby. Holy shit!" she suddenly exclaims, as if she has had a new thought. "You don't think he started having affairs around that time, do you?" Samantha's fists ball up and I can tell she's getting angrier by the second.

"I have no idea. But anyone who'd cheat on you is a fool, Samantha. You're the most amazing woman in this world. I'd be so lost without you," I offer as I pull her close once again.

Samantha holds me for a long while. Eventually, her breathing calms, her body loosens, and her mold to me intensifies somehow. Thousands of thoughts run through my mind. None of which are worth repeating, as they would only fuel the fire of discontent.

"Was I a fool for not knowing?" Samantha's voice is weak and breaks at the end, causing my heart to constrict. I fucking hate seeing her in pain. Devin's lucky she's my priority right now. Her self-doubt rips me apart and who the hell knows what I'd do if he and I were alone right now.

"This is on him, Samantha," I grit out as I pull her closer. What a bastard. Now she's doubting herself.

"Why wouldn't he tell me?" she asks, but I'm sure it's for her benefit, not mine. I sure as hell don't have the answer. How the hell is this her fault?

"We'll get to the bottom of this once Maddie's friends leave," I suggest, not wanting her to cause a scene.

I seriously can't wait to hear what Devin's fucking excuse will be when he's confronted. I hope she finds the anger she started with, rather than this self-deprecation. *Seriously, who the fuck gets a vasectomy and doesn't tell his wife?* Maybe he had something to hide or didn't want to risk anyone else getting pregnant. Fuck, Devin is such a douche. After a long moment, she takes in a deep breath. I feel her pull back to look me in the eye. Her expression surprises me as she says, "No, I don't think that's necessary."

"Why the fuck not?" I ask in disbelief. I would want fucking answers. He lied to her and should be fucking called on his shit.

"Some things are just better off not knowing. I don't want to know when he started cheating on me. Finding out about the affairs I do know about was hard enough to go through. It won't change anything, and I've spent years dealing with the hurt he put me through. I refuse to hang on to anger. It consumed me for so long." She pats her belly and stares at me lovingly. "I have too many other things that take priority."

I have no words. This woman continues to amaze me at every turn. I'd go fucking ballistic. Not only would I rip him a new asshole, but I'd tell him where to go and how to get there. There'd be no doubt about my feelings over this. But I can see where she's coming from. A little.

"I wouldn't hold it against you, if you told him off." I tip her chin so I can look directly in her eyes and she can't hide her feelings about this.

"I'm serious, Enzo. It won't do me any good to say anything."

"He deserves to know how you feel, Sam. It was shitty of him to not tell you about this. Not only did you experience month after month of misery, hoping your period would never come, but the fact that you longed for a baby for years is beyond words to me."

"Ha, I guess the joke's on him," she mutters.

What the fuck is she talking about? What joke? She

reaches for my hands to place them on her growing belly. "What do you mean, beautiful?" I whisper, trying to calm myself.

"I mean, if he hadn't cheated on me, I wouldn't have been content with my life. I would never have experienced this." She motions between the two of us to prove her point. "If he hadn't gotten a vasectomy, I'd have never thought the problem was with me."

"That's fucking bullshit," I seethe. "You never should have felt like something was wrong with you, Samantha."

Somehow, Samantha smiles. Her knowing look and the coy smile that follows almost knocks me on my ass. "If I hadn't thought there was something wrong with me, I would have never had unprotected sex with you, silly." She pokes me in the belly and almost makes me crack a smile. "I would have been on some form of birth control. That's the kind of responsible person I am. I'm a planner." She's quiet for a moment then adds, "Holy hell, I never saw you coming. Everything about you sets my world on fire and makes me feel things I never imagined."

I chuckle, but before I can respond, she continues, "With you, Enzo, I'm reaching dreams I never thought were possible. I never knew how much I wanted more kids until I saw those two blips on the screen."

"Me, too, beautiful," I whisper, suddenly choked with emotion.

"Of course, you and your super sperm had to do the job extra well." She shakes her head and laughs at the absurdity. "Just wait until Devin finds out we're not only pregnant, but having twins. He'll never experience this." She wraps her arms around my neck and pulls me closer. "He'll never experience the kind of love we share with one another and for our growing family."

When she reaches up on her toes, I lean down to close the gap, pressing my lips to hers. The warmth of her body as it presses against mine is something I never want to live without. I place my arms around her waist and revel in the moment. My hands roam her back and we stand here for a long moment, just enjoying one another.

Wanting her closer, I reach under her ass, lifting her to my height and kiss her for all I'm worth. Her baby bump rests against my stomach as her legs naturally wrap around my waist. Before getting too carried away, I suddenly feel something strange move across my stomach, causing me to instantly still. *What the fuck was that?*

I pull back from the kiss and stare into her eyes, hoping she will answer my unasked question. There's a slight movement again, as if something is slowly moving across her stomach.

I set her down and eye her suspiciously. "Did you feel that?" I ask in wonder.

"The better question is, did you?" She quirks an eyebrow. "I think these little monsters heard us talking about them."

"That's what they feel like when they kick?" I ask in disbelief.

She lets out a little chuckle. "That's not how it usually feels. I started feeling them flutter from time to time, but that was the first real kick." She places her hand on her belly to feel them again.

When I see movement, I quickly reach out to her and place

my hand right along with hers. Holy hell. It's like there's an alien inside her. There's a thump, thump, thump against my hand. It's not hard, but definitely movement. I'm in complete awe of this woman. She's had five humans grow inside of her. "How often do they move?" I whisper, not wanting to accidentally stop the action.

"It depends. I've never had multiples before. Usually I don't feel much movement this early, but maybe there's less space in there." She shrugs as if she's speculating at the end. Samantha couldn't be any cuter if she tried.

After a moment, the babies still. She presses on her belly, but no further movement happens. "I think they're done for now," she sighs wistfully.

A thud from downstairs interrupts our moment, and reality comes crashing back. As much as I don't want to leave this room, I suggest, "We'd better get back downstairs. We left a house full of teenagers on the loose, and Aubrey and Devin are alone."

"Yeah," is all I get in response.

"You sure you're okay?" I pull her close to me for a hug.

"I'm not pleased he kept it from me, but I'm not willing to let this ruin Maddie's party, or our happiness."

The woman is a fucking saint. I'm still pissed at the asshole. But if she's taking the high road, I'll follow her lead. *Even if I want to sucker punch him in the nuts.*

16

SAMANTHA

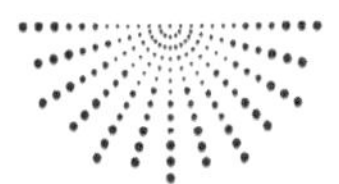

SOMEHOW, ENZO AND I MANAGE TO MAKE IT THROUGH THE PARTY without any further drama. Even though I'm incredibly irritated with Devin, having the two of them here was handy. By the time Enzo and I come downstairs, most of the kitchen's clean and leftover food has been put into tubs and placed in my fridge. Aubrey even took the liberty of doing the few dishes in the sink. Devin realizes something's wrong but is smart enough not to bring it up. Maybe Aubrey let the cat out of the bag to spare us from having to fill him in. When they leave, they graciously offer to take Declan and Frankie for the night. They know how loud slumber parties can be.

The next morning, as Enzo piles on pancakes to everyone's plates, I add sausage and eggs. Each girl's melancholy compared to last night and eats in silence. Occasionally, conversations continue about what had happened at the party, but for the most part, they keep to themselves.

As soon as they finish eating, the majority of the girls go

home, leaving only Nicole and Maddie visiting in the family room. Enzo's doing dishes and I'm sitting to eat while Maddie and Nicole curl up on the couch, deep in conversation, which is typical for them. I'm surprised when I hear Nicole mention, "Hey, Maddie, is your mom feeling all right?"

Maddie glances in my direction and I shrug, wondering where Nicole is going with this. "Yeah, I think so."

When Nicole realizes I'm paying attention, she directs her comment to me, "Sorry, Mrs. O'Reilly. No offense."

"None taken." I shrug, wondering why she thinks I'm sick.

"Well, it's just that." Nicole blushes and appears embarrassed, but I eye her skeptically to continue and she does without any further prompting. "Well... you seem to be really exhausted and there's something about you that's different. I don't know. I... I mean, you look great. Glowing even, but you're dressing differently and..." she trails off.

Holy fuck. She knows I'm pregnant. How the fuck can she know this? I take in a deep breath and slowly release it, trying like hell not to let my sudden tension show. I turn my attention to Maddie and see the wheels turning in her head. She boldly eyes me up and down. When she reaches my midsection, she stops and stares. Maddie's expression morphs from confusion, to shock, to what I can only describe as denial.

"Oh. My. God. You're not... Are you? There's no way you can be..." Suddenly, she grits out in a hiss, "You're such a hypocrite."

Wondering where the anger is coming from, I ask, "What do you mean?"

"You sat Soren and me down in this very room and lit into

us. You had the 'sex talk,' right here in front of him. It was beyond embarrassing."

Without thinking, I burst out a response to her, "Well, the timing was right. You came in here talking about one of your friends staying out all night with a girl. You and Soren have been together awhile. The odds are you were either A… Already having sex or B… At least thinking about it. I thought I would hedge my bets and take the side of safety."

"But you know we're not having sex," Maddie retorts.

"I know that, now. I would have had that talk with you no matter what. I've always been frank with you, Mads. You know that."

"But… But…" she mutters and I see the wheels still turning in her head.

I feel Enzo come to my side as I wait out Maddie, to find where she's going with this. He places a hand on my back, showing moral support.

After a long while, I quietly state, "I'm not a hypocrite, Maddie. You know that."

"But are you…" She looks between Enzo and me, then back to my belly. If I wasn't in the midst of having to defend myself, I'd almost think her ogling was comical. Unfortunately, this means I have a lot more explaining to do than I ever intended.

"But what?" Enzo finally breaks his silence.

"Are you guys… Um… Pregnant?" Maddie finally whispers, her eyes still wide in disbelief.

"Yes," Enzo's deep voice rings out. "But I want you to be clear on a few things before you jump to any more conclusions." His tone is one I've never heard before. It's commanding, and not to be messed with.

Maddie takes the hint and waits for him to continue.

Enzo reaches for my trembling hand. I'd been worried as to how to tell the kids, and didn't think we'd have to say anything until after the wedding. A pin drop can be heard throughout the house as we all wait for him to continue.

"First," Enzo's deep voice breaks the silence. "Like I told you when I asked if I could marry your mother, I love her more than life itself. Second, I love you kids, too. I never knew what I'd been missing until I met your mom and you kids. Did we expect to add more kids to the family? No. But are we ecstatic about it? Hell yes. I'm so happy I get to be a part of five kids' lives. I'm freaking scared to death I won't know what to do, but I'm hoping with all of your help, I'll be a great dad to all of you. Don't get me wrong. I'm not trying to replace your dad, but I want to be there for you, too."

He takes a big breath, then continues before anyone can say anything. "Your mom loves you. She does everything in her power to protect you, even if it means causing embarrassment to set things right. You need to get a few things straight. She's not a hypocrite and this isn't her fault." Enzo takes another settling breath and I swear, the tips of his ears turn a few shades darker, but only if you know him like I do. He continues with, "It... Uh... Takes two to tango. I'm just as at fault as she is for this unexpected pregnancy. Not that it's any of your business, but we were careful, and it still happened."

Maddie's mouth hangs open and my heart squeezes as tears prick my eyes. His words have my emotions reeling. I don't think I could love this man any more than I do right at this moment.

The torch of anger Maddie's been carrying is quickly put

out. She looks from me to him, then back to me. She approaches me with tears in her eyes. "I'm sorry, Mom." She reaches out for a hug and I squeeze her tight.

"It's okay, honey."

Maddie pulls back and looks me in the eye. "I'm really going to be a big sister again?"

"Yep." I smile widely with tears still blurring my vision. "You most certainly are."

She then turns to Enzo and holds out her arms to him. She hugs him as well. "I guess congratulations are in order."

"Thank you, Mads. It means the world that you're happy for us." Enzo's voice is thick with emotion at the end.

"When are you due?" Maddie asks enthusiastically.

"July," I state, not knowing how long I'll be able to last with two kiddos. Each of my other kids came a week early, so who knows with twins.

"Wow. That's just... Wow." Maddie eyes me over. She places her hands on my belly and I'm sure she can feel the bump that I've been trying to hide.

When she releases me with wonderment in her eyes, I look between her and Nicole. "Hey... Uh... If you don't mind, can we wait until after next week to tell everyone? I'd really like to keep the focus on our wedding."

"No problem," Nicole speaks as Maddie nods in agreement.

Nicole's face suddenly fills with confusion. "Wait... Enzo, you do know you're only going to be a father to four kids, right? You said five kids."

Enzo's eyes shine with delight. This eagerness rolls off him and his smile's infectious. "Nope." He pops the p at the end. "I meant five. Sam's having twins, can you believe it?"

Both Maddie and Nicole's jaws drop nearly to the floor. Maddie is the first to recover. "Wow. There's two growing inside you? That's. Just... Wow..."

Enzo wraps his arms from behind me, his hands cradle the baby bump that's the center of attention. Though I'd rather this be under different circumstances, I'm glad everything's out in the open. I'm sure Frankie and Declan will be shocked when they learn about the twins.

"When will you know if they're a boy or girl?" Nicole asks in awe. "I've always wanted a younger brother or sister. But now that I'm in high school, I'm fine with being the only child."

"Oh my God, Mom!" Maddie gasps. "People are going to think I'm their mom if I take them in public."

"We'll make sure you set them straight." Enzo chuckles. "We can get you an 'I'm the sister' t-shirt, so you never have to explain."

"Hopefully, it'll be a long time before you have kids of your own, Mads. I'm too young to be a grandma, officially. Besides, these two are likely going to be amazing birth control for you in the future. You're in charge of late-night feedings and diaper changes." Sarcasm drips off my tongue at the end, making us burst into laughter. *God, I hope she knows I'm joking, even if it might be the most effective birth control I could ever give her.*

17

ENZO

Whirlwind doesn't even describe what life's been like since I've been stateside. I can't wait to be married to Samantha. Not only will we get to tell the world I'm going to be a father, but she'll be officially mine. Four more days. Just four more days and Samantha will be my wife.

I love that woman more than I ever thought was possible. She handles things with grace and dignity. Between finding out about Devin's vasectomy and Maddie finding out about the twins, these past few days have taken their emotional toll on us. Though I would've punched his fucking lights out, Samantha, as usual, took the high road.

Tonight, Lexi has asked Sam to go out to dinner. I know it's going to turn into her bachelorette party since Erin let the cat out of the bag when she called to ask me for directions earlier. With it being a Wednesday night, the girls can't get into too much trouble. I'm heading over to my parents' and have dinner with Pops and my brother, Zane. We're on kid patrol, so Erin can go out.

I'm so fucking relieved none of the guys from my former unit are around for a bachelor party. We've done some crazy shit over the years to each man who took the plunge into matrimony. Being the perpetual bachelor, I'd be in some serious trouble if they'd had time to plan anything. Thank God for small miracles.

When I get to my parents', I let myself in through the kitchen. There's noise in the living room, but it doesn't sound like kids. The hairs on the back of my neck rise when I realize there's more than the sound of three men's voices coming from the other room. Who the hell are Dad, Nate, and Zane talking to?

When I enter the family room, I'm blown away when I hear, "Here's the man," from none other than Mack Gunderson, my buddy since basic. How did he get leave so soon after his vacation to London? He must have pulled some serious strings. But then again, he probably has plenty of time to spare as he, too, is single and nearing retirement.

"Holy shit, is that really you?" I shorten the distance between us to shake his hand before pulling him into a man-hug. After a few hard slaps on the back, we let go of each other. "What the hell are you doing here?" I ask, still reeling in disbelief.

"You think I was gonna let you get married without fuckin' being here? I have to report back to command that you, the king of perpetual bachelors, has fallen from his throne."

There's laughter from around the room and for the first time, I look to see who's here. Holy fuck. There's got to be about fifteen full-size men in Ma's family room. Where the hell did they park? Each of them has shit-eating grins plastered on their faces and I can't help but join them.

"Damn, you got me." I laugh, shaking my head. *I didn't see this coming.*

"Harps, we couldn't let you get away without a bachelor party." Nate Carson reaches out his hand and pulls me in for another back-slapping hug.

"Hell, it's great to see you, Cars." I feel like a tool to let them slip this over on me.

Before Cars can respond, Rowan interrupts, waggling his eyebrows, "I've taken the *liberty* of planning tonight's events. You can thank me later."

Oh, fuck. This could go so wrong tonight. "No fucking strippers. I've got all I need with Samantha."

"Oh, don't be such a sourpuss," Pops, of all people, chimes in. What. The. Fuck. I'd never take him for a strip-joint man.

Zane walks over to greet me with a handshake. "Hey, man. I distinctly remember, you were all about the strippers at my bachelor party. Payback's a bitch, brother." Zane's mischievous grin tells me he knows something I don't. Christ. I hope it's not what I think it is.

The next to greet me is Nate, my brother-in-law. He's flanked by my boisterous cousins. Each is about ten years younger than I, but are married nonetheless. Gabe, Mike, and Heath all have smug grins plastered on their faces. They know what's coming, but knowing these numbskulls, they won't let me in on the secret. *God, I wish I wasn't such a jackass to them at their bachelor parties. I have a feeling I'm going to pay for my sins tonight.*

Each of my cousins greets me with a handshake and slap on the back. They all have something snide to say that makes me worry my fears are coming true.

I'm pleased to see Riggs, Boone, and many of the guys from Riggs' barbeque here, too. Carson must have invited them. Sure, we've worked together before, but I guess nothing says bonding like a bachelor party. Christ, I hope I don't live to regret this night.

Holy shit, Brian Ford, my buddy from high school's even here. I haven't seen him since his wedding, about five years ago. I walk over to him and thank him for coming. He razzes me about finally taking the plunge, but before I move on to greet another guest, he sincerely states, "Congratulations, man. You're in for the ride of your life." I can't help but think of Samantha and everything that's happened since we met. It sure has been a ride, but it's one I never want to get off.

I take the time to introduce Jason Riggs and the members of the team I will soon work with to my family. I haven't worked with Trent Daniels, Drew Warren, or Ira Michaels much in the past, but from the way they're joking around, I'm sure to get along well with them.

Once I've greeted everyone, Rowan announces to the crowd, "Gentlemen…" Quickly, the crowd settles and he continues, "If you'll follow me, I've arranged for our night of festivities as we celebrate Enzo's end to being a bachelor."

Hoots and hollers erupt around the room. Comments range from, "Sorry, sucker," to "It's about time," and probably everything these bozos in front of me can think of. These guys let me know their thoughts on my impending nuptials.

We walk outside to find two large custom passenger vans,

with accompanying drivers, parked in my parents' driveway. They weren't here before when I parked. We each pile into one of the vehicles. Once inside, I find they seat fifteen, but with most of us being larger than average height, I'm sure Rowan took that into consideration when he ordered the vans.

Rowan takes a seat next to me. I turn to him, shaking my head. "How the hell did you pull this off?"

"You know me and secrets, Harps. Planning this was a walk in the park." Rowan waggles his eyebrows, causing me to sigh and shake my head.

"At least tell me this," I plead. "Will Samantha be speaking to me in the morning?"

The entire van erupts with laughter. I internally cringe at all the things he could have up his sleeve. Why the fuck did I get in this car?

Gunderson doesn't make it any better when he chimes in, "Oh, Harps. You should be scared."

"I've been looking forward to this night for the past few weeks," Ira Michaels pipes in. "Tonight's going to be legendary! It's sure to keep up with the stories Carson's told me about you."

Fuck a duck! I'm utterly screwed. I look out the window and wonder if there's a way to come out of this night without smelling like cheap perfume and lipstick on my collar. I used to pay the strippers extra to do that for my buddies. We're heading downtown. It's a little-known fact that Portland's the strip capital of the world, if I recall statistics from my youth correctly. I guess I can always Uber it home if necessary before things get out of control.

It's funny. As a single guy, I was never much into strippers. I have no problem with them, but I never got my kicks going into strip clubs. I did, however, love to act like it was my thing. I always was the one who paid for the bachelor's last lap dance and did whatever necessary to make sure he went out of the single life in style. Now, the thought of anyone other than Samantha being near me is completely repulsive.

We drive down a road known for its establishments, and my palms sweat. Why the hell did I have to be so rebellious in my youth? When I see we're passing a few of the better-known places, I relax my stiff muscles, *a little.* When we pull into a parking lot, all my tension returns.

To my relief, we've stopped at some food trucks. Not a stripper joint in sight. Thank God. We all pile out and look over various carts. I make my way to a place called Chicken and Guns, where I order wood-fired chicken with a Peruvian sauce made of cilantro, jalapeños, and sour cream with a side of sea-salt fries. There're tables between the vendors and I take a seat as I wait for my meal.

"Gotta get some grub before we hit the bars," Heath, my youngest cousin, says as he rubs his belly in anticipation of the delicious-smelling food.

"Eat up, sucker," Mark McGowen, my new teammate, teases. "You'll be doing shots before the night is through."

Oh, hell no. My days of doing shots with these crazy-ass people were done, the moment they mentioned strippers. I'll gladly go out of bachelorhood as a dud, if it means I won't have a hangover and actually remember my night. I've seen *"The Hangover"* enough times, as well as experienced the real-life version of that movie, to know what I *won't* be doing tonight.

When everyone finishes their meal, we get back into the car and head to the outskirts of town. Though we approach it from a different side of town, I quickly recognize our location as Riggs' headquarters. *We'd better not be getting in a plane.*

To my surprise, we end up at an underground shooting range. *Who would have known?* I guess with all the ops that he runs, Riggs needs a place for people to keep sharp. We break out into groups, taking turns at unloading at a target for the next hour or so. Of course, there's friendly competitions and side-wagers going on. After taking a bet with Ira Michaels, I know he's a guy I want on my six. *Damn, the man has a great aim.*

When we exit the building, I realize the night's still young. We pile back into the vehicles and make our way back to the city. Once downtown, my fears from earlier return with a vengeance. Music plays in the background and people have conversations. We make a large loop and end up in front of Allure, Rowan's restaurant and club. Relief once again washes through me.

Once inside, I'm surprised to see the club has been closed for a private party. Shit. It never occurred to me. Rowan might hire strippers and bring them here. The entire ride up to the club has my nerves on edge.

I nearly sing when I see tables set up for poker. Rowan even has dealers and a waitstaff to bring us drinks. When he announces, "Hey, guys, anything you want from the kitchen, just me know." I could almost kiss him.

"Let the games begin," Pops announces. "It's twenty-five dollars to join. Winner will take three-seventy-five home at the end of the night."

Once everyone gets settled with their chips in place and a drink in hand, I really start enjoying myself. I'm at a table with Drew Warren, another new teammate, Zane, Gunderson, and Brian, my buddy from high school. Between hands, we catch up with one another and shoot the shit. I end up doing pretty well, and when the tables consolidate, I move over. Eventually, I lose and continue to drink and visit with the other guys who are out of the game.

Carson comes over with shots for everyone. "Let's toast," he announces to the crowd.

There are various cheers heard from all around.

My brother Zane's the first to stand and raise his glass. "Zo, I never thought I'd see the day when you'd rather chase kids than skirts. I'm beyond thrilled Samantha came and knocked you on your ass. You have no idea what you've been missing out on. Here's to my big brother. May he find health and happiness and never have to use a blue pill."

I nearly double over when he tacks that last bit on without any warning. Holy shit. Did he just say that?

"Here, here," can be heard and we all take a drink.

Gunderson's the next to stand. "I have to say, I'm sad you won't be able to go on any more epic single adventures with me. You've been the best wingman through it all. I can't wait to meet the woman who's made you change your ways. Congratulations, Harps."

After more cheers, Pops clears his throat. "Son, I never in a million years thought this day would come. But I've been here from the beginning. I was there the day you laid eyes on Samantha. You've grown into a man I'm proud of. My only advice for marriage is, never do something once, you don't want to do for the rest of your life. Love with all your heart, and in the middle of the night, put the toilet seat down."

The room bursts into laughter and I just shake my head. As I look at the room. I'm so thankful for those who've shown up to support me. I've been through thick and thin with most of these men, and having them here is everything.

18
SAMANTHA

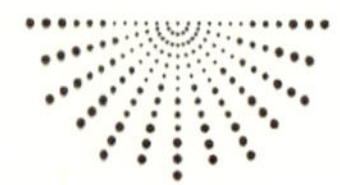

SHOCKED IS AN UNDERSTATEMENT TO DESCRIBE SHOWING UP FOR dinner at Lexi's, only to find a house full of women I know and love. Each of these women have been a part of my life over the years. Lexi has our dinner catered and I'm pampered beyond belief.

I have no idea how she managed to get Mom and my sister-in-law, Megan, here as a surprise, either. But I'm beyond ecstatic. I squeal with delight when I see them in the living room. They weren't due in until tomorrow, so they could be here for the rehearsal dinner.

After eating, the ten of us go to a day spa. Somehow Lexi's worked her magic and got them to stay open just for us to be pampered. When we arrive, we fill every pedicure chair available. As we chat about the details of the wedding, Lexi wanders off for a bit before returning with a huge smile on her face. She's up to something, but for the moment, she's not filling me in.

"How did Enzo propose?" my college roommate Brooke asks. Everyone in the room quiets as they await my response.

I know this question's inevitable, but I feel guilty for not being honest with everyone. There's no way I'm announcing my pregnancy, so I launch into my visit with Enzo in Germany. I tell them how he greeted me with a beautiful bouquet of flowers at the airport. Audible sighs can be heard as I describe how he swept me up into his arms, like no one was watching. I tell them about touring castles, seeing the sights, and of course, how utterly perfect he is. I omit the part about being sick or my stint in the hospital. There's a ton of laughter when I explain how I convinced Enzo to go to a bathhouse. Keeping things casual, I mention, "One day while we were out and about, he got down on one knee. And... Well... You know my answer." Everyone sighs at how romantic I made it sound.

Lexi catches my eye and winks, letting me know my secret's safe with her.

As soon as our toes are dry, most of us opt to get manicures, too. Just as I'm about to get a French manicure to match my toes, a woman comes out from another room and calls my name.

"That's me."

"Great," she says with a more than cheery smile. "Come this way and we'll get started."

Get started with what? I look to Lexi and her grin almost splits her face in half. *Christ. What has she done now?* I take a deep breath to prepare myself for the possibility of answers. "Started with what?"

"I've got you booked for a Brazilian wax. Just follow me to our back room and we'll get you all set up." I glower in Lexi's direction but with everyone in the room looking at me, I obediently follow the all too cheerful woman in front of me.

"Just think of this as my gift to both you and Enzo," Lexi hollers out.

"Ohmigod," falls from my lips in a whisper. "I'm going to kill her."

The woman leading me away tells me her name, but I'm not paying attention. When we're out of earshot from my bachelorette party, Little Miss Sunshine leads me to a room with a table set up in the middle like I'm going to my obstetrician. At least there aren't fucking stirrups for my legs. That would just be too much. "If you'll just remove your clothing from the waist down, I'll get everything ready."

"O... Kay," I draw out slowly as I look around the room. I guess it makes no sense in her leaving. It's not like she won't be up in my business in a matter of minutes. I drop my underwear from beneath my skirt and decided to just let it gather at my waist.

"So, when's the big day?" Miss Sunshine gleefully asks as I lie on the table, keeping the back side of my skirt around my waist, and the front covering me, for now.

"Saturday." For a second, I can't help the smile that forms. I'm dying to be Enzo's wife. I can't wait to tell everyone about our growing family as well as simply be with him. I adjust the pillow behind my head and get comfortable.

"Wow, that's exciting. I got married last year. We honeymooned in Italy. It was amazing." She rolls everything necessary on a cart and comes to stand behind me. "Have you ever had this done before?"

"Nope. I've only gotten my eyebrows and lip waxed," I let out slowly. My eyebrows I can handle, the lip on the other hand, never fails to hurt like a bitch. The sheer thought of waxing my nether region has sweat beginning to form.

"Just relax. It'll all be over in about fifteen minutes."

I reach down and pull up my skirt to let it gather at my stomach and my nerves tremble. I typically stay trimmed, so I'm not worried about my personal grooming habits. After having three kids, I'm not shy about having anyone poking around there either. I've been to enough gynecologist appointments to last a lifetime. No. What scares the ever-loving shit out of me is the thought of having each hair ripped out. I don't even want to imagine the excruciating pain.

"Why don't you pull up your knees, keep your feet together, and let your legs fall to each side," Miss Sunshine suggests. As she begins to apply warm wax to the crease at my inner thigh, she asks, "So, where's your wedding taking place?"

Next comes the paper being pressed against the wax. If I'm not mistaken, there's likely a sweat ring of my ass on the tissue paper I'm lying on. This next part will be the true test of whether or not I can handle this. I grip each hand with all my might against the edge of the table I'm on. "The lodge at Multnomah Falls," I grit out. I know she's getting closer to becoming a torturing technician, rather than the sunshine, unicorns and shit she's trying to portray at the moment. I mentally prep myself, in an attempt to convince myself I can handle this, all the while having a normal conversation with her.

"That's wonderful. Now on the count of three, you're going

to feel this." *No shit.* I close my eyes to prepare myself for the torture. "One..." My ass cheeks clench. "Two..." A bead of sweat trickles down my face. "Three..." I let out a strangled scream.

OH... MY... MOTHER-FUCKING... GOD. That fucking hurts like a son-of-a-bitch. How the hell am I going to be able to finish this? I look down and see one side of me is smooth, while the other's a jungle in comparison. There's no way I can go on my honeymoon looking like this.

"You okay?" Miss Sunshine sweetly asks.

No, I'm not fucking okay. I take in a deep breath and let it out slowly. *But I can't be seen like this either. Christ, what did I get myself into?* I nod my reaction, knowing that if I were to speak at this precise moment, I'd curse a sailor out of the bar, making him go crying home to Mommy.

All the while, she preps the other side. By now, I'm certain this flimsy paper beneath me will shred apart from the amount of sweat coming out of my pores. I don't even want to look at the aftermath when I'm done in this torture chamber. God, get me the hell out of here.

"Will you have a big or small wedding?" Miss Sunshine chooses the time right before she applies the paper again to ask. As she pats it down and smooths it over my skin, my entire body tenses, bracing for the impending agony. My knuckles are straining against my skin where I manage to grip the edge of the table even harder than before.

"Small," I grit out, while I do my best to keep this mantra running through my head. *You can do this. You will do this. You already know what it feels like. You will get through this.*

When she rips the paper off, it hurts even worse than before. FFFUUUCCCKKK!

I manage to keep my thoughts to myself, somehow. Goddamit, that hurts. Sweat covers my body, my breathing's short, and it takes all I can to nod in her direction, so she can finish and I can get the fuck out of here as soon as possible.

There's some relief with the gel she liberally applies afterward. It feels so good, I want to jump into a bathtub full of it. My body relaxes and after a while, she wipes me up and tells me I can sit up. I attempt to put my underwear on, but they feel itchy. When she suggests I leave them off, I gladly do so. There's no way I want to have anything rub on me in the near future. *Now I get to hang out with my friends and family commando. Just what I've always wanted.*

When I stand to put my shoes back on, the babies move like crazy. They must not like a tense Mama. When I cradle my hands around my belly, Miss Sunshine notices.

"You're pregnant?" she asks with disbelief.

"Yes," I whisper, but quickly add, "no one knows yet."

"Oh." Her mouth forms a perfect 'O' as she gasps in air.

"What? Did I harm the babies? Crap." I suddenly panic.

She shakes her head and places an arm on my shoulder. "No, not at all," she assures me. "It's perfectly safe. I just would've warned you that it is going to likely hurt worse than normal." *Well, isn't that nice.*

When I slowly walk out to the room, everyone's in various stages of getting their nails done. I make my way over to Lexi. "You are so going to pay for this," I grit out when no one can hear.

She has some nerve using a singsong voice as she says, "You may hate me now, but you'll thank me later."

"Don't count on it," I growl, as another woman comes to show me where I'll get my fingernails done.

By the next morning, I feel much better. I want to keep my waxing a surprise for Enzo. When Enzo came home late last night, I was nearly sound asleep. We managed to talk for a few minutes and I casually contemplated waiting to have sex for our wedding night. Surprisingly, he agreed. Knowing I'd been dead on my feet might have had something to do with it.

As we sit for breakfast, he tells me all about how the guys set him up. I was in on the plan, but I enjoy letting him sweat it out. Rowan informed me Enzo used to be the "wild one," and he needed payback. I tell him about my surprise, minus the waxing bit. He'll find out soon enough.

We spend the next two days preparing for our wedding, hanging out with family and other out-of-town guests. True to his word, I hardly had to lift a finger to prepare for our big day. When I went to the bridal shop to have my last fitting, I'm pleasantly surprised. It looks perfect. From most angles, you'd never know I was pregnant. The woman at the bridal shop is a miracle worker.

By Friday, everyone's eager for our rehearsal dinner. We drive out to Multnomah Falls in the afternoon, leaving plenty of time for sightseeing for those new to the area and to get to our dinner on time. The view's unbelievably gorgeous for February. It's bright, sunny, and clear in every direction for miles. Enzo insists on stopping to take photos at the Vista House, with the gorge in the background. Maddie, Frankie, and Declan ride with us, while our families and close friends travel in cars behind us. All stop to see what's wrong as we pull into a lookout.

As it turns out, Enzo couldn't have predicted a better place to take family photos. Enzo's mother insists on taking several pictures of different groupings of people once we arrive. Some of these photos will be cherished for years to come. I'm nearly brought to tears with the love Sara shares for my children and me. She insists on having the kids call her Granny or Granny Sara, just like her other grandchildren do. At the mention of how happy Sara is to include three more to the mix, Maddie gives me a conspiratorial grin. *Yeah, she'll be over the moon.*

Enzo catches our interaction and whispers in my ear as he holds me from behind during a photo. "She'll be out of her mind when she finds out she's getting more. I'm warning you, she takes being a grandma seriously."

I can't help but laugh and shake my head. "I'm sure we'll manage."

"Okay, but don't say I didn't warn you," he taunts as he kisses my cheek once more.

"Save it for your honeymoon, Harps," Gunderson hollers and the crowd laughs.

Without a moment's hesitation, Enzo replies, "You're just jealous. This fabulous life will happen to you someday, if you let it." He pecks me on the cheek once again, then steps away.

"Pops, has hell frozen over?" Zane chimes in.

Lorenzo chortles, "Just might have, Zane."

Enzo flips Zane the bird, everyone bursts into laughter. Once we've settled down, we finish taking our family photos.

By the time we get to Multnomah Falls, there's still time for people to hike and enjoy the scenery as those who are in the ceremony go to our rehearsal. Laughter comes easy with this group and I almost feel bad for Melanie who has worked so hard to pull this together. We get through the necessary obligations of the rehearsal. The guys Enzo's worked with over the years are a riot to be around. I can't remember when I've laughed so hard.

The night goes by like a blur. By the time we get to toasts at dinner, my cheeks hurt from laughing so hard. My emotions are in full swing and I can only hope people keep their speeches mild.

Lexi's the first to get everyone's attention by clinking her knife against her champagne glass. "We can't let the night go by without toasting the happy couple." Cheers erupt around the room. "I'd like to begin by saying it's an honor to be here."

Lexi looks to me and whispers, "Thank you," before turning her attention back to the crowd. "Let me start by saying I'm so thankful that Enzo swept into Sam's life and knocked her off her feet."

"Hey, now," I warn, but it's easily dismissed.

Lexi grin's infectious, even though I'm leery of what she's about to say. "I'd always known it would take someone special to make her consider dating again. Let's face it... I mean, we all know Sam's far too stubborn to have thought about dating seriously."

More laughter erupts and I feel my face flush crimson. How can she do this to me? It's not like I never dated.

"The day she came into work starry-eyed and zoning out was the day I knew something changed. When she told me she'd met a pilot, who lived on the other side of the world, I'll admit I had my doubts." She smirks at Enzo before continuing, "But since this was the first guy she'd even considered going out on a second date with, I encouraged her to let down her guard and have some fun."

"I knew I've always liked you," Enzo interrupts.

"Well... Thanks. I like you, too, Enzo," Lexi chides. "But seriously, you brought out a part of my best friend I've never seen before. Your actions spoke louder than your words and it's evident to all in this room, that your love for her is real. I wish you both the best and can't wait to share this journey with you." She raises her glass to the crowd. "To the bride and groom."

"To the bride and groom," the room echoes.

The arm Enzo's wrapped around my shoulders pulls me closer to him. He kisses me on my temple, sending shivers down my spine. God, I love this man.

As soon as Lexi finishes, Zane stands beside her. As the only members of our wedding party, they have the crowd's full attention. Before he begins, he looks over to Enzo and me. He shakes his head as his body rocks with silent laughter. "God, where should I start?" Laughter from the crowd continues. "Zo, I never thought I'd see the day you'd settle down. Before seeing you with Sam, I would've bet my next paycheck, you'd be a bachelor the rest of your life."

Jeers from his friends and family fill the room, but when they settle, Zane pins his eyes on me. "Sam, thank you for making him see the light. I'm sure you'll have your work cut out for you, but it'll be worth it. Enzo's a force to be reckoned with."

Boldly I state, "I'm sure I can handle it." The room fills with hoots and hollers.

"Ohmigod," Lexi bellows. "See, she's a changed woman."

Zane clears his throat. "But seriously... Samantha." Zane looks me directly in the eye, then looks to each of my children. "Maddie, Declan, and Frankie. It's an honor to have you as a part of our family. Enzo never stops talking about you and I can't wait to get to know all of you better." The fact he's included my kids in his toast brings tears of joy to my eyes. He continues, "I wish you all the best. Let's hear it for the bride and groom."

I get up to hug Zane. As he pulls me close, he whispers, "Love you, Sam. Thank you for loving my brother so much. He means the world to me." *Gahh, now I'm full-on crying. Damn hormones.*

When he releases me, Enzo stands and looks me over with care. I shake my head to assure him I'm fine. Zane reaches out and pulls him into a bear hug. "Love you the most, Zo."

"Hey, now!" Erin shouts as she comes to join them. "I'm your favorite sibling." They each reach for her and pull her into a group hug. When they release her, she announces to the room, "I have a few words I'd like to say..."

"This ought to be good." Enzo chuckles as Zane adds, "You're in trouble," simultaneously.

Enzo chuckles as Erin takes the attention from the room. "As the baby of the family, I've always looked up to my big brothers." She eyes them both before continuing, "Enzo has spent the last twenty years flying all over the world, but has always made a point to make family a priority. I love the fact that rather than a video chat, you'll be just down the street. What's even better is that I get a new sister out of the deal... No offense, Ann. I love you just as much." Ann nods her head in approval and Erin continues, "I knew you were special the day Enzo brought you home, Sam. Hell, he hadn't brought a girl home in twenty years. We all knew something was up."

"Seriously?" Maddie says in wonder and the room erupts with joyful noise again.

"Seriously," Enzo assures her.

"As I was saying..." Erin does her best to get control of this boisterous crowd. "I couldn't be happier for the two of you. I wish you both the best of luck and love. So, let's raise our glass to the bride and groom. Here's to the happy couple."

It was hard to sleep alone last night, but Sara insisted he sleep in her house the night before our wedding. Enzo only agreed because he knew he couldn't sleep next to me another night without making love to me.

As I lie in bed contemplating the day to come, I can't help but feel giddy. I'm getting married today. Sure, I've been here before, but this feels different. I get out bed, take a shower, and get dressed in clothes that can easily be slipped off, in place of my wedding dress later. Maddie, Frankie, and I are meeting Lexi at the hair salon to get our hair done in a couple of hours. Enzo melted my heart when he asked Declan if he would like to stay the night with him at his parents. He thought they'd hang out and get ready for the wedding together.

On the way to the salon, Frankie asks, "Mom, are you ready to get married?"

"I sure am, honey." I flip my blinker on to turn at the light.

"Well, how do you know you're ready?"

Maddie breaks in, "That's a silly question, squirt."

"No, it's really not," I defend. "I know I'm ready to marry Enzo because he loves me as well as you kids, more than life itself. He's proven through both his actions and words that he'll never do anything to intentionally hurt us and that he has all of our best interests in mind. There's also this undescribed feeling of happiness when I'm around him. It's been there from the start, and I doubt it will ever go away," I answer honestly.

"But didn't you feel that way with Daddy?" Frankie sincerely asks.

"Yes. I loved your dad." Not that I want to talk about this on my wedding day, but I have to be as honest as I can with my kids. "We loved each other for a very long time. But eventually, we wanted different things out of life and it didn't work out. If I'm being honest, a part of me will always love him. He gave me you kids."

Maddie surprises me by joining in the conversation, "Are you ever worried that might happen with Enzo?"

Geesh... it's not even nine in the morning and they're already bringing out the big guns. I take a deep breath and think of how to explain. "It's a possibility. But if I focus on the 'what-ifs' of life, I'll never be happy. I'm older now and so is Enzo. We've both had a lifetime of experiences that have made us who we've become today. We also both know how things can go awry if you don't have open communication in a relationship… I could get hit by a bus tomorrow, you never know. You just have faith and trust that love will get you through."

"I guess that makes sense," Maddie states and Frankie agrees. "I know that Enzo makes you happier than I've ever seen you."

"Thanks, Maddie. That means more to me than you'll ever know."

19

ENZO

I'VE BEEN WAITING FOREVER FOR TODAY. SAMANTHA WILL BE MY wife before the night is through. *Wife.* I never thought I'd see the day. If anyone had asked me a year ago what I'd be doing after retirement, I would have bet my last dollar it wouldn't be this. That's simply because I had yet to meet Samantha.

I've been up since before dawn, waiting to get the day started. I force myself to stay in bed until at least six, to keep from disturbing Declan and my parents. I haven't slept in my childhood room much over the years, except while visiting on leave. As I look around, I realize Ma hasn't changed it much. After enlisting, I either packed or took most of my personal belongings with me. Ma's changed the bedding and added a few pictures to the walls, but for the most part, it's how I left it over twenty years ago.

There's a light knock on my door and I answer, "Come in."

A second later, Declan's bright eyes peer through a crack in the door. "Did I wake you?" he whispers.

194

"I've been up for about an hour. Come in." I sit up and pat the edge of my bed since there's no other place to sit in the room.

Dec looks around the room and spots a few pictures of me that Ma framed and put up over the years. "Is that you?" He stands to take a closer look.

He looks at a picture of me right before I went to the Air Force. My hair is longer, nearly to the tip of my nose in front and tapered to almost cropped in the back. I was scrawny, compared to how I look now. "Yep. It sure is. That's taken right before I graduated high school."

"Wow, you haven't changed much. Well…. You're bigger, but not in a bad way." He shakes his head as a chortle escapes and bats his hand in the air at me. "You know what I mean… No offense."

"None taken. I didn't bulk up until after basic. Why are you up so early, anyway?"

"I couldn't sleep… And I'm a little hungry. Granny Sara said she'd make breakfast and I don't want to miss it." He shrugs impishly.

"Trust me, Ma won't let anyone miss breakfast. Let's go to the kitchen and see if we can get things started." I push back my covers and grab the shirt I'd worn last night, having slept in pajama pants. Ma keeps her house too damn hot to wear a shirt to bed.

We find Ma in the kitchen with her back to us, making coffee. I walk over and kiss her on the cheek. "Morning. Need any help?"

"Mornin', love." She turns and her smile widens as she sees

Declan. "You two take a seat at the bar and visit with me while I cook. Did you sleep well, Dec?"

Declan tells her he slept well, and our casual conversation makes waiting for breakfast go by quickly. It isn't long before Pops joins us, freshly showered and ready for the day. When he enters the room, he pats me on my shoulder.

"Here's the man of the day."

"Morning, Pops."

"What time do we need to be out at the lodge?"

"The photographer wants us there at noon. Melanie claims everything's under control and the only thing we have to do is show up."

"So, what do you boys want to do to fill our morning?" Pops looks at his watch, then to Declan and me before adding, "It looks like we have at least three hours to kill."

Knowing Pops, he has something planned. "What do you have in mind?"

"I want to take you somewhere. It's a place my father took me. I took your brother before his wedding, and now I'm taking you." He looks to Declan. "Of course, you're coming along, too. Maybe you'll get to go again someday."

"You and your traditions," Ma says knowingly.

I'd never heard of Pops going somewhere on his wedding day or him taking Zane. My interest is piqued, so I nod at Declan. "Are you up for it?"

He shrugs. "Sure. Why not?"

As we pull into the parking lot, I can't help but shake my head. Pops sees my response, and a smile spreads across his face. He knows this place always has a special place in my heart.

"We're going golfing?" Declan asks when he sees the sign.

"We sure are, kiddo. Wanna hit a few buckets of balls at the range before we get this guy married?" Pops gets out of his truck and we follow him inside.

Declan's eyes light up with excitement. "I've never done it before, but it looks fun."

"Well, let's get going." Pops places an arm around his shoulder and leads him into the building.

Once we're set up, the three of us stand side by side and take turns swinging into the range. Declan's never done this before, but after a few swings, you'd never know it. Talk about a natural athlete. I look over to Pops and he nods in agreement. Our time at the range is filled with laughter and casual conversation.

This calms my nerves by keeping me occupied. I'm not having cold feet or anything. I don't have a single doubt about marrying Samantha. I never thought I'd feel this way about anyone, but I can't wait to set my eyes on her and spend the rest of our lives together.

"Did Gramps really bring you here?" I finally ask, wondering what the connection to this place and getting married is.

"Yep." Pops swings, and his ball goes sailing out over two hundred fifty yards.

"Any particular reason?"

"I think there might have been a few. First, I'd been up pacing at the crack of dawn and needed to pass the time or drive Ma crazy. The second was to give me some life lessons." Pops shrugs.

"Oh, yeah? What's that?"

"Ever notice how you can't hit the ball in the exact same place twice?" He points out toward the ball he just hit.

I'd never thought about this before. "I guess you're right."

"Even the best of them get close, but hardly ever in the same exact place."

Where is he going with this? "Okay?" I prompt to help him get to the point.

Pops sighs after he takes another swing and looks me directly in the eye. "I guess I'm just trying to tell you that no matter how hard you try, no matter how prepared you are, life is sometimes going to give you a curve ball, and you just have to make do with what you've got. You need to focus on how to go from where you are, not where you think you should've been."

I think about Samantha, her kids, and the twins coming. I couldn't agree with Pops more. "You're absolutely right. Sometimes the best things in life come out of unexpected circumstances."

"Of course I am." Pops snickers. "There's also another reason to come out here..."

"What's that?" Declan chimes in. I hadn't realized he'd been paying attention.

"If you ever get really frustrated about something, it's better to take your aggravation out on these balls than to say or do something you'll regret. Trust me. I've only *had* to come out here a few times in my life, but it's probably kept me out of more trouble than I was already in." He quirks an eyebrow at me and I can't help but laugh.

Glancing at my watch for the hundredth time, I see there's less than thirty minutes before the ceremony begins. Samantha arrived earlier than us to take photos by herself and with the wedding party. Keeping to tradition, I haven't seen her since last night at the rehearsal dinner. It's been pure torture to know she's within a hundred yards of me and I can't see or touch her.

Zane finds me pacing in the room we used to change into our tuxes. "Want me to get the car ready? It's gassed and ready to go if you need it."

I stop pacing and glare at him. *How could he say such a thing?*

"What?" he asks defensively.

"Not funny at all, man."

He pats me on the shoulder. "Got you to stop wearing a hole in this carpet though."

"True," I admit. "Hey, will you take something to Samantha for me?"

"Like passing a note in grade school?" Zane teases.

"No, dipshit. Like deliver a gift."

He puts his finger to his chin, pretending to think about it. "I suppose I could do that."

I pull out an envelope and the long, skinny box I've had in my tux jacket. I'd picked this out when I'd bought her engagement ring. It's a charm bracelet she can add to through the years. I already picked out charms to represent each of her three kids: a soccer ball, ballet slipper, and a formal dress. I also got a heart-shaped charm with the inscription, *'You've held my heart from the moment we met.'*

Before Zane leaves, I ask him to bring Declan back when

he returns so we can get this show started. Zane nods and is out the door within seconds. And… suddenly, I'm back to pacing the room.

When the door opens, I expect Zane and Dec, but instead, it's Samantha's dad Randall and her brother Blake. Once they've both entered the room, Blake shuts the door. *Hmmm… this could get interesting.*

Randall's deep voice is the first to fill the room. "Just wanted to stop in and see how you're doing." He reaches out to shake my hand.

"I'm doing great, sir," I offer.

"Ha… I remember being a nervous wreck before my wedding," Blake chimes in. "You sure you don't want to go running for the hills? You look like a nervous wreck."

I level Blake with a stare that's been known to make grown men quiver in their boots. Instantly, Blake puts his hands up in surrender. "Just joking, man. I had to be sure you weren't going to ditch my sister on her wedding day."

I shake my head but have no words to reply appropriately.

Randall reaches out an arm and pats me on the back. "It'll be here soon enough, don't you worry."

I exhale the breath I didn't know I'd been holding and shake my head. "The hardest part's the waiting. I just want to start forever with her and it can't get here soon enough."

"I know the feeling." Randall exhales a loud breath as well. "I knew you were something special when you flew out to meet us before returning to Germany. When you asked for her hand in marriage, I was shocked with the timing, but seeing you together, I know you're perfect for Sam."

"Thank you. It means a lot to have your support." I look

them both in the eye to make sure they both clearly see how I feel.

"You have a long road ahead of you," Blake starts but back-peddles, "I mean… It's going to be hard adjusting to a life with three kids. But we've seen the way you interact with them and I can tell you've won over their hearts, too."

And we'll have two more on the way. That'll be one hell of an adjustment.

"Oh, I'm sure they'll have their bumps in the road, but they'll figure it out, Blake." Randall reaches in for one last handshake and clears his throat. "Well, we'd better get to our places. I hear there's a wedding happening today."

Standing at the altar in front of our closest friends and family is something I'll never forget. I've taken my place, waiting for Frankie, Lexi, and Maddie to walk down the aisle before Samantha. Zane and Declan are by my side, waiting for the girls as well.

Finally, it happens. The music changes and my heart picks up a few thousand beats. Maddie's the first to arrive in the doorway. She's wearing a sleeveless, red formal dress that flows to her knees. The part that makes it so her is the white Chuck Taylors with red stripes on her feet. She looks so happy as she enters the room, I burst with pride.

Next comes Lexi. She, too, has the same color dress, but it's a completely different style. She's also wearing red heels instead of Chuck Taylors. Frankie's right behind her. Her dress is similar to Maddie's, but it's white. She has a red sash tied around her waist, as well as red Chucks. The minute she sees me, she squeals with delight and my heart overflows with love. Her pace quickens and instead of going to her assigned spot, she comes straight to me, jumping into my arms with a hug. The room roars with laughter, but I don't hear a thing.

Now, I'm not a crier. I'm not. But I'll be damned if I can see straight for a few moments. I squeeze her tight and she whispers in my ear, "Love you, Enzo."

Before releasing her to her spot, I whisper, "Love you, too, Frankie."

When I look around the room, I'm not sure I see a dry eye in the house. Even Gunderson and Rowan's eyes shine from across the room when I spot them. *Who knew they could be sappy?*

When the music changes to the wedding march and people stand, I think my heart stops beating. Samantha steps around the corner, and it takes everything in my power not to run to her. She's the most beautiful person I've ever seen. Her dress fits her perfectly, and her beautiful mahogany eyes hold my gaze as she approaches on her father's arm. Her hair's partially down and flows with curls around her shoulder. She opted not to wear a veil, but her hair has something in it, similar to a tiara, that sparkles in the light.

I briefly remember her father shaking my hand and pulling me into a hug before handing Samantha off to me. I want to devour her on the spot. The knowing glance she gives me tells me she feels the same. Together, we walk to the altar and the minister we've hired for the ceremony begins. I can't actually tell you much beyond that. It feels as if I'm in a dream.

I'm so lost in Samantha. Her touch, her smell, everything about her pulls me into a trance. I can't wait until I actually get to kiss her.

When we get to our vows, I manage to pull myself out of

the trance she has me under. When she steps back and looks me in the eye, my heart stills once again. Her eyes lock onto mine and I can't look away. The entire church could go up in flames and I wouldn't be any the wiser.

She licks her lips and clears her throat before clearly stating, "Lorenzo Dean Harper. I have loved you since the moment you walked into my kitchen that fateful day. Little did I know the surprise would be on me. I've never been bold enough to ask a man out, but here we are, mere months later. So, it proves I was right about you."

I can't help but laugh along with the crowd. When we settle down, Samantha continues, "Enzo, you have made me unbelievably happy. You not only love me, but you cherish each of my children as well. I promise to love, honor, and cherish you for the rest of our lives... So, let's face it, buddy, you're stuck with me." She wrinkles up her nose as she scrunches her eyebrows, daring me to say anything different.

I can't help but mouth, "I love you," in her direction.

"I love you, Enzo, with all of my heart."

The minster then turns to me.

Crap. Everything I had planned just went out the window. I look into Samantha's eyes and speak from the heart. "Samantha Elizabeth O'Reilly, you've come into my life like a heat-seeking missile and I'm beyond thankful you won't let go. I, too, have loved you from the start. One of the best things I've ever done was surprise Pops at your house that day. Your kids have burrowed their way into my heart, and there's no way in hell I'm letting any of you go." I stop and look at each of them before continuing, "I will be with you all, through thick and thin. I promise to love, honor, and cherish you for all the days of my life. Thank you for doing me the honor of becoming my wife and making me the happiest man alive."

The minister then proceeds with the ceremony. We repeat the magic words, and the best fucking thing of the day is when he finally says, "I pronounce you man and wife. I'm happy to introduce to you, Mr. and Mrs. Enzo Harper. You may kiss the bride." And boy, do I ever. If it wasn't for some less than subtle throat clearing from the crowd, I may have taken her right there. When I pull away, I can't help but grin at the blushing bride beside me. I swear I hear, "Thanks. Now I'm all hot and bothered," but I can't be sure. *God, I love her lack of filter.*

We're ushered out to the reception area where we receive congratulations from all of our guests. We then go outside to take pictures before the sun sets. The staff Melanie's hired for the wedding changes out the ceremony chairs for dining tables, and by the time we return to the room, it's been completely transformed.

The night passes in a blur. We eat, cut cake, and once again, people toast in honor of us. We thank the crowd for spending their Valentine's Day with us, and this gets a roar of cheers. By the time I get to have the first dance with my wife, I think I'm about to die from keeping my restraint. When *Shape of You*, by Ed Sheeran begins, I'm so relieved to have Samantha in my arms. It's not a traditional song, but it's ours. The smile that lights up her face when the opening beats begin has me willing do just about anything for this woman. We show off a bit while dancing as we enjoy each other's company. Before the song ends, I tell her we have to dance more before the night is through.

We each take time to dance with our parents, each other's

parents, and of course her kids. For quite a few songs, the five of us try to top one another on the dance floor. I don't remember a time I've had more fun with them. Of course, Maddie dances with Soren for the slow songs. Everyone at our reception enjoys themselves.

The best part of the night comes when it's time for us to leave. Samantha and I have reservations at the Skamania Lodge, just on the other side of the Columbia River. Our friends and family shower us with love and handfuls of birdseed as we make our departure. God knows how I'm ever going to get all this birdseed out of Samantha's car. She shakes her head and more birdseed cascades over her body and into the seats of her SUV.

It's still relatively early by the time we make it to the Skamania Lodge. I've booked us a romantic couples' package for the next three days. It includes a couple's massage, though when I found out they offer prenatal massages, I switched hers to that. So far, I've kept it a surprise as to what our plans are for the evening. I simply told her to pack for cold weather for three days, not that I care if she ever dresses in that time, but I'm sure we'll have to eat at some point.

Samantha eyes me skeptically when I exit the freeway a short distance later. When she realizes we are going over *The Bridge of the Gods*, I suspect she's figured it out.

As soon as we enter the Gorge Suite I booked us, Samantha sighs.

"What's wrong, beautiful?"

She shakes her head and birdseed still somehow manages to rattle to the floor. "Ugg... As much as I've been dying to attack you from the moment we've been alone, unless I want birdseed in my nether regions, I need to get out of these clothes and take a shower. Would you mind helping me get the pins out of my hair? There are at least forty of them in here, or so I've been told."

Well, this is unexpected. But as she pulls at her hair, it's obvious it hurts to do it on her own. She peers at me in desperation, so I jump in to help. "Sure, let's go into the bathroom and I'll see what I can do to help you out."

Forty minutes later, she's de-pinned and ninety-nine percent of the birdseed is out of her hair. Honeymoons in real life are hardly like TV, I'm coming to realize. But one look at the relief on Samantha's face is worth every second and more.

Finally, when the pins are free, she asks, "Mind giving me a sec to get ready for bed?"

I'm so fucking thankful I'm sitting when she walks out of the bathroom about ten minutes later. She takes my breath away in the sheer negligee she's wearing. It's a cream color and leaves little to the imagination. The sexy garters and silk stockings make me instantly hard. Holy. Fucking. Shit. This woman's going to kill me. A growl escapes, as I'm at a loss for words. My instincts are suddenly pure primal.

Her eyebrows raise, and a feign innocent look appears on her face. "You like?"

"I fucking love," I growl out as I find my body moving on its own accord in her direction.

"I may have gotten a few surprises for our honeymoon."

"I'll take you dressed or naked, or any variation in between. I fucking love you, Samantha." When my hands reach her body, I pull her close and kiss her for all I'm worth. "God, you smell amazing, Samantha. I'm completely addicted to you."

I lift her and carry her to the king-size bed. My first mission of the evening is to taste her everywhere and draw out her pleasure as long as I can. As soon as I set her in the middle of the bed, I crawl up her body. I pepper her with kisses on the way. I pull back when we're eye-to-eye and stare for an unknown time. She completely unhinges me and the sheer thought of knowing she's officially mine has me wanting to shout from the rooftops.

"Are you just going to stare at me or are you going to do something about it?" she challenges.

"Oh, I'll do something all right, beautiful," I tease as I lean in and swipe my tongue along her lower lip, getting her to open for me, while simultaneously dragging one hand up her luscious body. I tease her sensitive nipples through the sheer fabric and I swear they've grown since the last time we were intimate.

When Samantha moans and pulls at my boxer briefs, I move back down her neck, trailing kisses, until I can tease her nipples through the fabric of this sexy get up. "Enzo…" she writhes. "I need more."

I reach down and glide my hands from her knees to her inner thighs. The silk stockings feel magnificent against her skin. She must agree because she audibly sighs. When I skim past the garter belt, and onto her silky, smooth skin, I'm forced to stop playing with her breast. I need to see what my fingers have discovered. Samantha's silky, smooth, and bare? *Holy shit, there's not a stitch of hair.*

"Did you?" I tilt my head in wonder.

"You like?"

I flip the scrap of material obstructing my view out of the

way. The sight alone nearly takes my breath and coherent thoughts away. There, in all its glory, is Samantha's glistening pussy fully on display. Not being able to control myself. I bend down and lick from her center to her clit. I vaguely hear Samantha stifle a deep moan when I do it again and again until I nearly have her coming in seconds.

Don't get me wrong, I love going down on Samantha, always have. But this brings things to an entirely new level of satisfaction. She seems to be hyper-sensitive and I can't get enough of her. Out of nowhere, an orgasm comes barreling through her, and I've barely begun to get my fill of playing with her. Once she's come down from her high, I start all over again, this time adding my fingers to the mix.

By the time I actually fuck her, my cock's about to explode in seconds. I do my best to make things last. This new sensation as I bottom out in her is a huge turn on for both of us. We finish together in an epic explosion, and I swear I almost black out. I don't think I've ever been so turned on. I'm not sure if it's because she's officially my wife, or she felt so unbelievable bare, but this is among the hottest nights of my life.

When I'm able to move, I flop onto my back until I can muster the energy to get up to clean us off.

I'm not quite sure what to think when Sam pants, "Lexi's right. This feels fucking fantastic." Her fingertips graze her bare mound. I cock an eyebrow at her and she smiles. "She's the one who booked the Brazilian wax. It hurt like a son-of-a-bitch, but my God, I think it was so worth it."

"Sam, you know I enjoy it either way. There's no need to hurt yourself in the process."

"So do I," she admits. "But wasn't this fantastic?"

"It's something I'll never forget, but I never want you in pain, beautiful."

"I think I just might have to try that again." She giggles. "For research purposes."

"I think I can handle that," I murmur and somehow, my cock has decided it's time to play again.

20

SAMANTHA

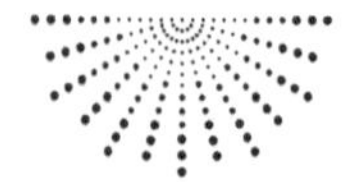

"Holy crap! Being married to Enzo's amazing," I tell Lexi one morning over coffee when it's just the two of us at our office. "The man's insatiable, but with my pregnancy hormones in full swing, so am I." I can't help but laugh. "Our honeymoon was unbelievable. When we finally ventured out of our room, we had the most amazing couples' massage."

"I'm so happy for you, Sam," Lexi says before taking another drink from the mug she's holding.

"He's so thoughtful. He even arranged for me to get a prenatal massage, so that I could be more comfortable," I add as I take a bite of the bagel she's brought me.

"How are the kids handling the adjustment?"

"Well, it's only been about a week, but I'd say it's going well." I shrug.

Lexi nods in agreement. "Yeah, you're all in the honeymoon phase. I'm sure shit will get real soon enough." She winks.

"Bite your tongue, woman. I don't need to borrow trouble. We're going to tell Frankie and Dec tonight about the twins. We didn't want them to have too much thrown at them all at once."

"That should be interesting. But, Maddie seems to be handling it well, isn't she?"

I nod. "Thank goodness. I just about died when Nicole figured it out." I place my hands on my belly and rub lightly. Just a matter of days until everyone knows. "Frankie, on the other hand, might be realizing the honeymoon's over." I shake my head, remembering their standoff last night.

"Why is that?" Lexi asks with interest.

"Well, last night, Frankie wanted Enzo to keep reading way after bedtime. It wasn't a big deal, but he had to firmly put her in her place, to let her know it was time for bed. I almost died laughing when he came to tell me her quivering lip almost worked on him. He had stayed firm for her sake, but once we were alone in bed, he was second-guessing himself."

"Did you tell him, welcome to the joys of parenthood?"

"Something along those lines."

"Well, it'll get easier for him in time. Just wait until you have two more to tend to. You guys are gonna have your hands full... How does he like his new job? Didn't he start yesterday?"

"He said most of yesterday was just training at their headquarters. I think he likes it, but he hasn't had to fly anywhere yet. The guys he works with are pretty funny and like to give each other a hard time. Apparently, he's worked with many of them before, so he's not the new guy, so to speak."

Lexi finishes her coffee and places her mug on my desk. "Will he travel with them often?"

I let out a deep breath to face reality. "It's a possibility. But most of what he'll do will have him home within a couple of days."

"If you ever need anything, you know where to find me." She stands and picks up her cup. "I'd better get to work if I'm going to meet with Abigail for her next book on time."

"Thanks, Lex. I'll see you this afternoon."

When she leaves, I send a quick text to Enzo.

Me: Hope your day is going good. Miss you.

His reply is almost instant and brings a smile to my face.

Enzo: Miss you, too. Wish we were still on our honeymoon. Adulting has lots of disadvantages.

Me: Welcome to reality, sweetheart. See you when you get home. XOXO

Enzo: Should be home for dinner. Want me to pick something up?

Me: Sounds good. Maddie asked to have Soren for dinner. Make sure you get enough for him, but not so much that we'll be eating it for the next week.

Enzo: Ha. I only made that mistake once. How does Thai sound?

The man knows my weakness. My mouth waters at the sheer thought.

Me: Delicious. See you tonight. Love you.

Enzo: Love you. Now let me get back to work. 😌

I force myself to stop thinking about Enzo and get some work done. With all the time off I've taken lately, I have plenty to catch up on. I spend the day on the telephone, touching base with clients. I even manage to read through most of a manuscript. By the time I leave to pick up Declan and Frankie from school to take them to ballet and soccer, I feel like I've got a handle on things.

Frankie and I pull into our driveway just as an unfamiliar vehicle does.

"Who's that, Mama?" Frankie asks as she hesitates to get out of the car.

"Not sure, honey. Let's find out." I leave everything in my SUV, but my keys and phone, should I need it.

By the time we get out, we see it's Enzo. *What in the world has he done now?*

"So... What do you think?" He gestures to the shiny silver SUV behind him. It's far bigger than mine, but still beautiful. As I take in the vehicle, I see it's a Toyota Sequoia, with dealer plates.

"Is it ours?" Frankie jumps up and down with excitement.

I notice he doesn't answer, but Enzo walks over and opens the passenger door. "Come on, let's go for a ride."

I have to step up onto the running boards to get into the luxurious vehicle. The seats are a soft-gray leather and it smells new. I easily relax into the seat as I watch Enzo walk around to the driver's side. *Damn, I will never get tired of looking at his sexy body.* He opens the door, meets my eyes, and gives me a knowing smirk. *Crap. Caught again.*

Frankie chatters a mile a minute about all the features she sees in this vehicle that our other car doesn't have, as Enzo pulls out of the driveway. He reaches for my hand but lets her continue. We pull out of the driveway and head toward the main highway. I learn how many cupholders, seat recliners, seat heaters as well as about a thousand other features Frankie finds in the vehicle as we drive down the road.

After a few minutes, Enzo breaks in, "So, Samantha, what do you think?"

"It's nice." I give him that. It has a lot of features. I shrug. "What do you want me to say?"

"Would you want this as your daily driver?" he hedges.

I glance around again. This car's huge. *Can I even drive a car this big? This vehicle's a beast compared to mine.* "Umm... I haven't driven it to know if I could handle this beast."

"Trust me, Sam, this is nowhere near a beast. It has a nineteen-foot radius and turns on a dime. Here, let me pull over and you can drive it."

As I drive down the road, I find that this car is magnificent. It handles like a dream. The fact that it seats seven, has a TV, and all the latest features is nice, too.

"So how much is this going to set me back?" I ask as I punch the gas in a straightaway. Holy crap. This has power!

"You'll get used to the V-8 engine, Sam. But unless you want to draw the attention of the local law enforcement, I'd lay off your lead foot," Enzo teases.

I ease off the gas and grin. "I could get used to driving this."

"Does this mean we're keeping it?" Frankie excitedly pipes in.

I glance at Enzo, who gives nothing away. "So, what are the monthly payments?" I repeat to get a straight answer.

"Nothing," he calmly replies.

Giving him my best mom tone, I glare in his direction. "What do you mean, nothing?"

"I mean, unless you completely hate it. It's already paid for."

What. The. Fuck? Who goes out and pays cash for a vehicle loaded with this many options. "Your prior job was for the U.S. Air Force, right? Not some secret agent shit or anything?"

He gives me a disapproving look. "Sam..." He glances to Frankie and doesn't say anything.

"She's heard worse," I glower, but am frustrated he's not explaining anything. "Talk."

He takes a deep breath, and slower than molasses in January, exhales. *Oh, this has got to be good.* "Samantha, you know I haven't had a lot to spend my money on over the years. I'm a simple man and live within my means. I've pretty much saved about half my money from each paycheck and invested it. Any money I got while on deployment went into that investment account, too."

"Don't you think we should've talked about this before you went out and bought it?"

"We talked about vehicles, and you said this was one you'd consider. I drove by this morning in Pops' truck and saw them putting this on the lot. I was off a bit earlier than expected and figured if it's meant to be, it would still be there. And here we are."

There's no point in arguing. He's right. But still. This is a huge purchase.

"Did you even think to run this by me first?" comes out before I can hold it in. *Crap. That sounded way snarkier than I meant.*

"Again, you had already agreed this was a vehicle you wanted. I found it, paid for it, and honestly didn't think it would be that big of a deal. I never meant to leave you out." He's quiet for a moment, then adds in a lighter tone, "By the way, I ordered Thai food. We just have to pick it up. I was dying to show you this, so I thought we could drive to pick it up."

"Being perfect isn't always polite, Enzo," I grimace and pretend to have some steam left for a fight.

"I'll work on that, beautiful." He laughs, but the look in his eyes tells me he thinks I'm being utterly ridiculous.

Men.

As we finish dinner later that evening, I look to Enzo, raise an eyebrow, and pat my belly. *It's time.* He nods in agreement and clears his throat just as Declan is about to ask to be excused from the table. "So... Guys, we have an announcement to make."

Maddie looks to Soren knowingly. By the look on his face, I'd bet he already knows what Enzo's about to say. Enzo and I have discussed that we need to tell the kids soon, but I haven't given much thought as to what we'd actually say. Enzo looks in my direction and I shrug.

"What is it?" Declan asks impatiently. He's about to go upstairs to finish his homework and I can tell he's tired, by his cranky demeanor at dinner.

Frankie's the exact opposite, her eagerness to know what's going on is almost comical. She bounces in her seat and says, "Yeah, what's going on?"

I glance to Maddie and she knowingly winks at me, smashing her mouth shut, making her lips form a straight line, just to keep from spilling the beans. I can't help but smile. She's good at secrets, but I can tell she's dying to tell this one.

Enzo reaches over to me and grabs my hand. "Well... I know that it's been an adjustment with me moving in here. But it's been okay, right?"

Both Maddie and Dec nod. Simultaneously, Maddie says, "It's the best," while Declan says, "Yeah."

Enzo nods and continues, "Since we're making changes... How do you feel about adding to the mix?"

Both Frankie and Dec stare at him in confusion, then glance at me for an interpretation. "Well, Franks," I say in a teasing tone, "I hate to break it to you, but you're not going to be the baby of the family much longer." I place my free hand around my belly and watch both of their eyes nearly pop out.

"Wait... You're..." Dec stutters.

Frankie finishes as she jumps out of her seat. "Pregnant?"

"Yes, I am." I reach out my arms to catch Frankie as she rushes in for a hug.

She places her hand on my belly and asks in wonder, "I'm finally going to be a big sister?"

"You sure are, squirt," Maddie chimes in.

"Congratulations," comes from Soren.

Enzo beats me to thanking Soren. I glance at Declan and realize he still hasn't said much. "You okay, bud?"

With a look of pure dread, he says, "Please don't let it be another girl. I can barely use the bathroom as it is." He groans in disgust. This makes the room break into laughter, with Enzo's the hardest.

Enzo pats Dec on the shoulder as he settles. "I can relate, Dec. If it gets too bad, I know someone who can make us a bathroom all our own."

"Grandpops can build you one," Frankie announces. "Then we won't have to smell your stinkiness."

Before this gets too out of hand, I put a stop to it. "Well, there's more…"

"Yes! And you're never going to believe it," Maddie shouts over me. "Mom's having TWINS!!!"

"You have two babies growing inside of you?" Frankie's round eyes and high-pitched voice make me smile.

"She sure does." Enzo's deep voice booms and the loving look he gives me completely melts my heart.

"I won't have to share a room, will I?"

"No, Dec. We'll make the guest room the twins' room," I announce. "They'll be the only ones sharing a room. Don't worry. Your room's safe."

"What will happen when we have company?" Frankie asks.

"We're not sure yet, kiddo," Enzo answers. "Let's just get through setting up a nursery first, then we can see what happens. If we run out of space, I'm sure Pops can help us figure something out."

How does the guy always have an answer to everything?

21

SAMANTHA

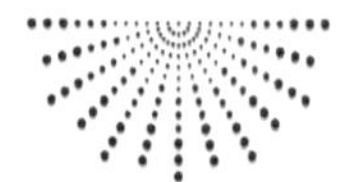

As the young ultrasound tech moves the wand over my stomach, I look to Enzo, who's holding my hand anxiously. His eyes widen and the tension in his body shows he's on pins and needles as he stares at the screen. The rapid heartbeats echo through the small, dark room and I couldn't be happier.

I turn my attention to the screen and I see the profile of a head. The baby's fist is curled and at its mouth. I can't help the sigh that falls from my lips. I never will get used to seeing something so precious. Just before the tech moves the wand, another hand reaches out and bumps into the baby on the screen.

"That's a little freaky," Enzo whispers. "They almost look like aliens."

"Wait until you see them move," I warn.

As if they hear, both babies nearly flip upside down. They've grown so much since our last ultrasound. They're now a bundle of arms and legs. Their spines zoom in and out of focus, and if I didn't know any better, I'd say Enzo's right. I've been taken over by aliens.

The technician measures each of the babies. She identifies each part as it appears on the screen, as well as which baby it belongs to. Right now, we refer to them as Baby A and Baby B. I think it's the cutest thing ever to watch their little bodies move all over the place.

After another sudden movement on the screen, Enzo asks in wonder, "Does that hurt?"

I shake my head. "No. I only feel the big moves."

The technician interrupts with, "Do you want to know the sex of each baby?"

I look to Enzo for reassurance and he nods. Since their arrival has been enough of a shock, we think it's best to prepare ourselves for the future. "Yes. We'd love that," I eagerly state, and Enzo grips my hand tighter. I'm just as excited as he is waiting to find out, now that I know they're both healthy.

The technician moves the wand around and suddenly, there's legs and a little bottom on the screen. It goes in and out of focus for a few seconds, then she freezes the screen. "See here." She uses the pointer on the screen to bring our attention to a specific area. "See these dots here…"

"What does that mean?" Enzo jumps in as she takes several screenshots of the image.

"Congratulations. Baby A's a girl!" She takes a moment and types it onto the screen as well.

"Wow… Just… Wow," Enzo murmurs. He looks to me and I swear I see his eyes shine as if they're filling with tears. He blinks a few times and they clear. He whispers, "I hope she looks just like you, Samantha." He bends down and presses a kiss to my temple. "I love you."

The cheery technician brings our attention back to her. "Now, let's see if we can find out the sex of Baby B."

After a few moments looking at a blurry screen, Baby B cooperates. Its bottom comes into view and I gasp, throwing my hand over my mouth. Enzo immediately turns to me. "What's wrong?"

I shake my head, pointing to the screen. "Look…"

He's silent for a couple of heartbeats and I hold my breath, waiting for his response. "Are you kidding me?" He shakes his head from side to side. "Is that what I think it is?" He turns to the technician, who nods in agreement, then to me for confirmation.

"That depends. What do you think it is?" I ask playfully.

Enzo's eyes are as round as saucers and his hand squeezes tighter against mine. "We're having a boy, too?"

"It appears so," I say, getting excited. He bends over and brushes a kiss to my lips. "Oh my God, Enzo! Can you believe it?"

Later that evening, we gather in our family room to update the kids on their new siblings. All are eager to see the ultrasound pictures. Each takes a turn enjoying the profile pictures, not believing how big they've gotten since the last ultrasound was done. When we announce Baby A's a girl, Frankie jumps up and down. Her hoots and hollers could probably be heard by our neighbors. Her reaction melts my heart and makes me realize everything's going to be okay.

Declan, on the other hand, groans until we reveal the sex of Baby B. Then he cheers right along with Frankie. "YES!" comes out as a hiss before he turns to Enzo and grins. "Five girls in the house would be crazy."

"You may live to regret that." Maddie reaches over and rustles his hair. Then she turns to Enzo and me, sitting on the couch together. "As long as they're healthy, I didn't really care."

"My thoughts exactly, Mads," I add as I instinctively cradle my belly.

"Have you thought about names?" Maddie excitedly blurts as she pulls her feet up and settles into the oversized chair beside us.

"What about Zelma, for a girl?" Frankie suggests.

"Zelma?" *There's no way in hell I'm naming my child that. Has she been watching Scooby-Doo?*

"Or Tapanga?" Frankie shrugs.

"We're not calling our sister that, squirt." Maddie laughs. "You've been watching too much TV." Her voice turns serious and she places her hand on her chin as she thinks seriously about something for a moment. "What about... Hayley? Hayley Harper sounds cute."

"That does sound good," Enzo agrees.

We spend the next twenty minutes discussing possible names. In my mind, many more were vetoed than considered a possibility. I've read too many books or knew someone with names similar to ever consider them as a possibility.

By the time we're getting ready for bed, I think I've heard at least one hundred names for each twin. Enzo takes it all in stride. He suggests a few, but I'm pretty sure we're going to go with Lorenzo Dean Harper. He'll be the fourth son to have this family name. I'd really like to continue this tradition.

As we snuggle into bed, I lay my head on Enzo's shoulder, in that special spot I've claimed as mine. "Would you be against naming our son Lorenzo Dean Harper?"

"No, not at all." He kisses my head lightly as he pulls me closer. "I just didn't want to presume anything. As much as I love tradition, if you have your heart set on something else, I'm fine with that, too."

"Are you sure? I really like Lorenzo. Everyone I know with that name is strong, handsome, and has a big heart." My voice becomes playful by the end.

He sighs deeply. "It's not really an easy name to have as a kid, though. Kids are kind of mean. Hey... What if we called him Loren, so it's not so confusing around the house? Dad and I only had trouble when I was called by my given name."

I sit up to look him in the eye "So, you're okay with Lorenzo?"

Enzo nods and pulls me in for a kiss. It's slow and consuming. Suddenly, we're no longer interested in talking about names.

The next morning, I come downstairs to find bickering in the kitchen. It doesn't sound too serious, but it's evident Maddie and Declan are in the midst of a disagreement. Enzo's already at work and Frankie's nowhere to be found. As much as I hate having to listen to them argue, over the years I've found when I intervene, it only gets worse. I know when to step in to stop things, but I want to see what they're arguing about before I jump in. From the tone of voices being heard throughout the house, Maddie is ticked at something.

"You're such a jerk!" Maddie shouts. "You used milk and put it back into the fridge when there was barely any left. Then you ate the last granola bar." When Maddie sees me enter the room, she shouts, "Mom, we need milk and granola bars!"

I notice Dec takes the opportunity to slink out of the room, shaking his head as he goes.

"I'll pick some up next time I go shopping," I reply.

"You need to pick me up from school today," she huffs. "Practice is cancelled and I don't wanna ride the bus," she announces like the entitled teenager she thinks she is. *I have to do this, huh. So... this is how today's going to go. Who peed in her cereal this morning?* I take a moment to calmly gather my wits and look to the ceiling for some guidance. *Please give me patience.* When days start like this, we are all in for a world of hurt. Maddie's a great kid, but when she's on the rampage, logical sense and reasoning go right out the window.

"I'll see what I can do," I nonchalantly counter. I've long ago learned not to engage with the enemy when she's setting up for a fight. She'll fizzle out faster if I just let it go and stay impartial.

"Ugg," she huffs and rolls her eyes. "Did you pick up that poster board for my project?" comes out in a tone that makes me cringe. *How can a fifteen-year-old sound like a toddler in an instant?*

"I didn't know you needed it," I reply.

"Mooomm! You know it's spirit week and I need to make a sign by Wednesday."

"Well, since today's only Tuesday. I'll see what I can do

about getting one for you tonight," I offer, in an attempt to keep the peace.

"Grrrr..." she actually growls. *Have I just stepped into the Twilight Zone?* "I guess I'll have to wait until tomorrow," she grumbles. I swear I also hear, "I can't wait until I can drive." *If she thinks she's going to be driving with that attitude, she's got another thing coming.*

Maddie forcefully opens and shuts a few cupboard doors before I've finally had enough. "Wanna tell me what's on your mind, Madelyn Mae? Or are you going to rip every door off the hinges before school?" I arch an eyebrow and wait for a response.

"Ugh." She turns to face me, steam still flows out her ears as her chin juts in my direction. "Can't I *just* have a bad morning?" She sounds like a typical prema donna. *God, I love teenagers.*

I glance at the clock. "Well, if you want to be fit for company at school, you'll need to adjust your attitude. Soren will be here any minute. So, unless you want him to see your horns come out, you might want to rethink this fit you're throwing."

She pants, "Uh. I'm not throwing a fit."

"Sounds like one to me," Frankie states all too cheerily. I quickly step between the two of them or we might just have World War III, right here in the kitchen. I place my hands up in the surrender position as I step toward Maddie and I curtly tell Frankie, "That's enough. We don't need comments from the peanut gallery."

Frankie shakes her head, but knows better than to respond at this moment. Instead, she walks to get her bag by the kitchen table and places her lunch pail into it. Once she has her things, she walks to me and gives me a hug. "I'm walking to the bus stop. Don't forget I need to bring snacks to school tomorrow for that party. I have twenty-five students in my class and we'll need to have it there by eleven. See you this afternoon when you pick me up. Love you."

"Love you, too, Franks. Grab your brother and walk together."

Declan walks through the kitchen to grab his things and heads out the door. Before he leaves, he looks to me and whispers, "Have fun dealing with…" he looks to Maddie, who's currently brooding as she looks for something else to eat, "that."

I roll my eyes and silently mouth, "Don't you start." Then add in my regular voice, "I love you, bud. Have a good day at school."

"Love you, too, Mom."

Once Frankie and Declan leave, I use this time to grab something for myself to eat and let Maddie cool down. She's still slamming things harder than normal, but it's not worth getting into it at the moment. Eventually, she settles and sits at the table to eat in silence. *Maybe she's calmed down.*

Unfortunately, that theory's short lived as she snaps, "So you'll be there after school?"

I take a deep breath and force myself to keep a civil tone. "Yes, I'll be there."

"You need to take me driving, too. I've hardly gotten any hours in this week."

"Madelyn, you **need** food, water, shelter, and air. Everything else is a want." She starts to say something, but I cut her off, in a strict, no-nonsense tone. "If you want me to do things for you, I suggest you change your attitude and check your words."

Before Maddie can say anything, there's a knock at the door. She rushes to grab her backpack, lunch, and open the door for Soren. The little twerp doesn't even say goodbye.

When Enzo calls a few hours later and asks about my day, I groan loudly. "Are you sure it isn't a Monday? Ugg… Anything that can go wrong, has today. I started off by getting into it with Maddie, our network's down at work and the IT guys are here fixing it, and a client I've spent the last three weeks planning with decided to go in a different direction."

"I'm sorry to hear you've had a bad day, beautiful."

I dismiss his kind words and continue with my rant about my day, "I now have to leave early, pick Maddie up from school, take her to get a poster board for a project, buy Frankie snacks for a school party, and since Declan has team pictures tomorrow, I also have to take him to get a haircut. Oh… and the snarky teen had the audacity to tell me she needed to go driving today, too. As if I want to spend more time with her after our morning."

"Samantha." Enzo's deep, sexy voice is the medicine I need after a day like this. "It'll all work out. Trust me."

"I know. It's just been a crappy day," I whine.

"I actually called to let you know I'm on my way home now. We're wheels up at zero five-hundred, and from the looks of the mission, I'll be gone a few days."

I know it's inevitable he's going to be gone from time to time, but I can't help the pang fluttering through my heart upon receiving this news. *Can today get any worse?* This isn't what I need to hear right now. "Seriously?"

"Yeah, it's just a routine mission, so get that worry out of your voice, Samantha." I know he can't tell me where he's going, but from what he's told me, he's basically their transportation as well as some behind the scenes intel, so I shouldn't worry. But I obviously do. It's in my nature to worry.

He's silent as he waits for me to respond. I let out a huff. "Fine. I'm just going to miss you." I've gotten used to him being around and I sleep so much better with him here.

"I'll miss you, too, beautiful." There's silence on the other end of the line for a few heartbeats and when he breaks it, the tone of his voice is back to business. "What do you think of this... I'll pick up the kids from school. We'll take Dec to practice and then get the things Maddie and Frankie need for tomorrow. I'll even let Maddie drive, and we'll grab dinner en route."

"Are you sure?"

"Samantha." His stern voice tells me not to question him.

I look at the pile of unfinished work on my desk and glance at the clock. It would be amazing to be able to work for a couple more hours without having to worry about the kids' schedules. "Sounds good. I'll pick up Dec to get his haircut before I come home."

2 2

ENZO

WORKING FOR RIGGS AND HAVING A FAMILY TO COME HOME TO every night these past few months has been a bit of an adjustment, to say the least. I'm not used to having people to check in with. These last few days, I've put in some long hours. We joined forces with the Department of Homeland Security, so they took over the rest of the operation once we got the girl we were after. DHS has a shitstorm on their hands after what we witnessed. I sigh and shake off the action of the day.

I pull into our driveway just a little after three in the morning. I do my best not to wake Samantha and the kids. Knowing it's late, I showered the grime off at headquarters before coming home. Samantha only has a few more hours of sleep until Frankie will be up at the crack of dawn, so I leave the lights off as I enter our room. I undress to my boxers, slip back the covers, and snuggle close to Samantha. God, having her in my arms and holding her close is what I need after the week I've had.

I wake up a few hours later to the feeling of being watched. Samantha's laying her head on my chest, so it can't be her. I open my eyes to find Frankie on the other side of Samantha. Her head rests on Samantha's pillow, but her eyes are bright and a huge smile is plastered to her face.

"Hi," she whispers.

"Hi," I whisper back, suddenly worried because Frankie's in our bed and I'm only in my boxers.

"I had a bad dream. Mama said I could sleep with her since you weren't home," she explains, as if it's no big deal.

"I see that. Are you okay?"

"Yeah. I'm going to watch TV," she says, as if this is a normal occurrence. Thank God, I decided to let Sam sleep this morning, instead of my usual sexy wake-ups with her.

"You do that. I'll come down in a bit and make breakfast." After I put on some pants.

"Okay, Enzo," she whispers.

She hops out of bed and goes to the door. Before she goes out, though, she turns to say, "Oh, Mama says she needs to sleep in, so be very quiet." She rushes back to my side of the bed and hugs the part of me that Samantha's not sleeping on. "I'm glad you're home. I've missed you."

This completely takes me back and I have no idea what to say. "You, too, kiddo," finally comes out as she rushes out the door.

I feel a soft kiss on my pec, right as the door clicks shut.

"Oh... So, you're awake now," I whisper to Samantha teasingly.

She giggles and her body convulses across mine. "Yeah, I

figured if I stayed asleep, I'd get a few moments alone with you."

"Did you, now?" I tease as I roll her onto her back. She's wearing a tank that has risen over the swell of her belly and her amazing boobs are barely contained in the top. Her pajama pants have settled below her baby bump and she's gorgeous as ever.

"Yeah, I've missed you." Her husky morning voice fills me with desire.

I bend to kiss her, being careful not to put pressure on the babies as I settle between her legs with the lower half of my body. "I've missed you, too, beautiful."

After I give her a scorching kiss, I make my way down her body by peppering her with kisses along the way. I swear in the last week of my absence, her boobs have gotten even bigger. I take the time to kiss the swell of each breast before I make my way down her protruding stomach.

When I get to her belly button, which is predominantly on display, I stop for a moment. I rub my nose along her navel back and forth. I can't help but whisper, "Hey, babies. I've missed you, too. I can't wait to meet you. Your ma and I are counting down the days until you arrive." I lay my cheek along her stomach and continue, "You're gonna have the best sisters and brother you could ever ask for."

As if they were talking to me, Samantha's stomach starts to roll. It almost feels as if they are stretching to wake up for the day. I see one ripple along Samantha's upper abdomen and another in the lower half. Yes, I've seen them move before, but I'm still in awe each time. Suddenly, there's a jab at my cheek.

"Damn, are you okay, Sam? That felt strong."

She chuckles, so I know she's okay. "You and your kids do nothing halfway."

Suddenly, she gasps. "Rib," comes out as a whisper. But then a beautiful smile appears on her face. "They're happy their daddy is home."

I sigh. "It's been a long week. I'm sorry I was gone for so long. The mission took longer than expected and I was their only way out."

My team had been assigned to help break up a human trafficking ring. When we found the girl that we were hired to recover, we learned there were more. There's no way we could walk away and not recover all that were in the compound. With the help of DHS, I am happy to say twelve other women and girls were reunited with their families.

"I know. You're a rock star in the air. I've missed you, but glad you were there to bring your team home safely." *If only she knew the details.*

Suddenly, Samantha gasps and a look of panic crosses her face.

"What's wrong?" I ask, wanting to jump into action to help.

"Bladder shot," she moans. "Help me up, so I don't wet the bed."

I immediately get off the bed. She rolls to the side, then throws her legs over the edge, as if it's a well-practiced move. I reach for her hand to assist her. She still has three more months until she's full term, but she looks like she could pop sooner.

She places one hand on the swell of her stomach and the

other at the base of her back. As she waddles though, I'll never tell her I'd describe her walk as that, I can't help but be in awe of the woman before me. She never complains, though I'm sure she can't be comfortable. I start to follow her into the bathroom, when I hear a light knock on the door.

"Enzo," Frankie whispers. "Do you think you can cook the pancakes I mixed up? I can't turn on the stove without you or Mom downstairs."

I glance at Samantha with a grin on my face. "Sure thing, sweetheart. I'll be right down." I grab a pair of pajama pants and a t-shirt. *The life of being a parent. Though I wouldn't have it any other way.*

"Okay," I hear Frankie say, and her feet retreat.

Samantha laughs. "Duty calls. Aren't you glad you signed up for this?" Just as I finish dressing, she waddles my way. She wraps her arms around me and says, "Thank you."

"I wouldn't have it any other way," I reply with complete honesty. I kiss her once more, then go off to make pancakes.

Once downstairs, I see Declan's already up and watching TV in the family room. He has blankets strewn about and breakfast dishes at his side. It appears as if he's been up for a while and he's completely engulfed in the show he's watching.

Frankie has the batter ready, so all we have to do is turn on the stove and warm up a pan. I cut some fruit while she focuses on making pancakes.

"How long are you home this time?" Frankie asks.

"For the next week or so, at least." I place the fruit in the bowl next to me and wash the cutting board.

"Why do you have to go away so much?" Her voice has a

slight quiver and she keeps her focus on the pancake in front of her, instead of looking me in the eyes, which instantly puts me on alert and makes my heart pang. I'm not used to having people care about me so much.

Though I can't go into specifics, I think of a way to explain. "Well... sometimes people need Riggs and his team to help them. I'm the one who gets them there safely and bring them back. I don't want to go away, but I'm needed. Lives literally depend on the work we do."

"Oh." Frankie's unusually quiet for a few moments.

I do my best to let her process whatever is on her mind, but finally, I can't take it any longer. "What's on your mind, Franks?"

"Well..." She plates the pancake and makes eye contact, finally. "Dad's out of town for the next two weeks and there's this father/daughter dance." She pauses and suddenly appears shy, but quietly asks, "Will you take me?"

Suddenly, my throat is thick, and I can't speak. When I don't answer right away, Frankie stammers, "If you don't want to go, that's okay... I just...thought..."

"I'd be honored, Frankie," I croak out before she can continue with her line of thought. Then I clear my throat. "Really. Tell me when and I'll be there." I'm not the only pilot Riggs employs, so it should work out, regardless of the date.

She rattles off the date, then goes on to tell me how we will need to dress up and find something that matches one another. Ugg... I see another shopping trip in my future. I guess that's the price for having girls in my life. But when I look at the smile on Frankie's face as she gushes over the details, I know I'd make a thousand more, if she reacts like that.

Samantha joins us in the kitchen, fresh from taking a shower. Her hair is still wet, hanging loose around her shoulders. There's no denying she's over six months pregnant in the yoga pants and fitted green t-shirt she's sporting. She couldn't look more beautiful if she tried. One hand cradles the babies growing inside instinctively while the other rests at the base of her back.

Frankie sets a plate in front of Samantha at the counter as she sits on one of the barstools. "Here, Mama, have this."

Samantha looks around the counter at the toppings I have placed out and narrows her eyes as she doesn't find what she's looking for. When she starts to stand, I ask, "What do you need, beautiful?"

"Just some powdered sugar."

"I got it," Frankie chirps and Samantha sets in to buttering her pancake.

"Where's Maddie?" Samantha asks the room.

I shrug. "Haven't seen her." I dish up Samantha some of the strawberries I'd cut up for this morning's breakfast.

Samantha turns her attention to Declan. "Have you eaten, Dec?"

"I'm good," he offers as he zones back into the television show he's watching. He mumbles something else, but I don't catch it.

Once we're through eating and there's no sign of Maddie surfacing this morning, we start to clean up. Just as we're finishing, Samantha calls over to Declan, "Can you bring in your dishes from this morning, Dec?"

He completely ignores her, entranced in his show.

I wipe down the counter as Samantha tries Declan again. "Hey, Dec. Bring your dishes in. I want to start the dishwasher."

I faintly hear Declan grumble something, but he ignores her once again.

"Declan," I sternly say to get his attention.

He turns to look in my direction. "What?" he replies as he looks to me defensively.

"Your mom asked you to do something." I give him a pointed look and he blanches like he has no idea what I'm talking about.

Samantha politely repeats herself, "Can you bring in your dishes? I want to start the dishwasher."

"In a minute," Declan mumbles, then focuses his attention back to his television program.

Oh, hell no. He didn't just say that. I straighten my stance and am about to stalk over to him to give him a piece of my mind and remind him of his manners, when I feel Samantha's touch on my arm, holding me in place.

"Give it until the commercial," she whispers so that no one but me can hear.

I wait the three minutes until the next commercial, then I pointedly look toward Sam. She rolls her eyes, puts the soap in the dishwasher, then she calls across the room, "Dec, it's a commercial. Time to bring me your dishes."

He groans loudly before mumbling, "Geesh. What's the big deal?" He begrudgingly grabs the plates and glass beside him and brings it to set on the kitchen counter. His attitude rolls off him in waves, and I'm completely out of my element. I look to

Samantha, who merely shakes her head and rolls her eyes behind his back. *As hard as it isn't to interfere, I'll take my lead from her. No sense in rocking the boat unnecessarily.*

Declan walks back to the couch and plops down. Just as he's about to cover up with a blanket he'd tossed down, Samantha asks, "Have you finished that biography project that's due on Monday?"

"Ugg..." He flops his head against the couch hard. "I'll get to it..." *What's gotten into him today?*

"You've finished reading the book, right?" She eyes him suspiciously and *I'm suddenly doubting he has much done.*

A snarl rips from his throat, as his eyes shoot daggers at Samantha. "I told you I'd get to it." He lets out a huff at the end and attempts to go back to watching the show. But Samantha has other plans.

She stomps over to the television and without the remote, turns it off from behind. This causes Declan to stand quickly. Now he's face-to-face, squaring off with his mother. He may only be ten, but he's almost as tall as she. "What's the big deal, Mom? I always get my work done. Why do I have to do it right this minute?"

"Because you likely haven't even finished reading the book and it's going to take hours to do the report, not to mention everything else that's required of it."

"I'll get it done..." He juts out his chin and crosses his arms in a stand-off.

Samantha takes a deep breath, closing her eyes for a second or two. When she opens them, they are calculating and narrowed at him. "You need to start. Now. You've had weeks to work on this and you've put it off until the last minute."

"Last minute would be tomorrow," rolls off his lips faster than I would've thought.

Steam can almost be seen coming from Samantha's ears. Her fists ball and her shoulders bunch. I immediately jump into action and put myself between the two of them. "Okay, buddy," I say in an attempt to diffuse the situation. "Why don't you go upstairs and get started."

"Why should I listen to you?" Declan seethes in my direction. *Wow. He's really going to go there.* I've never seen him like this, so this should be interesting.

I straighten to my full height and look him in the eye. In a tone that usually makes grown men quake in their boots, I quietly say, "Your mother told you to go upstairs and get started with your homework."

He stares indignantly at me.

I quirk an eyebrow in his direction. "Are you going to do this on your own, or will you need some help in getting there?" This is the first time I've had to lay down the law. I hope I'm not overstepping my bounds, but the shit he's trying to pull is ridiculous.

Declan's eyes bulge for a split second, then he recovers to his glare, but he says nothing.

The tension in the room can be cut with a knife. I cross my arms against my chest and let him know I'm not budging on this issue either. He *will* be respectful to his mother. I have no idea in hell what I will do if he doesn't listen, but I'm not backing down.

After a few more death stares thrown my way, Declan huffs. "Fine!" He turns and stomps up the stairs to his room, and just before his door slams, he yells, "I used to like you."

What the hell was that? I blink a few times and look to Samantha for confirmation that this has become my reality. She simply rolls her eyes and mutters, "Welcome to parenthood. I think you've officially been inducted."

I shake my head and mutter under my breath so Frankie doesn't hear, "Good times..."

23

SAMANTHA

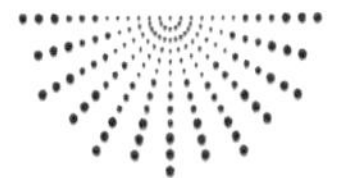

"Well, I can officially say Enzo's experienced into parenthood," I huff as I sit to have coffee with Lexi in her office the following Monday morning. I'm allowed one cup a day and after the weekend I've just experienced, I'm taking it.

"Really? Why's that?" Lexi states in disbelief. There's a slight upturn of her lips and I can tell she's on the verge of smirking at me.

"For starters, Declan was a complete turd this weekend. He waited until the last minute to do his biography report and then proceeded to act like we were the bad guys for asking him if it was done."

"Sounds like a normal pre-teen," Lexi deadpans.

I tell her how Declan went all-out into complete fit mode. He refused to work on his project for the better part of Saturday, which resulted in having to spend all of Sunday completing it. Bless Enzo's heart, he actually took pity on the kid and spent most of yesterday afternoon helping Declan put the finishing touches on the poster requirements.

"I'm telling you, Lex, even after Dec was a complete ass to him, Enzo still went out of his way to help him. They didn't finish until nearly ten last night."

"Wow. That's commitment."

"I know. I was done with Dec about thirty minutes into it yesterday. He's so infuriating, I just had to walk away. Enzo didn't know what to do with himself when Dec screamed, 'I used to like you' after the start of their argument. If I hadn't been so ticked at Declan's behavior, I would have laughed at the look on Enzo's face."

"But everything worked out?"

"Yeah. Enzo was a champ and seemed to know how to handle Dec and his shitty attitude."

"Is there anything Enzo can't do?" Lexi asks, her tone sarcastic. "I mean, did you order him from make *your-fantasies-come-true-dot-com* or something? Come on… He's gotta have some flaws. No man is that perfect. Dish, Sam."

"Of course he does." I shake my head at her absurdity. Is Enzo perfect? No. Far from it. But is there anything worth complaining over? I'm not sure. Sure, he wakes up at the crack of dawn. He's almost a neat freak. I hardly have to lift a finger around him, but those aren't things to complain about. "If anything, he's too attentive."

"Oh, that's a serious problem. We should report him to Bad Husbands R Us," she scoffs.

"Ha… Ha… Very funny." I roll my eyes at her ridiculousness. "He's got his flaws, just like anyone else."

"Whatever you say, Sam."

The intercom buzzes, interrupting our conversation. ” Lexi... I've got Marie on the other line. Do you want me to take a message or is this a good time?”

I nod in her direction and I get up to leave.

Lexi mouths, “We'll catch up later.”

I spend the rest of the day meeting with clients via phone conferences and reading over a manuscript for a prospective client. I'm relieved to find it intriguing, and I have high hopes we'll be able to sign her. I'm just about finished for the day when I get a text from Enzo.

Enzo: What's your ETA?

**Me: I'm just about to leave and pick up the
    kids. Why?**

**Enzo: I told Frankie I'd take her shopping. Meet at
    the school?**

The thought of seeing him still has the same effect on me as when we were first dating. Butterflies zing as tingles disperse along my spine. I hope I never get over this reaction.

Me: Sure. See you in 20.

I make it there with plenty of time to spare, but somehow, Enzo's waiting for me in the parking lot. He's sexy as hell as I see him step from his Range Rover to greet me. He's dressed in dark denim, a navy Henley, and brown-leather work boots. My mouth dries at the sight of him and I have to remind myself I'm in public.

He greets me with a sexy, dimple-popping smile, as if just seeing me has made his year. I roll down my window and he lowers his head to brush a kiss against my lips. He pulls back, all too short in my opinion, and a smirk forms on his face. "Hey, beautiful. How was your day?"

"It's been good. How about you?" He reaches out to push a loose strand of hair behind my ear. The sensation of the electrical current that is ever present, sends a shiver down my spine.

"Decent. I have the next few days off. What do you think about making use of the time and painting the nursery? I'll paint it while you're at work so the strong fumes will disperse before you return home."

I rest a hand on my protruding belly and grin. "That sounds good. These guys will be here before we know it."

As we wait for the kids to get out of school, we make plans for the room. We discuss paint colors and the furniture we'll need. He says he'll stop by and pick up some samples while he and Frankie are out this afternoon. I'm sure she'll have an opinion, too. That should be interesting. Last time she picked out paint, she was dead set on pink and purple.

Later at home, I find myself lost on the internet, delving deep into my favorite social media site. Who knew looking for decorating ideas would be so time consuming? It's then that reality sets in. *Holy crap! We have to buy two of everything.*

"Well, that is the plan, beautiful. What did you think having twins meant?" Enzo chuckles from behind me on the couch. *Shit. I didn't know he was behind me.* I turn to look in his direction and the beautiful smirk on his face has his dimple popping, which makes me lose all train of thought.

He sits beside me, placing an arm behind me to pull me closer. "Show me what you've got."

"Well, I have a few things tagged as my favorites. Let me know what you think."

As I show him my ideas, his eagerness gets the better of him and it turns into an all-out brainstorming session. All of a sudden, we're going from simply painting a room and putting some baby furniture inside, to building custom shelves that will also serve as changing tables. He insists on customizing the closet to utilize the space the best we can.

Enzo's eagerness is a sight to be seen. He's completely animated as he suggests adding on to our house to give Maddie a new room, and converting her room into a playroom for the babies since their rooms are adjacent to one another. Of course, I squash that idea like a bug. I insist the babies will be fine sharing a room. He reluctantly agrees, and I make him promise not to go overboard. Though his definition and mine of what overboard means are entirely two different things.

The next day when I come home from work, the room next to ours is unrecognizable. All the furniture has been removed, shelves are being made, and the walk-in closet now has a state-of-the-art organizer inside of it, which includes built-in dressers for each of the kids.

If I thought the room was impressive, that's nothing compared to what I see next. My jaw drops when I spot Enzo, with his shirt off, low-slung jeans resting on his hips, and a tool belt strapped around his waist. His carved, muscular back faces me as I feel my mouth go dry and all my breath leave me.

Holy freaking hell. If the kids weren't just down the hall, I'd let my fantasies run wild. *Who knew I had hot construction worker fantasies?*

"I'm happy to make all your fantasies come true, Samantha," Enzo states matter-of-factly. "Though, I'd prefer not to have company either."

Shit! Did I just say that aloud? I cover my face with my hands and laugh. "I'm blaming that on pregnancy hormones."

"If that's what makes you sleep better at night," he chides. "Though I'm pretty sure you always wanted to jump me before you were pregnant, too."

"You and your ego," I rebut.

"You love my big ego."

True. I love everything about him. But there's no point in letting his head swell.

He shakes his head as if he can read my thoughts as he reaches for my hand. "Come on, let me show you around before your thoughts get carried away."

24

ENZO

As I drive home from taking the tools back that I
borrowed from Pops, I can't wash the grin from my face. I can't
wait to show Samantha the finished nursery. I have kept her
out since that first night, and I can't wait to see the look on her
face.

Just as I'm a couple of blocks from the house, I spot a girl
similar to Maddie walking briskly down the street. She keeps
swiping at her eyes and it's obvious she's upset. My heart pangs
as I approach, hoping it's not Maddie.

As I get within a few yards, it becomes clear, it's her. *Fuck.
What's wrong with her?* I pull into an open spot just past her
and rush to get out. The tears streaming down her cheeks and
the blotchiness all over her face tells me she's been crying for a
while. "What's wrong, Mads?"

She stops dead in her tracks and looks the other way.
"I'm... fine," she mutters between breaths, "it's... Nothing."

The hell it's nothing. I've been around the block enough

times to know a woman is *never* fine. I square my shoulders and step into her path. "Seriously, what's wrong?"

"I... Don't... Want... To talk...About it," is panted out between breaths.

"Well..." Fuck. Obviously, something's wrong. I can't just leave her like this. "Are you hurt or angry?" I look her over with care, trying to assess any physical damage.

"Pissed," she croaks and relief washes through me.

"Pissed, I can handle. Come on. Get in the car." I don't wait for a response before walking to the driver's door.

I see her hesitate for a moment before walking to the passenger side of my Range Rover. Once she's in and buckled, I turn the engine over, flick my blinker, and do a U-turn.

Maddie doesn't say anything, but her breathing begins to calm. It takes a few minutes before I can no longer hear sobs coming from her chest. Whatever it is, she's pretty worked up. There's only one place I know to go when I need to let off steam and it sure isn't home.

After about five minutes of driving, Maddie looks around and finally breaks the silence. "Where are we going?"

I simply grin and state, "You'll see."

Within twenty minutes, we arrive at my intended destination. Maddie's a lot like her mom and keeps her thoughts to herself when she's upset. She eyes me suspiciously when we drive through the gates. Unlike Sam, Maddie has a filter, so I have no idea what's going on in that head of hers.

We walk into the building and head down the elevator. As we arrive at my intended destination, Maddie's eyes widen bigger than ever. Her mouth drops open and she sputters, "Wh... Wha... What are we doing?"

I walk over to my lockbox and open it. I set things down with precision so I can explain how to use everything safely when she's ready. "Have you ever used one of these?"

"No…" comes out faintly. "I can't say that I have."

"Would you like to learn how?" I eye her cautiously to make sure she wants to learn.

"Sure." She shrugs.

"Before I begin, I want to stress to you that you must always treat this gun as if it's loaded. Never point it at anything you don't intend to shoot, and keep your finger off the trigger until you're ready to shoot. That means you're aiming at your target and you're ready to fire."

Her eyes are on the semi-automatic pistol for a few moments before her eyes return to mine. "Okay."

Before I'll let her shoot anything, she needs to know how it works and the things she must do to use the weapon safely and efficiently. We discuss the frame, barrel, and action and how those components work, as well as how the features of the gun range itself works. I specifically point out the external safety and explain that it has to be disengaged before the gun can fire as well as the internal safety feature of this particular Glock. She asks questions freely and by the time I teach her how to load it and unload it, as well as make sure it's clear, I can see her eagerness growing. I show her how to load shells into a magazine, then make sure she knows how to keep her thumb clear of the slide.

"You'll only do it once if you forget this step." She smiles in response and instinctively flexes her fingers, imagining the pain. Finally, I let her practice with dummy rounds to get the feel of it before firing a live round.

Then I show her how to stand so she has a stable platform while she shoots. She laughs it off at first, but once she fires her first round, I'm sure she'll be thanking me. I point out how to line up her sights, and the importance of breathing.

"Once you have your breathing under control, take a deep breath. When you're halfway through your exhale, hold your breath, then pull the trigger slowly." I demonstrate this a few times before firing a shot.

"Okay, got it."

Finally, I gather the protection for our eyes and ears. I encourage her to use earplugs as well as the ear muffs, then we walk over to lane three and I show her how to set up. She walks me through each step I've taught her and when we've covered everything, she eagerly asks, "Can I shoot now?"

"Sure." I can't help but join in her enthusiasm. "Wait until I clear your lane, then you can fire at will."

Once I'm in lane two, I see her nod in my direction to see if it's okay. I give her the 'all clear' sign and she fires a round. She jerks slightly from the recoil, but she immediately adjusts her stance and takes aim again. Before I know it, she's emptied the entire magazine.

I enter her lane and show her how to bring her target back. I notice she actually has a decent shot. Her shots are grouped tight in the bullseye, just above the center. "Impressive, Mads." I whistle. "If you want to have them more centered, keep your wrist firm as you fire."

She simply nods, then refills her magazine like a champ. Before I know it, she's unloaded and getting another target. After a couple more rounds, I'm relieved to see a permanent smile that's etched into her features. I'd do just about anything to keep it that way.

While Maddie's target practicing, I shoot off a text to Samantha to let her know we'd be home in a while.

**Enzo: I have Maddie. We'll be home in a couple of
hours.**

Samantha: Everything okay?

Enzo: It is now.

Samantha: ???

Enzo: I'll fill you in when we get home.

Samantha: You'd better. LOL

I give Samantha a thumb's up in my reply and return my attention back to Maddie. By the time she's finished, she's unloaded quite a few magazines. She's rubbing her shoulders. She'll feel this in the morning. I show her how to clean up our area and put everything where it's supposed to go.

As we walk out of the gun range, we meet Ira Michaels coming in. He's met Maddie before, but quirks an eyebrow in the direction we came from. "Hey, man. How's it going?" I ask, keeping things casual.

"Just here to keep sharp." Michaels smiles. "What kind of trouble are you getting yourself into?"

"I brought Maddie to learn how to shoot and let off some steam. She seems to be a natural."

I look to Maddie to show her how proud of her I am, as a blush colors her face. She mumbles, "It was fun."

"I'm here to let off a bit of steam myself." He smirks. "Did it do the trick for you?" he asks Maddie.

"It sure did. I just envisioned the bullseye as the center of my anger, and you wouldn't believe how many times I hit it." She chuckles.

Okay... Remind me to never get on her bad side. "Wanna grab some pizza on the way home?" I still want to get to the bottom of what was bothering her. Something serious had to make her cry like that.

"Sure." She smiles like she hasn't cried a drop today. I'll count this as a win.

When each of us has a slice of pie in front of us, I choose this opportunity to find out what was wrong with Maddie. "So... What's the deal with the tears earlier?"

Maddie finishes her bite of food before groaning. "Ugg... Sophia Jones was making fun of me at school."

What the fuck could she tease Maddie about that had her that upset? "About what?" I grit out, picturing the worse-case scenario I could imagine.

"Well, Soren's at an away match today, so he wasn't able to drive me home from school." She takes another bite of her pizza.

"Okay..." still not seeing the problem with this.

"Right before school got out, Sophia started teasing me about being such a young baby and not being able to drive... Since I'm only fifteen and she's seventeen, like Soren."

"I see…" But I don't. Why would this make her cry?

"Well… then Caroline, the girl I told you about in my driver's ed class said, 'You should see the way she parallel parks. God help us all if she actually gets her license.' Everyone laughed, calling me 'curby' because I hit a curb one time. One time, Enzo. It wasn't even that big of a deal. I've never done it before and I wasn't used to driving the driver's ed car. Now the entire school is making fun of me for it. I couldn't even get on the bus. I forced myself to walk home, just so I could avoid the kids who were making fun of me." By the end, tears fill her eyes. Crap. This isn't something to cry over.

"Maddie, tell me more about Sophia. Have you fought with her before or is this a new thing?" There's gotta be more to this.

"Well, I never really knew her until I started dating Soren last fall. She used to hang out with him a lot before we started dating."

Bingo. "Well, if I had to place my bets, I'd say she's jealous of you. She probably likes Soren and wants you to not feel good enough to be with him."

She looks at me as if my head just spun around twice and popped off. "Me? You think she's jealous of me?"

"Well, why not? You're smart, beautiful, funny, and easy to get along with. You also got a great guy you're dating. Does she ever pick on you when Soren's around?"

Maddie thinks about it for a few moments. Placing her hand on her chin and looking to the sky for answers. "I guess not. It's usually just a snide comment when we're alone."

"I'm sure it has something to do with jealousy. Trust me. Girls used to do that to my high school girlfriend Vanessa when I wasn't around. But they'd be as sweet as honey if I was around. It used to piss her off." Boy, did it ever. I remember many a fight over my "so-called friends."

"Maybe..." she concedes.

"And about the thing with parallel parking... we're not going home tonight until you can do it with one arm tied behind your back," I tease at the end, making her laugh.

"If you say so." She rolls her eyes.

As soon as we finish with our meal and get a 'to-go' box for the leftovers, I take Maddie back to Riggs' place. It's the only place I know that I can set up an obstacle course for her to drive through. As we pull into the parking lot, I see Michaels and Riggs are still around. Once we get out of our vehicle, I quickly fill them in on my idea. Soon, they're both helping me create a course for Maddie to drive.

Once it's set up, I drive through it once, pointing out how to turn at specific points, to keep the cones in place. Then I sit beside Maddie as she maneuvers it. I've ridden with her a few times. I know she's a good driver, but like most fifteen year olds, she just needs practice and experience. Confidence is the biggest factor holding her back.

By the time we go through it three or four times, I actually hop out and let her drive it on her own. I want to see if she can do it without someone correcting her or warning her of things to come.

I walk over to talk with Riggs, while she drives the course.

"Hey, Harps. I heard you were in the range earlier, but I missed you," Riggs states as he leans against the hand railing to the stairs. He's balancing on one foot and the other is propped against the wall of the building.

"Yeah. I wanted to help Maddie let off some steam."

When Riggs cocks an eyebrow at me, I explain the entire situation. He nearly doubles over when I explain how I didn't have a fucking clue as to what I should do with a crying teenager who was so pissed at the world, she couldn't see straight. The gun range was a knee-jerk reaction.

"Holy shit. You may be new, but you're going to make an awesome dad. Not only will your girls know how to protect themselves, but word will get around that you regularly take them to the gun range. Half your battles will be won."

We watch as Maddie makes the last turn, then attempts to parallel park on her own. She pulls up to the car we have placed in front of the designated spot and without a single correction, she perfectly parks the car on her own.

As soon as she's in the spot, I hear a "Heck Yeah!" come from Riggs beside me and a "Omigod, I did it!" screech across the parking lot. Maddie ejects herself from the car faster than I ever thought was possible and runs toward me. I close the distance to give her a high-five, but she catches me off guard by throwing herself at me, in a gigantic bear hug. I get so excited, I pick her up off the ground and spin her around, making her squeal with delight.

By the time we settle down, Riggs and Michaels are there to congratulate her. Maddie beams with pride. After what we just witnessed, I highly doubt anyone will be calling her "curby" in the future. They each give her a high-five or fist bump and tell her they'd be happy to help her practice again anytime.

Maddie's on cloud nine as we walk into the kitchen that evening. We quickly find Samantha sound asleep on the couch, and since it's as quiet as a church mouse, I'm pretty sure Frankie and Dec are in their rooms asleep, or close to it. When Maddie sees Sam asleep, she whispers, "Thank you for an amazing afternoon." She reaches out for a hug again.

"You're welcome, sweetheart. Anytime."

Maddie turns to go upstairs, but not before she whispers, "Goodnight."

"See you in the morning," I quietly return.

When I look to Samantha, I see that she's out cold. She's curled up on her side, with one arm under her face, the other cradling the twins. Her shirt has risen, giving me a peek of her belly. I walk over and bend to kiss the swell of her stomach. I can't help but whisper, "Love you guys," as I pull away.

When I look to Samantha's beautiful face, I see she's smiling down at me. "Don't let me ruin your moment," she whispers. "I'm quite enjoying it, too."

I reach in to kiss her, too. She pulls me down to her. Instead of attempting to get comfortable on the couch, because let's face it, there isn't room for the four of us to snuggle in this position, I end the kiss and help her to a standing position.

"So, did you peek at the nursery?" I ask eagerly.

"No, I promised I'd stay out of there until you could show me," she groans in frustration. "Will you show me now? I can't take the suspense any longer. I wouldn't even let myself go upstairs because I'd have been too tempted," she grumbles at the end.

"Oh, Samantha, what am I going to do with you?" I shake my head at her, but pull her toward the stairs, turning off the lights as we go. I make one last stop to check the front door is locked and swoop her up in my arms so we can take the stairs at a faster pace. Her pregnancy waddle is just too slow.

When we get in front of the nursery, I set her down in front of the closed door. She looks to me for permission to enter, and I nod. When she steps in, it's dark, so I hit the lights. I adjust the brightness, so she can see there's a dimmer switch.

"Ohmigod, Enzo. We'll be able to sneak in here and keep it fairly dark. I wish I'd had one of those with the other kids."

She stands in the middle of the room and looks around slowly as if she's taking everything in. I've installed white wainscoting and painted the walls a shade of blue that's apparently called Blue Birds Feather. I have no idea what nut job names paint that, but it's what Samantha wanted.

I've assembled the cribs, shelves for toys, and replaced the carpet with light gray flooring. The two-toned cribs are gray and white, matching the floors and walls perfectly. My sister came over to help me hang pictures on the walls of baby animals, as well as set up the cribs for each child. Samantha had picked out blue and gray sheets for our baby boy and the same pattern, but accents of purple, blue, and gray for our girl. We still need to get the rest of the baby gear, but the room looks as if it can be lived in, if I do say so myself.

When Samantha turns to me, her eyes shine bright and her mouth is covered by her hand, so I can't tell if they are happy or sad tears. "Did I do okay?" I ask, needing reassurance.

"It's perfect, Enzo. Simply perfect," she whispers, then throws her arms around me in appreciation. "I don't think I've ever seen a more perfect room." She reaches up on her tiptoes and I take the hint to close the gap. When her lips taste mine, she's greedy and her kiss soon becomes filled with want.

Knowing that Maddie's right next door, I reluctantly pull back to whisper, "Why don't you thank me appropriately in our room."

I don't have to say any more. Samantha quickly takes my hand and leads me to our bedroom. The minute I shut the door behind us and click the lock for safe measures, Samantha reaches for the hem of her shirt and tosses it over her head.

Not to be outdone, I do the same, then toe off my shoes as I reach for the buckle of my belt. Before I can do any more, she whispers, "Let me show you how appreciative I am for all that you do for us." She reaches out to pull me close to her. Her breath tickles my neck, sending an electric current across my body. When her lips reach mine, my body explodes with desire.

I instantly take control of our kiss and show her just how turned on I am. I fist her hair at the base of her neck and guide her mouth as it moves against mine, like I know she loves. She lets out the sexiest moan I've ever heard and she presses her body to mine. Now that she's pregnant, she can't get as close as I desire, so I lead her to the bed. Once the back of her legs presses against the bed, I guide her slowly onto her back. She quickly breaks our kiss and scoots to the center of the bed.

I follow her, kissing every part of her along the way, starting at her ankles. I kiss her waist, and as soon as I feel her writhe beneath me, I pull down the leggings and panties she's wearing, quickly letting them land on the floor. She wiggles her arms behind her, and suddenly, her bra goes flying across the room, too.

I spread her thighs apart and kiss my way along the inner seam until I reach her center. She arches her back to meet me as my tongue licks slowly across her slit, driving her wild. I reach up and press my thumb to her clit and she practically detonates in an instant. I keep up this steady rhythm until she explodes with ecstasy. I keep right with her as she peaks and comes down from her high. Seeing Samantha come apart has got to be one of the sexiest things I've ever seen.

When she recovers, she grabs at my hips and leads me right to where she wants me. *Who am I to disappoint?* I push my tip inside and allow her time to acclimate. I move in and out of her ever so slightly, feeling each and every inch of her delicious body as she takes me in. "I love you. I want you. I need you, Enzo. More... Just like that," comes out in pants as I bring her to another pinnacle of her high. Warmth spreads across her body as her body convulses once again. Her coming apart is one of the things I have come to love. I pump in and out of her at a steady pace until I know she's through her orgasm. Then I follow her into my own release, letting out a string of low curses when I finally crest the wave of ecstasy I've been riding. *Holy shit. I don't think it can get any better than this.*

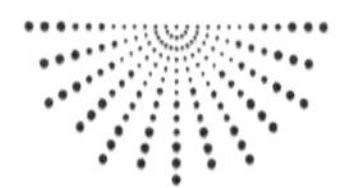

2 5

SAMANTHA

By the Fourth of July, I feel as if I'm thirty-five years pregnant, instead of weeks. I walk downstairs, if you can call my distinct waddle walking, and catch Enzo eyeing me up and down. The fool still thinks I'm sexy, but I feel anything but. He, of course, still makes my mouth water and hasn't gained an ounce since I've met him. In fact, with each passing day, I think he somehow gets hotter. *How the fuck does that happen?*

I catch Enzo's eyes, and he's smiling wickedly at me as he shakes his head. "I haven't changed since the day we met, beautiful."

"Damn filter," I mutter under my breath.

He looks me over once again, but stops at my feet. "Uhhh..."

"What?" I say defensively.

He seems a bit sheepish as if he isn't sure how to say something. "Are you going for a patriotic look?"

"What do you mean?"

His lips turn up at the edges, as if he's trying to hold back a smile. "Well, you're wearing a red and white top, blue shorts, and two different colors of shoes."

"Are you kidding me?" I can barely put my shoes on, unless I can slip into them, let alone see them once they're on.

"Which color did you mean to put on?"

"The red ones," I moan in disgust. Now I have to go back upstairs to get them. Which, of course, means another trip to the bathroom before we can leave. The twins think it's fun to bounce on my bladder with each vertical step.

Enzo must read how I'm feeling. "Stay right here. I'll get the red one for you. Do you need anything else while I'm up there?" He points to my right foot as I slip off what I hope is the white shoe.

"No. I just need that. I'm ready to go otherwise."

He kisses me lightly on the lips before leaving the room. I use this time to gather the salads I've prepared for the barbeque at Riggs'. We'll be staying through the fireworks tonight, so I also gather my sweatshirt and travel blankets from the hall closet.

When Enzo returns, he drops to one knee, and with a formal accent, he presents the shoe. "I believe you're looking for this?"

"Why, thank you, goofball," I tease. He slides it on my foot and stands to kiss me once more.

"Don't get any ideas, buddy. We have to leave in a few minutes or we'll be late picking up the kids from Devin's."

"I know, beautiful. I'm just making the most of our time alone together. In a matter of weeks..." He places his hands around my ginormous belly. "We won't be alone much more."

"Somehow, I'm sure you'll figure out a way."

As we pull up to Riggs' place, the driveway is packed. SUVs and trucks line the driveway, letting us know it will be a crowded house. Enzo assured me there'd be kids here, but once we get inside, I realize it's mainly couples and a few younger children. We were guaranteed this is the place to be for fireworks, so hopefully the kids will entertain themselves. Since Soren agreed to come with us, at least Maddie will be entertained.

Riggs has a slip-n-slide set up on one side of his house. Though, at the moment, there are many more grown men than children using it, which is quite comical. Immediately, Dec and Frankie take off in that direction. Soren and Maddie head with lawn chairs in tow to a shaded area, where they will likely hang out until it's time to eat.

After we greet Riggs and his wife Stella and visit for a while, Enzo insists I sit in the shade and put my feet up. I don't put up a fight. Being on my feet is killing me at the moment. Between the heat and being a hundred years pregnant with twins, I feel as if I'm about to pop. I still have a few weeks until my due date. But I've always delivered a week earlier than expected, so I'll take the reprieve when I can. The pressure on my lower back and abdomen is crazy with two in there. But as my doctor told me a few days ago, I am not dilated at all, so who knows how much longer these two will want to incubate in there.

We find a spot on the back deck where I can take in all the

action. We're next to Drew Warren and his date for the afternoon, Hannah. I spent some time with Drew at our wedding. He's quite the character and never fails to make me laugh.

"So, how much longer before those two make their debut?" Drew asks as he points to my belly.

"Not soon enough," I groan as one of them makes a painful jab to my ribs and decides to hang out there for a while. I gasp and rub my hand, trying to get them to move. But no such luck.

Drew reaches into the cooler beside him. He pulls out a bottle of beer and wipes it down with the towel next to him. Then he hands it to me. "Here."

"Warren, she's pregnant. She can't have that," Enzo snaps.

Drew sighs and shakes his head. "No shit, sherlock. I meant for her to put it on her rib cage. I'll bet you five bucks it makes the baby move."

"Seriously?" Hannah asks.

With a knowing look in my direction, Drew juts out his chin as he passes the bottle to me. "Trust me."

"What makes you so knowledgeable about kids?" Enzo inquires with a cocked eyebrow in Drew's direction. "Last I checked, you're still single and don't have any of your own."

Drew rolls his eyes. "Well, my sister had four. Every time the little booger wanted to stay in her ribs, she'd insist on getting a bottle of beer. We used to tease her on hot days when we came to her house to visit. There would always be a cold beer nearby, for just these emergencies. She claimed it worked fast and stayed cold longer than an icepack."

Hell, I'll give it a try. I place the bottle sideways, along my rib cage and sure enough, it makes the squirming baby move from my ribs. Ahhh, relief. "Drew, I think I love you."

"Hey, now," Enzo comes to the defense and gives me the most pathetic look ever, as if he wants to mark his claim.

"Oh, stop." I swat my arm in his direction. "You know I love you the most, but Drew might just have become my new best friend." *How did I not know about this beer bottle trick?* I settle into my chair and relax even further. This is pure heaven.

"You just make sure you always keep a few cold ones in the fridge. You'll be her knight in shining armor soon enough, Harps," Drew teases.

"Don't worry, Enzo. You already are," I tease in a dreamy voice, which makes his dimple pop as he smiles. My skin tingles as electric currents run up my spine from that look alone. Will I ever get immune to his sexiness?

By the time we're ready for fireworks, I've gone to the bathroom more times than I can count. The kids keep teasing me, but I kindly remind them they are to blame for this new problem as well. Having five kids will do that to a woman.

We've gathered near the edge of the clearing Riggs has set up to shoot off fireworks. As the first explosions ignite, the babies inside me jump. I reach over and grab Frankie's hand to place it on my belly. When the next firework goes off, the babies don't disappoint.

"They're moving like crazy!" Frankie exclaims. "Come feel this, guys."

Within seconds, I have about five hands placed on my belly. As soon as another explosion is heard, the babies move around like they're dancing at a disco.

"I don't think they like the fireworks," Declan announces.

"Are they going to be okay?" Maddie asks.

"They'll be fine. I promise," I say as I rub the spot that was kicked the hardest. "You did this, too, Maddie, at a New Year's display."

"Really?" she asks in disbelief.

"Sure did, kiddo. You also liked to dance to anything with a loud bass."

"No wonder you like to dance," Soren adds.

Soon, the babies settle down, and we all go back to watching the beautiful display of fireworks Riggs has provided for our entertainment. We leave right after, not only is it late, but Enzo has to work tomorrow. We say our goodbyes, and I can't help as I look at the tired kids in our car, how blessed we really are.

It's two days later that I come to find out how good we had it on the Fourth of July. I'm sitting in my office when I get a call over the intercom. Brenda's voice is full of concern when she states, "Sam... You have a Jason Riggs here to see you. Can I send him in?"

SAMANTHA

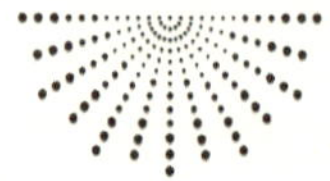

Instantly, my body goes cold and I'm filled with dread. There's no good reason on this earth why Riggs would show up at my office. *What the fuck has happened to Enzo?* Tears suddenly fill my eyes and I'm frozen in place.

"Sam... Can I send him in?" Brenda asks again, breaking me out of my panic for the moment.

"Sure..." I somehow manage to say.

I'm still frozen to my chair and can't do anything. It feels like hours have passed and there's no sign of Riggs at my door. Finally, there's a slight tap, and the door's pushed open.

The unreadable expression he has plastered in place leaves me little hope. If I thought that was bad, the stern, "Samantha, we need to talk," has me in near hysterics. The ice that fills my veins has me trembling on the spot.

Riggs doesn't wait for me to say anything, but sits in the chair across from me on the couch. He doesn't relax, but sits on the edge as if he's going to destroy my life in a matter of minutes. "I've got some news you need to hear."

Oh. My. God. This is it. Something's happened to Enzo. Suddenly, Riggs is out of focus and I can't see his expression clearly. *I need to be able to read his expression. I have to really hear what he is saying.* I wipe at my eyes to concentrate on him, and my hand is met with wetness. Christ, I'm crying and I didn't even know it.

"Breathe, Samantha," he whispers. "You've gotta breathe."

"Okay," comes out as barely a whisper. I take in a deep breath and force myself to let it out.

"Samantha." He reaches for my hand. He can't be dead. Please, God, don't let him say Enzo's dead.

"There was a situation in the field."

I gasp and do my best to remain upright.

"Enzo's team has lost all communication after being fired at twelve hours ago."

Tears roll down my face. I don't even bother to wipe them away as I shake my head in denial. This cannot be happening.

"We're fairly certain they weren't hit, but we're unable to locate them at this time."

"Wh... What does th... that mean?" I stammer.

"They followed protocol and went radio silent. They made it to their first checkpoint, but we haven't heard from them since."

This gives me a glimmer of hope. But I still don't understand. Since I can't seem to find my voice, I stare at him, desperately waiting for him to continue.

He takes a deep breath, and in the time it takes for him to

exhale, it takes everything in me not to come out of my chair and throttle him. *Why won't he just say it already?*

Just as I'm about to find my voice, he begins again, "We're not sure if anything's been compromised, and until we have any definitive news, we'd like for you to come to headquarters. We'll be able to keep you informed of all updates, as well as provide for anything you need."

At first, I don't comprehend what this means. I replay his words in my mind until I finally realize he's waiting for me to respond. "My kids are at their grandparents' for the week in Montana. They left yesterday and won't be back for a week. Do we need to get them?"

He shakes his head. "No. I just didn't want you to have to drive anywhere or have to juggle their schedules while we wait for word on our team. I'm simply trying to make things easier on you." He does his best attempt to give me a reassuring smile, but until I see for myself that Enzo's okay, I doubt anything will comfort me much.

Riggs looks around my desk and clears his throat. "Uh… Harper's mentioned you can work from virtually anywhere. Do you want me to give you a minute to gather what you need, then we'll go to HQ?"

I look around, unaware of how to start. I doubt I'll be able to concentrate. As I stand, I get a karate kick to the bladder, so I rub my lower abdomen. "I'll just use the bathroom and we'll be on our way."

When we get to the waiting room, I notice another man with Riggs. When he reaches out his hand to greet me, I realize it's Nate Carson. We've met a few times since I've known Enzo, but I can tell some serious shit is going down.

Gone is his ever-present overzealous attitude. He pulls me into a hug as he whispers in my ear, "Everything's going to be okay."

If that doesn't freak me out, I don't know what will. A fresh batch of tears streams down my face. I don't even know what to do or say. I'm so overwhelmed with emotion, I can't think of a way to respond. *What the fuck am I going to do without Enzo?*

As we exit my office, I gasp when Sara and Lorenzo flash through my mind. "Have you notified the rest of his family?"

Riggs shakes his head. "As soon as we knew the severity of this situation, we came straight here. We wanted you to be the first to know." He looks directly at me, then turns to Carson. "Do you mind taking Sam to HQ while I stop at his parents' house? I'll meet you back at HQ in less than an hour."

Carson nods, then turns to me. "Sam, do you mind if I drive your vehicle? We rode together, so you wouldn't have to drive."

Completely numb, I state, "Sure." I rifle through my purse and pull out my keys. "I'm parked right out front." Carson gently takes my arm and leads me to the vehicle. I faintly hear one of the girls in the office saying they'll be here if I need them, but I can't be certain who voices it.

Carson goes above and beyond to help me into my SUV. When he realizes I'm unable to do much more than stare into space, I feel him buckle my seat belt around the babies and me. Then he makes his way to the driver's side, gets in, and takes me to Riggs' HQ.

Once we're on the road, he reaches over for my hand. I hadn't known I'd been rubbing my legs until he stops me.

"What can I do to help you calm down? Have you eaten recently?"

"I'm not hungry," I mumble, but I'm sure he hears me.

The entire ride to HQ, my heart aches with the thought of not knowing what's happening with Enzo. I rub my belly and hope like hell he's safe and that I'll see him soon. I can't let the reality of him possibly never coming home sink in because that's a guaranteed way for me to break to pieces. To hold myself together, I force myself to keep a cycle of thoughts repeating through my mind. *He's going to be fine. He will get through this. I won't lose him.*

It doesn't take long before we're pulling into the HQ parking lot. I find myself being ushered into a conference room by Carson. Once again, he asks if there's anything he can get me. *Besides my husband, I don't want anything.*

It doesn't take long before Sara and Lorenzo come swooping through the doors. As soon as their eyes meet mine, they rush to hug me. I'm swallowed up in their arms for an unknown amount of time. My ears feel like cotton has been stuffed in them, and I don't quite catch what is being said, but I can feel the love they have pouring from them. I squeeze them each harder to let them know just how much I appreciate them.

It's Lorenzo's deep baritone voice, thick with emotion, that finally breaks through my fog-like state. "How are you holding up?"

"As well as can be expected," I mumble.

Sara pats me on the arm and states, "I'm sure it'll be just fine. Riggs got an update on the way here and there may have been some activity at the second checkpoint. They're verifying it now."

"What do you mean?" I ask for clarification, not sure I can let myself have hope, until I know for certain.

"I'm not really sure. I just overheard it as we arrived. They said they would come in and tell us in just a few minutes." Sara pats my arm and gestures for me to sit next to her in one of the conference room chairs.

We walk into a room and find three other women sitting at the conference room table. I faintly recognize them as some of the girlfriends or wives of the guys at the party a few days ago. I'm quickly re-introduced and reminded which man is their significant other. Instinctually, my heart reaches out to each of them because they must be in the same state as I. Other than a quick greeting, we each steer clear of the unfathomable topic as to why we've been brought to this room, waiting on pins and needles to find out more information.

After what feels like an eternity, the door to the conference room opens. This time, instead of more family members being brought together, Riggs himself enters alone. His stoic expression is unreadable. His strides are steady and he gives no indication as to which type of news he'll be delivering in just a matter of moments.

Enzo will be okay. Enzo is fine. Relax, Sam. You will get through this, runs on repeat through my head as I absent-mindedly rub my belly to comfort both my babies and myself. Their bodies twist and are just as tense as mine at this moment. As if they know there's a threat, each baby stands on alert as they stretch in what little room is left in my womb.

I keep my focus on Riggs as I feel Sara's arm wrap around my shoulders and pull me closer to her.

As soon as Riggs sees everyone's attention is on him, he doesn't waste any more time. "Thank you all for coming. I'll share and update, then I'll be happy to answer as many questions as I can." He looks around the room before taking a breath and continuing. "As you know, we've lost communication with our Delta team some hours ago, after shots were fired. As per protocol, they went radio silent and made it to their first checkpoint, which wouldn't cause alarm. But when they failed to clear the second checkpoint, we grew concerned. Their last location was a small village outside of San Salvador. I can't go into specifics of the mission, but I do know they were on their way out."

Sara squeezes my hand and Lorenzo places an arm on my back as we wait for him to continue. I feel myself tremble and I lean in heavily toward Enzo's parents for support. *I don't know what I'd do without them at this moment.*

"After several hours lapsed and they had yet to make it to their second checkpoint, we grew concerned. With their coms down and their tracking devices remaining stationary, we sent another team to get eyes on the ground for us. At this point, we are waiting for an update and we will let you know as soon as we know more."

"Mark has worked with you for years and scarier things than this has happened. Why have you brought us here?" a woman's voice whips out. "What are you not telling us?"

My eyes are drawn immediately to the icy voice sitting at the end of the table. She's a woman in her early thirties with light-brown hair. Her eyes are wild, pinning Riggs with a look that shows she's not to be messed with. I'm not sure I'd want to be on the receiving end of that glare.

Riggs exhales deeply. "Well… We wouldn't typically pull you all in on this but in this circumstance, we thought it best."

"What circumstance?" Daggers are shot in his direction again. There's a clear no BS vibe coming from this woman.

"Well… Since my team has apparently taken upon themselves to personally populate Portland, I thought it would be best to have all you expecting mothers here at one place. This way we can keep you up to date, keep an eye on you, and have a doctor on hand, if necessary." Riggs shrugs as if we should know this.

I take a closer look at the women at the table around me. Sure enough, each of us have stomachs protruding and if I had to guess, are pretty far along in our pregnancies. *How did I not notice we're all pregnant?*

Lorenzo clears his throat. "When Sara and I arrived, we overheard something about making it to checkpoint two."

"You're right. You did." Riggs nods in agreement. "It seems the team has made it to checkpoint two, but there's a mechanical failure, so they were not able to extract themselves in a timely manner."

Sara leans forward and places her arms on the table in front of her. "What does that mean?"

"We were right to send in a second team. They've made contact and will be extracting the entire Delta team as we speak."

"So… They're… Safe?" I mutter, not wanting to have false hope, but desperately needing something to cling on to.

"They're not out of the woods yet, but within the next hour

or so, we'll know if they've made it out of the hostile territory safely, and are on their way home."

Loud exhales can be heard throughout the room. For the first time since Riggs' arrival in my office, I take a full breath. There's still a weight on my chest that I know won't clear until I see Enzo for myself, but the pressure's not as deep.

"Ohmigod," I whisper in relief as I throw myself into Lorenzo's arms. Tears rush down my cheeks and my emotions are out of control.

"It's gonna be all right," Lorenzo whispers as he wraps his arms around me, giving me his strength.

"We'll know soon enough." Sara embraces the two of us and we sit here, tangled together.

When we finally break apart, Riggs clears his throat. "I'll be in command. You're welcome to make yourselves at home. I've made this conference room as well as our lounge available to you, so you won't be without the comforts of home. If you need anything, feel free to ask." With that, he walks out of the room.

Once the door to the conference room closes, Carson grabs everyone's attention. "Are any of you hungry? I'm ordering takeout and would love to get you something while we wait." He places a variety of takeout menus on the table and says, "I'll be back shortly to place the order." With that, he, too, walks out of the room.

Out of habit or perhaps it's nerves, I grab a menu off the table and peruse it. I can't for the life of me concentrate on the words printed before me. It's as if they are jumbled and in a foreign language. I'm not even sure how long it takes for me to realize the menu I'm reading is for a Thai restaurant.

The moment I do, thoughts of asking Enzo out for the first time flood my mind. I'd been so nervous and I had no idea what I was doing. I hadn't expected him to be outside my door that day. As far as I knew, he was long gone with his father and the only way I'd be seeing him again was in my fantasies. He'd taken me off guard with his deep, green eyes, sexy smile, and dimple that made me swoon. No man has ever made me react the way he does.

My heart still flutters as I recall him approaching my walkway. His complete sexiness had rendered me speechless. Of course, he'd been there to thank me for letting his dad take off for lunch. When his stomach rumbled, I'd seen it as a sign. I had no idea that one little move on my part would have set so much in motion.

There's a sudden jab to my stomach and the menu I'm resting on it nearly falls from my hands.

"You okay, Sam?" Sara reaches over to place her hand on my arm.

"I was just remembering the first day I met Enzo and couldn't believe I'd had enough guts to ask him to dinner."

"If I recall, his stomach did the asking for you." Lorenzo chuckles.

"Yeah," I say wistfully as I recall each and every moment of our dinner. I still can't believe the way he made me feel and the instant connection we shared. That evening when he dropped me off, I truly didn't want him to leave.

"I'll never forget the day Enzo came home with that suit." Sara laughs. "I knew something was up right away and I didn't even have to resort to my usual tactics to get him to spill his guts about you."

"Oh, come on, Sara. You've never had to do much when it comes to interrogating the boys. Erin… That's another story. But if there's ever a story to be told, it doesn't take you long to get it out of them."

"Ohmigoodness," Sara gasps. "Do you remember when Zane and Enzo tried sneaking out when they were in high school? Those fools thought they could actually push the car out of the driveway and we wouldn't be any the wiser."

"You're kidding me," comes out of my mouth before any further thought. *This must be interesting.*

Sara shakes her head and levels me with a stare. "You'd better believe it."

Becoming the perfect distraction for our current situation, Sara continues the story of how she just so "happened" to go out to the garage as they were pushing Enzo's truck into the driveway later that evening. She'd known they were gone and wasn't all too worried because they were together, but from what she tells me in her story, I would have paid millions to be a fly on the wall.

Stories about Enzo from Lorenzo and Sara are just what I need to pass the time. They somehow manage to get me laughing about Enzo and the antics of his youth. I don't even realize almost two hours have passed when Riggs makes his way back into the conference room we chose to stay in.

As I look up, I realize the other women are nowhere in sight. Riggs comes and sits beside me. "How are you holding up?" Concern is etched in his voice, which puts me back on alert for Enzo.

"Is he… Do you know anything else?" I manage to mutter,

all the anxiety I'd pushed away rears its ugly head and is back in full force.

Thankfully, it dies away as soon as I see relief fill his features. His eyes soften and a smile forms on his lips as he nods in my direction. "Yes. We've gotten word everyone made it out. They were wheels up hours ago. There were some injuries, but nothing sustainable. It's an estimated nine hours of flying, so they should be here late this evening."

"Is Enzo…" I take a deep breath and steady myself. "Was he injured?"

"He might have some bumps and bruises, but from the sound of it, the injuries were to someone else."

Instantly, the women I met earlier come to mind. "Ohmigod, what happened to them? Anything serious?"

"I'm not privy to specific details as of yet, but it appears as if McGowen's calf was grazed with a bullet. Nothing entered his body, but it slowed them down before they got to checkpoint two."

"But he's going to be okay?"

"Yes. There's also a medic. He's assured us he's fine."

"And nothing's wrong with Enzo?" I can't help myself by asking. *He did just say a grazing bullet wasn't a big deal after all. Is Enzo going to be covered in bruises and unrecognizable?*

"Seriously, Sam, he's fine. In fact, he's the pilot. We wouldn't have him flying if he's sustained any injuries." Relief washes through me and my chest loosens immensely. I want to scream and shout my relief from the rooftops.

Unaware of my intent, I throw myself into Riggs' arms, hugging him fiercely. "Thank you. Thank you. Thank you," I repeat into his ear. When I pull back, I find my eyes filling with tears.

"Are you sure you're okay?" Riggs has a cross between a deer in the headlights and there's a bomb about to explode expression down pat.

"Happy tears, I'm sure," Sara explains for me.

Lorenzo reaches out to shake his hand. "Thank you for letting us know." He looks to Sara and me. "Now that we know Enzo's safe and sound, we'll be able to relax some."

"Feel free to hang out here to wait for their arrival. Let's get out of this conference room, so you all can relax a bit while you wait."

Without even looking to Enzo's parents, words pour out, "Thank you, we will." There's no way I'm going anywhere until I see Enzo for myself.

A few hours later, Sara and I visit on an extremely comfortable couch in the lounge Riggs had let us use. Lorenzo took off to run some errands and will return before Enzo arrives.

I take a deep breath and I find myself getting sucked deeper and deeper into the cool leather surrounding me. I may need a forklift to get out of this thing, but for the moment, I simply don't care. The stress of the day has made me exceptionally tired, but I'm too wired to sleep. I absentmindedly rub my belly as my muscles turn liquid.

"Are you doing okay, love?" Sara asks as I exhale heavier than normal.

"Yeah," comes out as a sigh. "Now that I've calmed down, I

think this couch may be a little too comfortable, if you know what I mean. You'll probably have to send an SOS just to get me out of it."

Her laugh reminds me of Enzo, making my heart clench in longing. "Oh, don't be silly. We'll get you out of it just fine. In the meantime, why don't you rest. You don't need to stay awake for my sake. I've got my Kindle right here in my purse and I can tell you're exhausted."

I sigh heavily. "I'm wiped, but my brain's still whirling ninety miles a minute."

"About anything in particular?"

I shake my head. "No. The moment I think I've captured it, it flies out the window."

Sara gives a low chuckle. "I was like that right before I had each of my babies."

"Really?"

"By the time Erin came around, Lorenzo swore it was a part of my nesting ritual. Did you nest with your other pregnancies?"

"More with Maddie than the rest. I had time to dote on the details. With Dec and Frankie, I think I was too busy to focus on anything but what was in front of me."

"That's completely understandable. Once these two make their appearance, I'm sure you won't have any time to worry either. I've had two close in age, but obviously not twins." Sara shakes her head before adding, "If they're anything like Enzo, I'll pray you keep your sanity."

I can't help but smile at her rolling eyes. "Oh, come on, he couldn't have been that bad."

"No, he wasn't. But he was all boy. If there was something

tall, he'd climb it. If it moved, he rode it, and if it was even remotely edible, he ate it. Why one time, I had to pry dog food from his grip because he wanted to be just like the puppy we'd gotten him."

I shake my head in disbelief. "You're kidding." *Thank God, I've yet to experience that.*

"Nope." She smirks. "Parent of the year. Right here. Don't worry. It was only the one time. If I'm ever lucky enough to watch your little angels, we no longer have pets." Somehow, she manages a straight face until the end. Her downfall is when I make eye contact. Then we both erupt into fits of laughter.

"You'd better be careful what you ask for," I say when we've calmed down. "I'll be working part-time from home after my maternity leave. I may just take you up on babysitting if things get too hectic."

"Seriously, Sam, if you need me, I'm only a phone call away. Even if it's just for the chance to talk to a living, breathing human being with the capacity to respond, I'm always here for you."

As the hours tick by, I find myself losing the battle to stay awake. After a lull in conversation, I find my eyes waging a battle against gravity and losing terribly. They stay closed for longer periods of time and before I know it, I feel a blanket being thrown over me as I sleep on the couch.

The next thing I know, I hear the sound of familiar voices. "They're making their final approach." Then some silence. Since no one speaks, I figure it must be a part of the dream I'm having. Then in the distance, "How long has she been out?" from a deep, husky voice I try to recognize asks. Maybe this isn't a dream. I open my eyes to find Sara talking with Lorenzo and Riggs.

"About an hour or so," Sara whispers barely loud enough for me to hear.

I stretch and let out a big yawn. "I'm awake. What's up?"

Sara's eager eyes pin me. "Good. They're making their final approach. They should be landing in less than fifteen minutes."

Ohmigod! I can't wait to see Enzo. Instinctually, I attempt to throw myself out of the couch I've been lounging on. But these babies have other plans. I find myself stuck about halfway there. I rock myself back and try to extract myself again. This time I make even less progress. Holy crap. I think I really am stuck. *How the hell does one get stuck on a couch?*

Maybe if I scoot to the edge and use the armrest as leverage, I'll be able to stand? As I attempt to do so, I happen to look up. I find three sets of eyes staring at me with amused expressions of their face. *Great, here I am doing a beached whale impersonation and they're just watching?*

Riggs, stoic as ever, walks over without missing a beat and offers a hand. "Can I help you?"

As humiliating as it is, I reach out my hand, as it's likely the only way I'll ever get out of this couch. "Yeah. Thanks."

The second I'm upright, the weight of the babies crushing my bladder's astronomical, causing me to gasp. All eyes look to me. "I'm fine. Just pregnant," I mutter. I step toward the restroom and suddenly, the pressure increases. I take another step, determined to get to the bathroom and a gush of fluid runs down my legs. *HOLY SHIT! I just wet myself at Enzo's place of employment. This cannot be happening to me.*

A moan escapes as I do my best to look down at the mess I've made. As I turn around, I feel distinct movement from within my belly. It's sharp, and very much like an arm or leg moving across the middle. It's unlike their other movements as my skin feels tighter around their bodies.

I look to Riggs and find his eyes as big as saucers and his mouth hanging open. "Um... Sam..." he sputters.

"Oh, my!" Sara exclaims. "Your water just broke!"

"I figured it was that or she wet herself," Riggs manages to stay unflappable as he looks down at the puddle he's currently standing in.

A mixture of emotions overwhelms me. Mortification isn't quite strong enough, and panic doesn't fit either. As I survey my situation, it hits me like a brick across the face. *Holy shit, my water just broke!* I'm weeks until my due date, and Enzo isn't here. This cannot be happening! I'm not even in labor. Ohmigod... will the babies be okay?

Lorenzo's soft touch to my shoulder brings me out of my downward spiral. "Samantha, sweetheart. Are you okay?"

"Uh..." I take a moment to assess the situation. There's still fluid flowing down my legs, but at a slower trickle. It is probably one of the grossest things I have experienced, but nothing I can't live through. I haven't had any contractions, just some pressure on my lower back that's been there for days. Placing my hands on my belly feels weird. Without the amniotic fluid, they're more defined. It's almost like I can feel their actual bodies in my belly. I press tenderly along each baby as I take in their shape.

"Do you want me to call an ambulance?" Riggs pulls out his phone and waits for my response before dialing.

"I'd rather call my doctor first."

"Why don't you sit and I'll get your purse, honey," comes from Sara.

"Yes, please sit," Riggs strongly suggests as he reaches out to make sure I'm steady.

"Uh... I can't sit on that leather couch!" I scoff in disgust.

"Why the hell not?" Riggs' voice booms.

Isn't it obvious? "I'm disgusting. It's too nice and comfortable of a couch to ruin it," I argue.

"So what... Am I supposed to tell Enzo when he walks in here, 'Dude, your wife's water broke and I'm the ass that made her sit in an uncomfortable chair?' I don't think so."

"Your water broke?" comes from the voice I've been craving to hear all day.

I turn to the door of the lounge we've been camping out in and see the sexiest man alive in the doorway. His face is a mixture of awe, wonderment, and shock. My heart melts.

IT'S BEEN A SHIT DAY. ANYTHING THAT COULD HAVE GONE wrong, has. I've been flying for the past nine hours straight after getting shot at and having to rendezvous at another location. I'm dead on my feet and just want to crawl into bed next to Samantha and forget about this entire day.

Apparently, life has other plans.

As I round the corner to the lounge I was told my family is waiting for me, I hear Riggs' deep voice. "Do you want me to call an ambulance?" This has me picking up the pace to see what's going on. His tone is serious and a bit eerie. By the time I get to the door, I can tell Samantha's okay because she's arguing with him over sitting.

Just as I'm about to enter, the words, "Dude, your wife's water broke," register and I take in their full meaning. *Holy shit! She's going into labor?*

Needing to clarify, I ask in disbelief, "Your water broke?"

The minute Samantha turns, her rich, mahogany eyes lock

onto mine. I can see her visibly relax, just by my presence alone. I absolutely love having this effect on her.

I close the distance between us in mere strides. I wrap my arms around her and bring her in for a hug. When I pull back, she pulls in her lower lip and suddenly looks sheepish. "Yes. Just a few minutes ago."

"Have you been having contractions?" Ma interrupts. *Thank God, she is thinking clearly. I'm stuck on being near Samantha again.*

"I don't think so. There's been some pressure in my back, but lately, that's a daily occurrence."

"Have you called the on-call-doctor to find out what you should do?" I finally get my wits about me.

She shakes her head, but before she can respond, Riggs cuts in with a pointed look to Samantha, "She was just about to do that."

Samantha lets out an exasperated huff. "Great. Now we're all standing in this mess. Is there a way we could get some towels to clean this up so we don't continue to traipse through this everywhere?"

"Why don't we focus on the doctor, beautiful," I say, hoping to find out what to do next.

Samantha points to her purse next to the side of the couch that is clear from any liquids. "My phone's right there."

Pops is quicker than I can blink because he reaches out and hands it to us from a distance. I grab hold of the purse and open it for her. She reaches in and immediately calls the on-call doctor. After being on hold for what seems like an eternity, she talks to someone. The room waits on pins and needles for direction.

"Okay... Yes... No, not yet... Of course. I will see you when we get there... Okay. See you then."

She puts her phone back in her purse and a huge smile crosses her face. "Time to go to the hospital."

I'm instantly filled with about ten thousand emotions at once. I can't wait to get my family to the hospital, so I can guarantee they're safe. I'm just about to swoop them all off, until I look down at my dirt-sodden clothes. There's no way I can go like this. "Is there any way I can grab a quick shower?" I look to Samantha to judge her response first. "I promise, we will be on the road in ten. Sooner, most likely."

"Go ahead. Since I'm not in active labor, the nurse I spoke with told me to take my time and safely arrive when I can." She may have just had her water broke, but she's remaining calm and level headed. *How does she do this?*

I quickly pull her to me and plant a kiss on her lips. "I'll be back before you know it." Not wanting to waste any time, I look over to my parents. "Do you think you can walk her to our vehicle and I'll meet you out front?"

"We sure will, son." Pops smiles. "You look worse than what the cat dragged in. Get out of here and change. I want to meet my grandbabies." I hug him and Ma on my way out the door before he scolds me with, "Get movin', son."

We finally arrive at the hospital forty minutes later. Of course, Samantha put up a fight about riding in our new vehicle and ruining the seats, so I had to get plastic bags for her to sit on. Ma and Pops meet us at the labor and delivery entrance and we register at the nurses' station. Samantha keeps mentioning that she's not ready for this and all the things that are still on her list of things to do, but me being the smartass I am, just keeps telling her, "Samantha, our kids obviously don't care about the schedule. They're just ready for the world."

Once we're assigned to a room, Samantha's asked to change into a hospital gown. She asks if she can shower off the gunk and the kind nurse, by the name of Kate, offers to assist her. I pace the small space between the hospital bed and what looks like the couch I'll be sleeping on at some point. I hope to hell these babies make their entrance safely. The possibilities of unforeseen circumstances run through my mind. Thankfully, Samantha's into the room before my horrific imagination gets the best of me.

They hook her up to an IV and have monitors on her within minutes. The doctor comes in and greets the two of us. "I'm Dr. Allison. What seems to bring you in tonight?" Her warm smile and confidence puts me at ease. I reach out to Samantha's hand to find her muscles relax, too.

"Uh…" Samantha says as she sits up to shake her hand. "My water broke."

Dr. Allison does a thorough exam of Samantha. I try to wait patiently, anxious to hear what she has to say about Sam's progress.

When she's done, she explains, "Since you're at 35 and a half weeks, we're going to wait another hour or so to see if you go into labor naturally. We will induce you if they don't get things started on their own. Either way, you will be having these babies within the next twenty-four hours." She takes a step to the side toward a fetal monitor and pulls out the wand. She quickly does an ultrasound and we can still see two babies moving around. "Good. Things look good. I'd suggest you rest while you can. As you're only dilated to a three, we may have a long road ahead of us, and in this particular case at the moment, it's a marathon, not a sprint. I'll be back in a bit to check on you."

With that, she leaves the room, and Samantha and I are left alone. She couldn't look more beautiful. I reach in and kiss her tenderly. I love this woman more than life itself.

When our kiss breaks, she whispers, "I'm so glad you're here. It's been a hell of a day waiting to know if you're all right." Her eyes well up and I can tell she's about to break down into tears.

"Shhh…" I kiss her lips lightly. "I'm here now. That's all that matters." I kiss her once again and the love she has for me is felt throughout my body.

"I love you, Enzo," she whispers as I pull away.

"Love you, too, beautiful," I whisper.

There's a knock at the door and the nurse comes to check her vitals. I take this opportunity to go out to my parents in the waiting room and invite them into the room to wait a while.

My mother hugs me tight upon my arrival to the waiting room. "Oh, Enzo. I love you so much. You gave us all such a scare."

Pops joins us in a hug and adds, "Sure glad you're here."

"Sorry, Ma. I wasn't really in any danger. Plans just changed and I had to adapt. I'm so relieved I made it back before you all had to come here." I look to each of them. "Thank you so much for being here for Samantha."

"We would do that for any of our children," Ma sates, but holds my gaze as if I should know better than to say something like that.

"I know. But I want you to know how much it means to me for you to be there for Samantha. I know you love her, too. But to me, it meant the world walking in the room tonight and seeing you already there."

"Anytime, Enzo. Anytime." Pops claps me on the shoulder. "Let's go see how Samantha's doing."

Not even thirty minutes later, Samantha nearly squeezes my hand off. *Holy shit, the woman has more strength than I could've imagined.* Apparently, she'd been in labor and mistook her back pain as simple discomfort. Now she claims there's no guessing. These babies are on their way.

Before I know it, the doctor comes in and says she's dilated to a six. I feel completely helpless as she has contraction after contraction. I do my best do give her whatever she needs, even if it means I will never feel my fingers in my left hand again.

Since childbirth is the only time Samantha insists she's saying yes to drugs, a team of people soon arrive to give her an epidural. Though I want to freak out when I see the size of the needle they place into Samantha's spine, I may have to kiss the anesthesiologist because he takes the pain away from her quickly.

By the time they leave, Samantha is back to her beautiful self. She's laughing, joking, and in good spirits, considering the amount of pain she endured. We visit with Ma and Pops and I assure everyone I wasn't in any serious danger. I also take this time to call the kids and let them know their brother and sister are on their way. Samantha's parents decide they'll return tomorrow, instead of waiting the rest of the week because they can't wait to meet their new grandchildren.

I'm surprised when Dr. Allison comes in about an hour

later and asks, "Okay, Mom. Are you ready to have these babies?"

"Is it time?" Samantha asks in disbelief. "This epidural's a miracle maker because I haven't felt anything."

Ma and Pops excuse themselves before things go any further.

Dr. Allison helps Samantha settle at the end of the bed and lifts the blanket covering her legs. "Yep. I'd say you're about ready."

Words cannot express my admiration for Samantha as she spends the next hour pushing with all her might. Yes, there are plenty of disgruntled curses being sworn under her breath, and her filter's off the charts for comments, but as usual, I give her a free pass. I love knowing what she's thinking. It's the best part of her. There even comes a time when she thinks she can't push any more. If I had to push a watermelon out of a lemon hole, I'd probably feel the same. But somehow, she manages to keep going.

Nothing can describe the birth of our daughter when she arrives at eleven forty-three that evening. It's a mixture of awe, wonder, and a bit of disgust when her slime-covered body finally decides to make an appearance. The scream that comes from the tiniest body I've ever seen makes me think she'd rather have stayed inside. I'm offered to cut the cord, which is the craziest thing I've done yet, then a nurse quickly cleans her up and offers to let either Sam or I hold her.

I'm suddenly overwhelmed with emotions as I take in the beauty of my daughter. She's absolutely perfect. Her skinny little hands and feet move excitedly as she enters Samantha's arms. My eyes fill with water as I bend to kiss her lightly. Life can't get any more perfect than this.

I'm taken aback when her expressive green eyes meet mine. She may only be minutes old, but the look she gives me melts my heart instantly. She looks as if she holds all the secrets of the world with her pensiveness as she checks out the room around her.

"She's so tiny," Samantha whispers and our daughter reaches out to touch her face.

"She's beautiful," comes out in almost a croak. Clearing my throat, I continue, "I love you both so much."

"We love you, too," Samantha whispers, then groans in a sound of discomfort.

"Hey, guys, let the nurses examine that bundle of joy. Baby number two's roaring to get out of here."

On cue, a nurse whisks our baby girl away.

As I put my other hand in Samantha's, a contraction hits and the doctor tells Samantha to push. As if his sister has cleared the way for him, with the first push, we can already see the head crowning. When Samantha pushes once more, his entire body comes right along with it.

I stare in disbelief as my naked son in all his glory lets out a murderous scream, much like his sister's arrival. *Holy crap. If we ever piss the two of them off together, we are in for it.* I assist in cutting the cord, then the doctor whisks him off with the nurse to get him cleaned up.

As my son is handed off, the nurse introduces her name as Rosalie. She offers to get him cleaned, weighed, and most importantly, into a diaper. Knowing both children are in capable hands, I turn my attention to Samantha.

I look at her skeptically when the doctor says push again. *What the hell is she pushing out? There'd better not be a third baby in there.* Then I see it... and suddenly, I wish I'd been looking anywhere but at the doctor and her at that moment. It's fucking disgusting.

"One more push and the remaining afterbirth will be out," Dr. Allison cheerily announces. How can she be so upbeat after touching that?

Immediately, I blink my eyes a few times, trying to rid myself of the sight I can't seem to unsee. I may have been in and out of war zones, watched my buddies have some near-fatal injuries, but nothing has prepared me for the strength a woman must have to go through during childbirth. Holy fucking shit. Hands down, Samantha's the strongest person I know.

I reach down and brush the hair off Samantha's forehead. "God, you're incredible, beautiful. I love you so much."

She pants as the doctor pushes down on her stomach in various places before saying, "I love you, too."

As soon as I'm sure Samantha's in the clear, I rush out to the waiting room to tell my parents our exciting news. "Everyone's perfect!" I exclaim when I see their eager faces. They both nearly jump out of their chairs and rush to hug me.

"How's Samantha?" Pops asks.

"She's doing as well as expected, having just delivered babies. That woman is stronger than any person I know. Add to the fact that she's still smiling. I think she's a saint."

Both my parents chuckle as we make our way down the hallway to our hospital room. "I felt the same about your Ma," Pops whispers once he stops laughing.

I look to Ma and have a newfound respect I'd never known before. She's done this three times. And that was when epidurals were unheard of. This world would cease and fucking be extinct if men had to bear children.

We enter the room to find a nurse holding one of our children while Samantha has the other. They are in multi-colored pastels at the moment, so I have no idea which child is which. With them being swaddled like little burritos, all you can see are their squishy little faces and mops of golden-brown hair on top. We'll have to figure out a color system or something.

"Who've you got there?" I singsong as I reach down to the baby our nurse is holding.

"This is your son," the nurse beams. "He's quite handsome." She hands him over and I cradle him in my arms.

Ma rushes to my side. "Oh, Enzo. He looks just like you as a baby."

"God, help him," I tease as I stare into his big, green eyes. He has the most adorable thick patch of golden-brown hair that's all clean from his bath. His rosy cheeks pop out of the blanket swaddling him and his mouth is formed into the perfect little 'O.'

"Oh, hush." Ma swats at me.

"Do you have names picked out?" Pops asks from my other side.

"Yep. We sure do." Samantha draws our attention. "Let me introduce you to Lorenzo Dean Harper and Lorainne Marie Harper."

Ma oohs as Pops slaps me on the back. "You're straddling him with that name?" Pops asks in disbelief.

"Yep," I proudly say. "We'll call them Loren and Raine."

"How precious," Ma states as she walks over to see Raine in Samantha's arms. She reaches in for a hug and kisses Samantha on the cheek after doing the same to her granddaughter. "How are you holding out, Sam?"

"I'm doing as well as can be expected. I'm a bit tired, but I'm not sure we'll be sleeping much in the near future." The smile that lights up her face makes my heart clench. I don't think I can ever love her more than I do right now in this moment. She looks so natural. "Want to hold Raine?" she offers to Ma.

"You bet I do!" Ma almost squeals with excitement.

I look to Pops who's in awe of Ma holding our baby girl. "What about you, Pops? Want to hold Loren?"

He beams at me with delight and reaches for his phone in his pocket. "Can you get a picture of us?"

I stare at him in disbelief. He of all people is the one to think of a camera. I'd been so out of it, I'd missed everything. Crap, I'm a fuck up as a father already. "Only if you do the same for us," I say as I try to recover from my earlier mistake.

We each take turns holding the babies, and several cameras have made an appearance to capture the moment. I send a picture of Sam and me holding the kids to Maddie, as well as my sister and brother. It's too late to video chat since it's nearly one in the morning when Ma and Pops decide to call it a night.

A lactation specialist comes in right as my parents are leaving and introduces herself as Piper. She assists Sam in getting the kids to nurse. To my relief, Samantha's well at ease with someone grabbing her breast and positioning it into

Loren's mouth. Piper is up close and personal, and I've never seen anything like it.

"Before you know it, you'll be walking around the house, a kid on each breast and still managing to get things done," Piper teases. "You're a natural at this, Samantha." Do people really do that?

"Ha… I don't think I'd go that far, but I distinctly remember reading manuscripts and binge-watching TV series with my previous children."

One thing I'm coming to learn is there's an entire vocabulary set I haven't been privy to before having children. Words like lactation, latching on, unhooking, football position, and much more are discussed between Piper and Samantha.

I decide to make the most of my time by acquainting myself with Raine in the rocker. She's wide awake and ready to conquer the world. I undo the swaddle of blankets so that her hands are free and I can touch them. They are unbelievably tiny. Wondering what her feet look like, I un-swaddle her entirely. I can't believe her feet are smaller than my thumb. When I brush my fingertips against her toes, she kicks at me and makes a cooing sound. She's still curled up like she's been in her Mama's womb and it's incredible to see the miracle of life up close and personal.

Suddenly, Raine straightens her body as stiff as a board and her face turns fire-engine-red. Did I break her? What the hell's happening. "Uh… Sam… What's going on?"

Both the lactation specialist and Sam stop immediately to see what's going on. Each are frozen in place as Raine makes a grunting sound. I immediately stand and walk to them. "What do I do? Is she okay?"

Before either of them can say anything, I feel a rumble in her diaper. She grunts again and again. My hand feels more movement in her diaper and suddenly, there's a loud farting noise that has me scared to check what's coming from that precious girl of mine.

"Um... Not it." Samantha laughs.

"Did she really just do what I think she did?" I ask in disbelief. There's no way this precious angel can sound like that.

"Let me see." I bring Raine over to her and she pulls back the top of the diaper. "Yep. You're in luck. The meconium ones are the nastiest."

I blanch at the thought. "What the hell is meconium?"

With a straight face, Samantha simply states, "It's the babies first poop and it's usually tar black and stickier than all get out to get off. They will usually only have one or two, then it will pass, and it will turn a liquid, yellowish color."

I take Raine over to the changing table, and holy shit. Sam's right. This stuff sticks to her butt like glue. It also has a sandpaper texture, so I do my best to clean her up without causing her too much fuss. My sweet girl screams like she's cursing me out the entire time. Thankfully, I'm a pro at diaper changing, so I'm able to get her settled quickly.

"Bring her to me. It's her turn to eat," Samantha directs as she gets Loren ready for a handoff. "You'll need to burp him."

Once I get Loren and Samantha settled with Raine, I move to the rocker and glide back and forth as I pat his back. Soon, a loud burp erupts in my ear, followed by a series of toots. "I see how you're going to be," I tease Loren. Samantha giggles at my response.

"Well, I'm sure he's not to be outdone by his sister." Samantha's sass is back in full swing. It warms my heart to see her at her best.

Within minutes, Loren does his best, but Raine's still the champion. I clean him up just as the lactation specialist leaves the room. Raine's nearly asleep. I offer to take her and lay her in the clear-walled bassinet next to Samantha. Samantha's awake, but it's evident she needs some rest.

"Why don't you try to get some sleep, Sam? I'll take our looky-lou here and hang with him until he falls asleep. You've had quite a day and could use the rest."

"So have you, mister." She eyes me suspiciously. "But I'm fading, and they will need to be fed before I know it." She pushes a button to make the bed recline.

I walk over and kiss her lightly on the lips. "Thank you, Samantha. You have made me the happiest man alive today. I love you all so much."

She yawns and reaches her hand out to push the hair off Loren's face. "We make beautiful babies."

"We sure do, beautiful. Now get some rest." She closes her eyes and I walk to the rocking chair. I maneuver it with one hand, so that my legs can prop on the bench-like couch next to me.

Since the lights are dim, I grab the u-shaped pillow Samantha called a Boppy and place it on my lap. I let Loren settle down on it, so that he's facing me and I do the only thing I can think of. I tell him the story of how his mother and I met.

"One day, I came home from leave. I wanted to surprise Pops, so I went to his job site. That's the day I met and fell in love with your ma. I didn't know it then, but that one decision was the best I've ever made in my life..."

As I talk, Loren listens intently. His tiny hands wrap around my index finger and we have story time until his eyes grow heavy. When I think he'll fall asleep, I stealthily maneuver him to the bassinet and lay him inside next to his sister. I can't wait until they meet their brother and sisters. I know Maddie, Declan, and Frankie will be over the moon when they come tomorrow to meet their new brother and sister.

Not wanting to disturb either of them, I stare at my sleeping family and think to myself, life can't get any better than this.

EPILOGUE

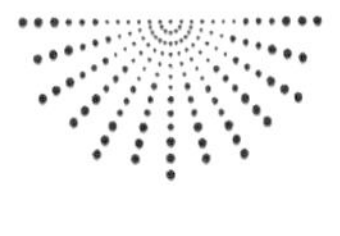

SAMANTHA

The next December...

OUR LIFE HAS BEEN A BIT OF A WHIRLWIND SINCE THE TWINS arrived, but we have done what we do best. Adjust and enjoy each new milestone. I'll never forget the day Maddie, Frankie, and Declan arrived at the hospital. Both Maddie and Frankie squealed and couldn't get enough of their new brother and sister, while Declan held back and waited for the commotion to be over.

When they were through, he went over to each of the twins and introduced himself as their big brother. He swore to protect them and always be there for them. I still get tears in my eyes when I think about it.

Now that the twins are five months old, they can roll over, so I can't leave them unattended for long. "Hey, Frankie, can you watch Loren while I hop in the shower?" Raine is sleeping and this might be my only opportunity to get a shower before Enzo comes back from picking up Maddie at a friend's house. All of us are looking forward to her getting her license in February.

"Sure, Mom."

I make a mad dash upstairs, check on Raine, and get in the shower. Enzo doesn't know it yet, but we're planning a surprise birthday party for him this evening. To make things even better, his parents have invited all the kids for a sleepover. And when I say all the kids, this includes the twins. It's our first night without them. Each take the bottle just as well as breast milk. I'm stoked to have this time with Enzo. He has no clue as to what I have planned for this evening.

When I get out of the shower, I dress in my sexiest panties and matching bra. Unfortunately, it's still a maternity one, but things have come a long way in fashion since Maddie was a baby. I also put out a change of clothes I will wear for this evening. He knows we're going to dinner, but has no idea everyone else will be there. I also take the time to blow-dry and straighten my hair.

When I get downstairs, I find Maddie and Enzo home. The sight of him still sends shivers down my spine. You'd think that after a year or so, I'd be used to him entering the room. But no such luck, my heart still flutters and my mouth dries at the sight of him. Add that delicious dimple that pops when he smiles as he sees me and I'm still swooning.

"Hey, beautiful," he whispers in my ear as he pulls me in for a kiss in greeting. The tingles that race up my spine have me shivering.

"Hey yourself, handsome." I pull him closer and increase the intensity of our kiss.

In all too short of time, he pulls back. "We'd better stop, Sam."

"Must you always be so responsible," I plead.

He lets out a huff. "Someone around here has to be. Besides, we need to decorate the tree today."

"Why yes, we do. Someone's gotta hide the pickle we got in Germany," I tease. "Let's do it as soon as Raine wakes up."

Decorating the tree with two five month olds proves to be a challenge. As Maddie, Declan, and Frankie try to put up decorations, the twins have found they want to be in on the action, too, and keep rolling themselves under the tree to look at the lights. We laugh and enjoy our family the best way we know how.

"Hey, Mads, do you remember this?" Declan holds out a picture she'd drawn in a tiny frame as one of her Christmas gifts to me from school. It had just the two of them in it as stick-drawn figures.

"Oh, yeah. I drew that before Frankie was born. I think I might have been in kindergarten or preschool. What about this one, Dec?" She points out a picture of them as kids in a Christmas ornament.

As a tradition, I've taken pictures of each of the kids each year and put it into a photo frame ornament. I pull out my phone and decide if I want to keep up the tradition, I'd better take their picture.

Frankie rolls her eyes and sighs. "Why do we have to take pictures now, Mom?"

"Because I told you to," I tease. "Besides, we don't have any with the twins yet."

"Come on, Franks," Enzo encourages. "I know you've got a smile in you." He reaches over and grabs her by the waist to tickle her. She full-on belly laughs.

"Enough!" she gasps. "Enough! Okay..." Giggle. "I'll take the picture."

Each of the kids takes turns to get their picture taken as we finish decorating the tree. When it's all decorated, I ask all the kids to pose in front of it. Maddie holds Raine and Declan holds Loren. I take about twenty pictures because God knows, with five kids, if they will ever look in the direction of the camera at once.

Enzo has his phone out and takes shots at the same time. Hopefully between the two of us, we'll have a decent photo. By the time we're done decorating, it's time to go out to dinner.

I send everyone upstairs to change into nice clothes and tell them to meet us downstairs within the next half hour. Enzo and I take the twins to their room to get them ready. I'm sure to load the diaper bag with everything they will need for their trip to their grandparents. Maddie, Frankie, and Dec have already packed and have their things in the back of our SUV. They are in on the surprise tonight and miraculously haven't spilled the beans to Enzo yet.

When we get to the restaurant I'd rented out, we're immediately ushered to the back room. Maddie carries Loren and I have Raine in my arms as we enter the building. I let the kids go first and then I say, "Oh, Enzo. I forgot the bag of wipes. Can you go back to the car to get it?"

He looks at me suspiciously, but being the amazing husband he is, he simply says, "I'll be right back."

I walk into the room I've rented for this evening and see his entire family and some of our closest friends waiting. Everyone remains silent as we wait for Enzo to return. As soon as he enters the doorway, everyone shouts, "Surprise!"

Pure shock fills his face, letting me know our surprise is genuine. His eyes are wide and his mouth hangs open.

As people wish him well for his birthday with hugs and birthday wishes, Enzo eyes me. "You did this, didn't you?"

"What can I say? You know I love birthdays," I singsong.

When Enzo finally gets to me, he shakes his head and laughs our surprise off as he mutters, "I should have known something was up. You look way too good for just a night out with the kids."

Since his family swooped the babies up as soon as we arrived, I reach out to hug him. "Happy Birthday, Enzo. I love you."

"I love you more, beautiful," he growls into my ear. "I can't wait to get you home tonight." He plants a kiss on me in front of everyone.

"About that..." I whisper.

He cocks an eyebrow at me. "Yes?"

"We're not going home tonight."

"Where would we be going?"

I shrug as if it's not a big deal. "Well, since your parents offered to take *all* of the kids tonight, I thought we'd go to a hotel where you can open my other present."

His eyes darken with desire. "What kind of present are we talking about?" comes out gruff and filled with need.

"The kind you can only open in front of me. Let's get through dinner and then you'll get to see."

"Are you sure we have to wait? No one will miss us if we sneak out the back door."

"Enzo…" I nudge him. "Yes, they will. You're the guest of honor."

"Look over there." He points to his mother showing off Raine and then to his brother showing off Loren. "No one will miss us."

In the sexiest voice I can muster, I show him my final card. "If you stay through dinner and don't complain, I promise to make this one of your most memorable birthdays. I've plenty of surprises for you and it'll be well worth your while."

He pulls me to him and I feel the result of the promise I just made. He's silent for a moment as he holds me close to him. As I look him in the eye, the sexiest dimple known to mankind makes its appearance. Then he growls in the sexiest voice, making my panties wet with desire, "You've just made this the Best. Birthday. Ever!"

The End

Want more of Sam and Enzo?
Check out Mistletoe & Mayhem
Only available at:
https://amandashelley.com/books-by-amanda-shelley-2/

Want more from Amanda Shelley? Be sure to subscribe to her newsletter: https://geni.us/AmandaShelleyNL

Keep reading for a peek at **Making the Call.**
If this is your first book by Amanda Shelley, you'll be happy to know she writes primarily in one world - so this won't be the last you hear from Sam and Enzo. Chronologically, **Making the Call** is the next book in her world.

SNEAK PEEK OF
MAKING THE CALL

Chapter 1 - Luke

For players, girls are a dime a dozen; the coaches, not so much.
I must keep my eye on the game. I've worked for this my entire
life. I played college ball and was even offered a pro contract.
But when a misguided tackle ended my career by blowing out
my knee, I changed gears, switched my focus and spent the
last six years working my ass off. I became the assistant coach
to one of the best in the nation. My entire life's been devoted to
learning what I can to help make my dream a reality. When
Ray Carson chose to retire due to health reasons, my name
was at the top of the list as his replacement. I never actually
thought I'd be starting this next season as the head coach for

the Rainier Renegades, a team I've always wanted to be a part of my entire life. But, in a matter of weeks, that's what's happening.

I'll never forget the day I walked into the owner's office. I rushed in to be early, unprepared to find everyone already waiting. I'd thought we were meeting to discuss the plans for summer camp. Little did I know they had something else in mind. Thank God, I'd been sitting down when I received my life-changing news.

"Hey, Luke," Mike Townsend greets, shaking my hand as I enter his office and gestures to the large conference table where I find both Tony Marcelli, our team's GM, and Ray Carson, the head coach, already sitting. "Why don't you have a seat. I have some things I'd like to discuss with you."

Instantly, my gut churns. Being under the impression we're meeting to discuss the summer camp training schedule and the logistics of getting everyone to camp, the expectant looks on each of their faces makes me think otherwise.

"Okay," I slowly draw out. "Aren't we meeting to discuss training camp?" I look from person to person already seated at the table, seeking clarification. But all of their faces remain stoic, giving nothing away. *The sorry fuckers. Couldn't they at least give me a heads-up as to what was coming?*

"We'll get to that," Mike bellows out as he takes a seat at the head of the table. He rubs a thick hand through his short, graying hair and rolls his chair forward to lean his elbows on the table. Okay, this is serious.

I take in a deep breath wondering where he's going with this. "All right."

I'm surprised to find Ray is the next to speak. "Son, you

know I had a valve replaced last spring after the championship game, right?"

"How could I not? You nearly gave me a friggin' heart attack right alongside you, when I found you that day," I tease in return. Ray Carson has been my hero since I was a kid. To work with him has been a dream come true. I've followed his career since he took over for the Renegades. When I began coaching, he took me under his wings and showed me what it takes to coach a team to be champions.

Ray's gravelly voice begins an explanation, "Well," he draws in a long breath, "I thought I'd try to make it through another season, but my wife has other ideas. She wants to travel and make the most of the time we have left together." Ray looks a little sheepish, which is completely out of character for him.

"You're not going anywhere soon, Ray," I eagerly remind him. "Your doctor gave you the green light months ago, and I know you work out, so you're healthy. You have years left in you," I argue to refute his response.

"Well, I have a couple of championship rings, and more money than I could ever spend. Who knows how much time we all have left? I could be hit by a bus tomorrow, you never know," Ray states with a shrug. "You know I'm a hard-ass on the field, but when Vivian wants something, she's ruthless. I'm smart enough to give her what she wants."

Mike clears his throat. "That being said, I wanted to tell you how much we appreciated you stepping up to fill in for things last spring, while he was recovering."

"It was nothing any of you wouldn't do," I respond automatically. "Just doing my job."

"Well," Tony Marcelli interjects, "it didn't go unnoticed."

"What would you say to being the youngest head coach in the league?" Mike's deep voice suddenly fills the room.

The fuck? Did he really just say that? No fucking way. I. Am. Speechless. As my mama would say, I could catch flies with my mouth. Now that my jaw's dropped to the floor, I may need a shovel to pick it up. *Fuck... and CPR to catch my breath.* Crickets could be heard from miles away; the room is that silent as they await my response.

"Luke?" Mike says as he places his arm on my shoulder, breaking me from my trance.

"Excuse me?" I manage to get out. *There's no fucking way he just offered me the head coach position. I'm only twenty-nine years old. I won't even turn thirty until August.*

"What do you say, Luke? Do you want to be the youngest head coach in the league?"

"Seriously?" Apparently, I say it aloud.

The room fills with laughter from everyone. "I think you shocked the shit out of him, Mikey," Ray bellows out. "The boy doesn't know what to do with himself."

"I'm as serious as a heart attack," Mike says again. "No offense, Ray."

"None taken."

"Wow. That would be an honor." I finally manage to get my wits about me. "I thought it would be years before Ray retires. I love the Renegades."

"We know you do, Luke," Tony Marcelli states. "We've been thinking about this for the past few weeks, and you're the only one we want to lead this team. You stand out above the rest."

I take in another deep breath. This is certainly humbling. "Thank you for even considering me."

"Do you not want this?" Ray asks in disbelief.

"Hell, no! I want this. I'm just thinking aloud, what an honor it is to be considered in the first place. There's no way I'd pass up this offer!"

I stand and gratefully shake everyone's hand. I receive congratulations and slaps on the back as I make my way around the room. This is the job of a lifetime. I know I can do just as good of a job as Ray. I know the members of the team, and the inner workings of the Renegades, better than anyone else in the running.

"Glad to keep you around," Tony states to me as I shake his hand. "I'll have my secretary send you a new contract, and we can hash out the details later."

After another round of congratulatory handshakes that morning, we do discuss the logistics of training camp as well as some of the added responsibilities required of me in the coming weeks, since Ray will leave before camp begins. Ray had a lot more responsibilities than I did over the past few years, but I know I can handle it.

Since that meeting, my life hasn't been the same. The weeks have flown by in a blur. I'm up well before six each day. I work out on my own, eat breakfast then meet with the team by seven. I have meetings all day, work with the team during practices, and plan for the next day with my coaching staff before returning home late at night.

I prefer to get away from it all when I go out to my house on Anderson Island, but since becoming head coach, I've stayed in town more often. There's a ferry that gets me to

Steilacoom, just before six thirty a.m., but I've been too tired to make the forty-five-minute commute.

Thankfully, this year's training camp went by without any major complications. Our practice schedule was rigorous, and the team feels in good shape, just coming off the championship win last season. Most of our team consists of returning players, with only a few rookies we'll test out in the pre-season games as well as some pivotal trades pushed through to help strengthen our O-line and special teams. Our hard work will pay off this fall, once the season officially starts.

To give everyone a break after our grueling schedule during summer training camp, the team has five days off before we come back at full force to gear up for the season. Many players will use this time to be with their families. It's an unspoken rule that each will continue their workout regimen on their downtime, but they don't have to be at our practice facilities for the next five days. Most of the members of our team are superstitious as fuck, so I'm sure they'll continue whatever gets them into their 'zone' as a professional athlete.

Myself, I'm looking forward to spending some time away from it all. I've been working my ass off around the clock to ensure nothing gets dropped through the cracks as the season begins. I know I need to prove myself not only to my team, but to the entire league, as I'm the youngest to ever do this. There's been a lot of hype and speculation, but I know the Rainier Renegades are ready, and I'll be there to ensure they keep the steady momentum we've built these past six years since I began working for the team.

I'm not spending the entire five days out at my home on Anderson Island, but I'll happily spend the majority of my time there. Sure, I'll review film from last season for the teams we're playing in the upcoming weeks. Since everything's digital nowadays, I can do it from the comforts of my couch, just as well as my office at the stadium. But I'll also spend time enjoying the remaining days of summer in the Pacific Northwest. There are a few projects I want to complete while I'm home, since I'll have free time to finally get around to them. The team's charity auction at the local children's hospital is the Saturday before we report back, so I must head back earlier than I'd hoped.

I pull off the ferry from Steilacoom just after four in the afternoon, and I quickly make my way to my home on the northeast side of the island. I love the land I purchased when I first was hired by the Renegades. I have a phenomenal view of the Sound as well as Mt. Rainier on clear days. I can hear the breeze as well as the water lapping against the shore when I sleep with my windows open at night. Sure, I have central air with my heat pump, but living in Washington, you don't need AC that many days of the year. Being on Anderson Island, it's nice to relax and take a break from the hustle and bustle of the city. The back side of my property is lined with trees, so I'm secluded while I'm here, which is a perk. Privacy is something I never thought was a luxury until I took this head coaching position, and my name was thrown into the limelight.

Anderson Island is the home to approximately a thousand residents. Most homes are vacation homes, so during the summer, the population raises to nearly four thousand. The island itself is just under eight square miles. It has a few restaurants and some stores if you need the basics, but if you want an item from a box store, you'll have to go to the mainland.

Thankfully, I have Evelyn, a woman who lives in the apartment above my detached garage, do my shopping and errands for me. Her young grandchildren live on the island full-time and when her husband passed away a few years back, she was looking for a part-time job close to her daughter so she could help her. I was looking for a housekeeper at the time and with my needs being flexible, it worked out for both of us. I don't have time to shop or clean for that matter and living on a remote island, it's necessary to keep things stocked up if I plan to spend any amount of time here.

Within a few minutes of exiting the ferry, I pull into the garage attached to my home and park my Mercedes next to my Jeep. I quickly unload the few things I brought with me and change into a pair of cargo shorts and a black t-shirt from back in my college days. Pulling a beer from the fridge, I prepare my dinner. I'm pleased to find Evelyn has the fixings for steak, corn on the cob, and a baked potato. Not wanting to waste time, I head to my back deck overlooking Puget Sound as well as Mt. Rainier in the distance to turn on the barbeque. Within fifteen minutes, I'm enjoying a delicious meal in complete solitude. I can already tell this is going to be just the break I needed before the season starts.

Chapter 2 - Luke

I may be on vacation, but my body's trained to wake up before the sun each day. I manage to sleep in until six, but beyond that, I might as well be wasting the day away. I get up, change into some shorts and a t-shirt, put my running shoes on, and begin to stretch. I don't have a state-of-the-art gym out here, but I do have the open road. Well, I do have a weight bench and a few free weights in a spare bedroom, but not much more than that.

I'm out the door within minutes, making my way across the island in no time. Since it's not a big island, I have a route planned that takes me along the outskirts, maximizing the amount of pavement, so I can get a good run in. The sun's bright in the sky, and the weather's warm. As I run, I take in the stillness of the island, since its inhabitants are still enjoying their Wednesday morning from the warmth of their beds. I make my way up and over hills, sharing my morning with the few deer and the birds chirping in the distance. I have one earbud in, and my favorite playlist beats out a rhythm I easily keep pace with.

Rounding the last bend, my heart clenches in my chest as I witness a bad accident. Ahead of me, a bicyclist flies over their handlebars at the bottom of the hill. They go ass over end and skid across the pavement, to an abrupt stop. *Fuck, that had to hurt.* From the looks of it, they must've hit the large pothole on the side of the road. Their tire's now bent and twisted in an unusual shape. *Damn, they had to be cruising down this hill.* I pick up my pace to see if I can be of any assistance.

The closer I get, the more I realize it's a woman who's fallen off her bike. Thank fuck, she's wearing a helmet since her head bounced across the pavement a few times. By the time I arrive at the scene, she's sitting up inspecting the gravel embedded into her knees, palms, and elbows. *Christ, that looks awful.* Her curly brown hair spills out from her helmet, and her back is to me as I approach.

"Are you okay?" I ask, so I don't scare her.

"I'll live, but I don't think my bike will." She glances to me then winces as she pulls a large pebble from the palm of her hand. She points in the direction of her bike, and I can confirm for myself, it won't be in working order anytime soon. "Do you have a phone I can borrow? I seem to have lost mine in the wreck." I look around the area but have no luck spotting a phone. She takes off her helmet, and her brown hair springs free. It distracts me for a moment because she suddenly takes out her ponytail, shaking her locks free. God, even with dirt in it, it's beautiful. Her curly hair comes to life with each movement, catching hints of auburn in the sunlight. It's almost mesmerizing, but eventually, I remember my manners.

"Um, I live just two driveways down. Would you like come to my place to clean up, or maybe I can call someone for you? I left my phone at home this morning, so I'll have to go home either way before I can help you." I walk over to her and hold out a hand. "Do you think you can walk?"

"It'll just be easier if I come with you." She lets out a groan as pain radiates across her face. I immediately reach out to assist her into a standing position.

"Are you sure you're okay?" I ask as I steady her. She immediately begins hobbling as weight is put onto her feet. "Here, let me help you."

As if on instinct, I reach behind her back and under her knees to pick her up. Standing at her full height, she comes only up to my shoulders. She's a slender woman with curves in all the right places. If I had to guess, I'd say she's around my age, and she can't weigh more than 140 pounds. I can easily carry her to my house and get her fixed up in no time.

"Wha… What are you doing?" she stammers as I walk in the direction of my home.

"I'm taking you to my place to get you cleaned up. Then I'll come back for your phone and bike, to take you wherever you need to go," I say as I reach the entrance to my driveway.

"But I don't even know you. You could be an axe murderer for all I know."

I can't help the grin spreading across my face. She's adorable as she attempts to get stern and pin me with her ocean-blue eyes. There's a girlish presence about her, but her body tells me she's fully a woman. The short riding shorts she's wearing have crept up her thighs, and I can tell she works out regularly by the firmness of her beautiful body. Her loose tank has risen as well, revealing a toned abdomen. *She's definitely all woman.*

"Well, I'm Luke. I'm pretty sure if I were an axe murderer, the community would've found me out by now. It's a small island. I can promise you, I have nothing but good intentions. I'll let you sit out on my back deck and tend to your wounds without making you step foot in my house. I have a housekeeper, who lives in the apartment above the garage over there. So, if you'd like to have someone present, I'll gladly wake her if it'll make you feel more comfortable."

Heat creeps up her face, making it turn slightly red. *She is adorable.* "I don't think that'll be necessary. Besides, you didn't have to help. You could have just left me on the side of the road," she says as she shakes her head to hide her embarrassment. Her hair brushes my bare chest, and my senses go on overdrive. *Calm the fuck down, Luke. She's injured, and you're only helping her out.*

"What kind of company do you keep, if you think I'd just leave you out alongside the narrow road with no shoulder?" I ask incredulously.

"It was a figure of speech," she deadpans, her eyes narrowing.

"Just checking," I reply, not knowing what to say. I walk up the steps to my back deck and set her down on a lounge chair.

"Wow, you have an amazing view," she whispers as I set her down.

"It's incredible," I say before I open the French doors to go inside. "I have a first aid kit, I'll be right back."

I rush upstairs to my bathroom and return only a few minutes later to find the mysterious woman on my porch beginning to pick out rocks from her palms. *She sure is stubborn.* "Here, let me help." I open the kit and look for a pair of tweezers. She appears to just have major road rash, but I should look things over as I help her clean her wounds. She may need a trip to the mainland to an urgent care clinic if anything needs stitches.

We spend the next few minutes cleaning out her gashes. It's just as I expected, only road rash. It'll hurt like hell for a few days, but she doesn't have any major injuries. She does her best to control her winces as I clean out each area. I try to distract her with conversation, though I'm not sure how effective it is.

"So, do you have a name?" I ask as I go through a particularly gnarled piece of skin on her knee.

Embarrassment floods her features. Her face flushes with color, and her ocean-blue eyes are suddenly hidden beneath her long lashes. "Uh, it's Dani?" she states, making it sound like a question and causing me to narrow my eyes at her. Before I can say anything, she continues, "It's short for Danika."

"Well, Dani…" I draw in a deep breath as I attack a stubborn piece of debris from her left knee. "What brings you barreling down the road this early in the morning?"

"I was trying to wake up by getting a workout in. I stayed up late last night working on a project, and I need to get into the zone, so I can continue today." A look of apprehension flickers across her face, as if she's revealed too much.

Not sure if I should pry further into what she's revealed, or let it go, I stick with a safe line of conversation. "Well, let's get you cleaned up so you can get back to it."

Dani lets out a groan, and I'm unsure if it's in frustration or from pain. "There's no way I'm going to be able to work today," she says as she shakes her head in disgust. *Well, at least she solved that mystery. Her project must be important.*

"Why is that?" I ask, genuinely interested in her answer. There's a look of determination that I don't find on many others. It's as if she's internally kicking herself for getting injured, and I'm not entirely sure why. It was obviously an accident.

Letting out a huff of breath that washes over my chest like a live wire sending electric pulses throughout my body, she states dejectedly, "I have a deadline in the next few weeks that

I need to meet. There's no way I can work on my computer, when I can barely use my hands. God, I was just getting ahead, too. Nancy's going to kill me."

"Is Nancy your boss? I'm sure she'll understand," I offer, trying to show sympathy.

"No, she's my editor."

Before either of us can say anything else, Dani's distracted by the hydrogen peroxide I pour onto her knee, and she instantly gasps. "Fuck! Give a girl some warning. That shit hurts like a sonofabitch!" She lets out a low hiss, then lowers her voice as "DAMN! FUUUCK! SHIT!!!" come out in a slur of words. She takes in a deep breath and holds it, while I press on the cloth to take the sting away. I can't help my smile when I realize this sexy woman could curse a sailor out of a bar with that mouth of hers. She'd definitely give the boys in my locker room a run for their money and would certainly make them stand up and listen. I nearly lose it when she suddenly turns tomato red and covers her face with her hands. "I am so sorry," she mumbles from behind her splayed-out fingers.

"No worries, Dani. I didn't mean to hurt you." I can't help when the corners of my lips tip up. "I'm honestly quite impressed you weren't cussing up a storm when I arrived on the scene. I watched you go airborne and skid across the pavement." I can't help but cringe at the image that replays in my mind.

"God, this is so embarrassing." She shakes her head and refuses to make eye contact.

I reach my hand under her chin and guide it to make her look at me. "Dani, you have nothing to worry about. Seriously. I just want you to be okay."

When our eyes lock, I'm not sure what comes over me, but I find myself sucking in a breath to steady myself. *What the fuck was that? Focus, Luke. This isn't the time. She doesn't seem to be like a girl who is into one-night stands, and that's all the fuckin' time you have these days. And let's face it, you don't even have time for that.* I shake my head and regain control of myself. *Sort of.*

"I know," she whispers. "I do appreciate your help. Please know that."

I release my hold on her chin and try to focus on getting her left elbow clean. It only has a bit of debris in it, so it cleans up quickly. When the last of her battered body is bandaged up the best it can be, I offer her some ibuprofen to reduce the swelling and pain. I quickly make my way into my kitchen for a glass of water and the bottle of pills. Upon my return, she quickly gulps it down and rests back on the lounge chair I had placed her in.

"Would you like to sit here for a bit while I fetch your bike and look for your phone? Here, put your number into mine, so I can search for it easier." I reach my arm over, handing her my phone.

Without any hesitation, she dials her number. When she places it back in my hand, I notice she's already pressed send and hung up. "I'll be right back," I say to her as I hop off my porch and jog down my driveway.

Making the Call is available everywhere. Continue reading about Dani and Luke today! https://books2read.com/Making TheCall

ACKNOWLEDGMENTS

First, I want to thank you, the reader, blogger, and reviewer for reading this book. There are plenty to choose from and I want you to know I appreciate you choosing mine to spend time with. I hope you have enjoyed Sam and Enzo as much as I have. They've been a part of my life for the past few years. I've spent countless hours with them. They've become like family. It's bittersweet to see their story end. I hope you have enjoyed their world as much as I have. I'd love to hear from you. You can find me on social media or at www.amandashelley.com. If you care to share your thoughts on this book with other book lovers, please feel free to leave a review at any of the retail sites or on Goodreads.

I'd like to take this opportunity to thank Amy Queau at QDesign, for creating the amazing cover of this book. She went above and beyond my expectations and even kept me sane when I found out it had to be changed. You are such a talented person and it's an honor to work with you, Amy.

To my editor, Susan Soares at SJS Editorial Services, thank you for your time and patience. I appreciated your feedback and this duet wouldn't be what it is today without your help. I'm looking forward to working with you more in the near future.

To Julie Deaton at Deaton Author Services, your proofreading is top notch. Thank you for making this as beautiful as it is. There's no way the quality would be as great as it is without your assistance.

To my beta readers, Jackie, Cara, and L.G. Thanks for all your help and support along the way. Your willingness to read and give me immediate feedback was invaluable. I couldn't have written this book without you. Some of my favorite memories while writing this book were calling or texting you and asking if you could choose your own adventure, which would you prefer when it came to twists in the plot. Thank you for being there for me and being a sounding board as well.

There are some people I'd also like to thank for special help along the way. To Andy for being my "go to" man. You answered the most random questions, but you still let me come back for more. To Curran for letting me run some hypotheticals your way to see if what I'd written was accurate. Leela, thanks for reaching out to answer my questions as well. I appreciate your help and hope you found my L&D to be accurate.

Last but certainly not least, I'd like to thank my four girls. Your love and support allowed me to finish these books, meet my deadlines, and get this published. I know you often wondered and verbally voiced why I write my books, but please know that I love and appreciate you more than you'll ever know. Thank you for letting me finish just one more page or holding that thought until I finished my sentence. I love you to infinity and beyond. Your love and support mean everything!

If you enjoyed this book, you will be happy to discover Amanda Shelley primarily writes in one world. For a complete list of the series reading order as well as a chronological time line, please visit:

https://amandashelley.com/reading-order/

Featuring Sam & Enzo from the Resilience Duet

When I met Samantha, my life flipped on a dime.

I'm still piloting missions, but no longer for Uncle Sam.

I used to think I was happy being single, but Samantha proved me wrong.

Thanks to her and our children, I'm certain I'm the luckiest man in the world.

Who knew my life could be filled with so much love, laughter, and utter chaos?

I'm looking forward to stealing some time with my wife before the holidays, but with all the mayhem of Christmas, will we be able to get away?

https://geni.us/AmandaShelleyBooks

Making The Call

Dani

As a bestselling romance author, most assume my life's glamorous, filled with combustible chemistry, and most of all, romance. Ha! I can only wish. With a deadline looming, I've escaped to my family's cabin on Anderson Island to free myself from distractions. My plan's great, until a man, who could pass as a cover model on one of my books, comes to my rescue. Is there chemistry? Sure. Is he everything I'd look for in a guy? Absolutely. But will my career be at risk if I give into my desire?

Luke

For a player, women line up outside the locker room. For coaches, we're lucky to get in the game. As the youngest NFL coach in the league, I live, eat, breathe, and even sleep football. To gear up for this season, I return to my home on Anderson Island for a much-needed break. When Dani literally crashes into my life, my mind's suddenly on the sexy brunette with a sailors mouth, rather than my team's next play. She has me dusting off another playbook entirely, making me wonder, did I make the right call?

https://geni.us/AmandaShelleyBooks

The Boy Upstairs

I ran into Derek while trying to escape the neighbor from hell.

Instantly, we hit it off. Since he's only here for three months and the microbrewery leaves me little time for commitments, it's the perfect setup for a fling.

He's adventurous, challenges me, and he just gets me from the inside out.

With our expiration date quickly approaching, I'm left to wonder… Will my heart ever be the same without the boy upstairs?

https://geni.us/AmandaShelleyBooks

He Saved My Boy

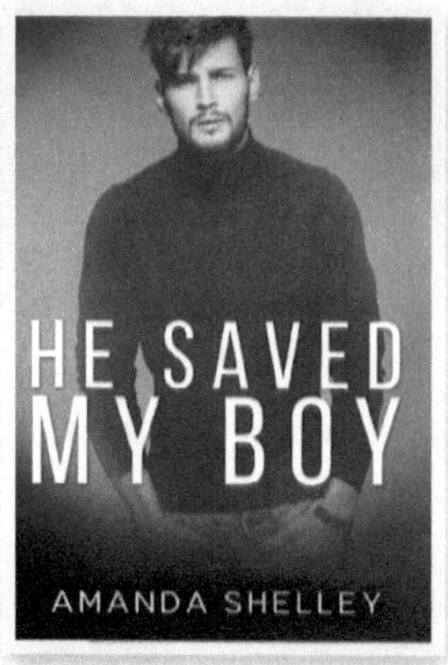

Davis is the first guy to catch my attention since… hell, I don't even know.

Instantly, he makes me think and feel things I've forgotten existed. It has been forever since I put my needs first, so I take the chance and let him light me up from the inside out.

Our night is the kind that will ruin me for all others.

But then I get the dreaded call.

I rush out without a second glance, knowing I'll likely never see him again.

My son will always come first—Always.

Imagine my surprise when Davis walks in, and I find he's the only one who can save my boy.

This cannot be happening—*I guess it's time to pull up my big girl panties and see what happens.*

https://geni.us/AmandaShelleyBooks

Zander: A Perfectly Independent Series Novella

Zander's known for being a player both on and off the court. When his name shows up as my next client, my heart stalls, and not in a good way. There's no way I'll survive the semester with him. I just don't have the patience.

However, when I need help, Zander makes a proposal I can't refuse. He'll be my fake date to my best friend's wedding so I don't have to face my ex and his new girlfriend alone.

The weekend goes off without a hitch as we effortlessly pretend to have the time of our lives.

All is perfect... until I realize my feelings for Zander are no longer an act.

What will I do when our arrangement comes to an end?

https://geni.us/AmandaShelleyBooks

Drew: Book One of the Perfectly Independent Series

Of all people, why him?

He didn't EVEN bother introducing himself, just assumed I knew him from his fame on the court.

I nearly died on the spot when our professor announced we were permanent lab partners. Between his arrogance and the constant

interruption from basketball groupies, there's no way I'll survive this
semester.

Sure, he's hotter than anyone I've ever seen in a science lab with his
sexy blue eyes, cute dimple, and muscles for days - but I can't
afford *his* kind of distractions.

Okay. Deep breath.

I can do this.

After all, it's only one semester.

Just when I think my self-control is in check, he does something to
show me that he isn't the egotistical, self-centered jerk I thought
he was.

How can his stupid smile suddenly make my mind melt, heart race,
and palms sweat?

If I take this chance on Drew, will my perfectly laid out plans disappear?

https://geni.us/AmandaShelleyBooks

Vince: Book Two of the Perfectly Independent Series

It's funny how one night can change everything.

As a bartender near campus, I'm certain I've heard it all. Rarely a shift passes without some guy taking his best shot, hoping I'll end my self-proclaimed dating diet.

Of course, this is exactly how I meet Vince.

Except, he isn't the one running his mouth.

No, he simply shuts down his idiotic friend, then stops my heart with the simplest of smiles and walks away.

Just when I force myself to forget him, he bumps into me on campus.

Our connection is consuming, and my world is knocked off kilter. It's far beyond physical attraction. He's smart, sexy, and feels like—home?

Wait, that can't be right...

Whatever it is, Vince has me breaking my rules to spend time with him.

My entire life I've prepared for meeting the wrong guys.

What the hell should I do when I find the right one?

https://geni.us/AmandaShelleyBooks

Damien: Book Three of the Perfectly Independent Series

Beautiful girls are not hard to find at Columbia River University.

The coeds on campus are great to look at but I was over that scene after graduation three years ago.

These days, outside of being part of the largest civil engineering job on campus, all I'm searching for is a decent meal and some peace and quiet. It's why I'm happy to have found what I consider a hidden gem in the diner I frequent.

All I need to do is finish this job and move on to the next by year's end.

Should be easy enough. Only when Vanessa walks up with a sexy smile and a mouth full of sass, she does more than take my order. She completely takes my breath away.

Next thing I know, I'm here every morning, making every excuse to dine with this intriguing woman. Not only is she smart and sexy, but she's laser focused on reaching the goals she's set for herself.

The more I get to know her, the more I'm convinced she's the one. I just have to find a way to get her to deviate from her perfectly laid plans and take a chance on me.

https://geni.us/AmandaShelleyBooks

The Vegas Pitch

This pitch could make or break my career.

Not only will it set a personal record for the biggest account I've ever landed, but it could set my newfound company three years ahead of schedule for expansion.

Thank god I've got Nate Bellinger on my team.

Even though I had my reservations hiring the sexiest man I've ever laid eyes on – he more than meets my expectations with his hard work and determination. Together, we've formed a solid team and play off each other perfectly.

As we wait for the final verdict, I begrudgingly take Nate up on his offer for a night on the town. After all, this is Vegas and I need to let the chips fall where they may.

Imagine my surprise when I wake up the next morning to find we've not only won the campaign, but I'm apparently married to the man I've only ever let myself fantasize about.

The kicker of it all – he has no intentions of letting me go.

But what will it mean once we leave Vegas?

https://amandashelley.com/books-by-amanda-shelley-2/

The Summer Dare

Leave it to Nana to think of everything.

After a grueling semester, I'm ready for a peaceful summer in Seaside with my sisters.

Imagine my surprise, when I'm woken by the screeching sound of a saw coming through my wall, the first official morning of break.

Not only did I come flying out of bed swinging, but I gave Ryan, the unsuspecting carpenter the surprise of his life, when I came wielding my killer coat hanger and all.

Too bad, I was only in a tank and undies and it wasn't nearly as effective as I'd hoped.

Of course, he insists he's only doing his job. Since it's Nana's last request to care for us, I can't refuse.

However, I won't let a tall, pesky, sexy as sin, know-it-all get in my way of my summer plans. I pretend I ignore him – that is until my youngest sister pokes her nose in my business and throws down a dare I can't back down from.

Kiss the next single guy who walks up to the bonfire – or explain to my sisters why I get riled up over the contractor.

When Ryan suddenly appears, I know I'm screwed in more ways than one.

Not only will my sisters learn my secret, but from the determined look on Ryan's face, I'm afraid he's eager to reveal it to the world as well.

What have I gotten myself into?

As I walk toward him, one thing is certain – this summer dare will either make or break me.

https://geni.us/AmandaShelleyBooks

The Summer Ultimatum

Watching my sister fall in love last summer gave me something I hadn't expected—hope. It gave me hope that there might be someone out there for me and hope that I might get past my misguided fears and finally let someone in.

With my help, Ryan's planning the most epic proposal. I just have to get the know-it-all musician I work with to fall in line to make it work.

Jax is wicked smart, extremely talented, and sexy as sin. But he can't see the forest for the trees when it comes to his potential. He'd rather keep playing in dive bars along the coast than take a real shot at success.

When the Seaside festival has a music competition, I present Jax with an ultimatum that will either make or break both our careers.

I've laid it all on the line, but can he?

https://geni.us/AmandaShelleyBooks

The Summer Proposal

My sisters are dropping like flies.

They're falling in love and having the time of their lives.

Don't get me wrong, I'm ecstatic for them. I love seeing them happy.

But I'm not ready for that type of commitment.

I can't even keep a plant alive, let alone find someone worthy of getting past a third date.

As the only sister done with school and single as a pringle, I have to do something fast, or I'll be my matchmaking aunt's next victim.

When Jax's drummer joins him for the summer and needs some help with his image, I make him a deal he can't refuse.

All is perfect—until I realize my summer proposal has one minor flaw.

Our relationship may be a sham, but there's nothing fake about my feelings for Finn.

https://geni.us/AmandaShelleyBooks

The Summer Arrangement

One, two, three—it's all down to me.

As the youngest and only single Lancaster, I'm eager to spend my summer in Seaside, Oregon, with my sisters. It's something I've looked forward to all year, and I'm determined to make every minute count. After all, I've only got one year before I graduate from college and have to adult for real.

However, if I want to graduate debt free, I need to work. I have a lead on the perfect summer job with the nanny agency I've spent the last three summers catering to.

I just have to win over an adorable three-year-old and convince her single dad I'm the right one for the job.

Simple enough, right?

Except when I show up at his door, I'm shocked to find he's the guy I hooked up with a few times last semester.

This cannot be happening.

I need this job. There's too much on the line to walk away. Maybe we can put the past behind us and make some sort of summer arrangement?

https://geni.us/AmandaShelleyBooks

The Summer I Found Home

Being a pilot is all I've ever known.

I served my country and I'm damn proud of my career.

But sacrifices were made, especially when it came to family.

I've missed first steps, first days of school, and first dates to name a few.

My kids grew up. They're having families of their own.

Was it worth it?

When an opportunity brings me to Seaside, I jump feet first no questions asked.

It means experiencing all those firsts with my grandkids.

With family as my focus and my guard down, I don't even see Faye coming.

She's a force to be reckoned with and has me holding on for dear life.

I thought our ship had sailed, but now that I'm home for good—I just might get more than one second chance.

arrangement?

https://amandashelley.com/books-by-amanda-shelley-2/

Collide: A Sweet Romance

Falling head over heels was the last thing I expected.

Literally.

Coffee is everywhere – and more than my ego is bruised.

When the handsome stranger I plowed into calls me by name, mortification sinks in.

He rushes off to class. I run home to change, hoping to forget the whole incident.

If only I could be so lucky.

I quickly find it's a small world and Gavin Wallace is completely unavoidable. Everywhere I turn he's there. In my classes. Hanging with my friends.

I've got his full attention and I have to admit, I like it a lot more than I should.

https://geni.us/AmandaShelleyBooks

ABOUT THE AUTHOR

Amanda Shelley loves falling into a book to experience new worlds. As an avid reader and writer, sharing worlds of her own creation is a passion that inspired her to become an author. She writes contemporary romance about characters who are strong and sexy with a twist of sass.

When not writing, Amanda enjoys time with her family, playing chauffeur, chef and being an enthusiastic fan for her children. Keeping up with them keeps her alert and grounded in reality. She enjoys long car rides, chai lattes and popping her SUV into four-wheel drive for adventures anywhere.

Amanda loves hearing from readers. Be sure sign up for her newsletter and follow her on social media. Join her reader's group Amanda's Army of Readers to talk about her books and stay up to date on her latest information.

www.amandashelley.com
Readers group: https://www.facebook.com/groups/Amandas
ArmyofReaders/
Newsletter: https://geni.us/AmandaShelleyNL
Goodreads: https://www.goodreads.com/author/show/19713563.
Amanda_Shelley

facebook.com/authoramandashelley

instagram.com/authoramandashelley

amazon.com/author/amandashelley

bookbub.com/profile/amanda-shelley